Books by Ki Longfellow

China Blues
Chasing Women
Stinkfoot, a Comic Opera (with Vivian Stanshall)
The Secret Magdalene
Flow Down Like Silver: Hypatia of Alexandria
Houdini Heart
Shadow Roll: A Sam Russo Mystery Case 1
Good Dog, Bad Dog: A Sam Russo Mystery Case 2
The Girl in the Next Room: A Sam Russo Mystery Case 3


Follow Ki Longfellow on the Internet:

Blog kilongfellow.wordpress.com
Facebook Ki Longfellow
Twitter @KiLongfellow
Official Website www.kilongfellow.com
Sam Russo www.eiobooks.com/samrusso

# Good Dog, Bad Dog

by
Ki Longfellow

## A Sam Russo Mystery

### Case 2

Eio Books

This is a work of fiction. Though based on the known facts of people and places mentioned, the events and characters inscribed herein spring from the author's imagination. No descriptions of public figures, their lives, or of historical personages, are intended to be accurate, but are only included for the purposes of writing a work of fiction, and are not necessarily true in fact.

Copyright © Ki Longfellow 2013
All rights reserved.

Published in the United States by

Eio Books
P.O. Box 1392
Port Orchard, Washington, 98366 U.S.A.

www.eiobooks.com

Library of Congress Cataloging-in-Publication Data

Longfellow, Ki
 Good dog, bad dog : a Sam Russo mystery CASE 2 / by Ki Longfellow.
    p. cm.
 ISBN 978-1-937819-04-0 (pbk.)
 1. Private investigators--Fiction. 2. Murder--Investigation--Fiction. 3. Staten Island
(New York, N.Y.)--Fiction. I. Title.
 PS3562.O499G66 2012
 813'.6--dc23

                                            2012029795


Cover designed by Shane Roberts
Book designed by Shane Roberts
Cover Photo by Chad J. Kainz

Dedicated to
Jimmy Cagney & Silky Sullivan

(And to my grandson, Kit Longfellow, the King of Upside Down.)

# Good Dog, Bad Dog

## A Sam Russo Mystery

### Case 2

It was seven p.m. on a cold evening in early November and I was still in my striped pajamas chain smoking Luckies. Where I was lying was on the old Murphy bed reading Gypsy Rose Lee's *The G-String Murders*. Not bad writing for an ex-stripper. Maybe I should write a book? It beat taking your clothes off for a pack of drooling mugs or getting seriously plugged three times by one of the funniest, most inventive, most adventuresome kids I once called "friend" back in the days of our old alma mater: the Staten Island Home for Children, aka the Staten Island Lock Up for Lost Little Kiddies.

Jane was lying up against my side, her knife wounds healing as well as my bullet holes, but she'd be badly scarred for life. I could hide mine but Jane's would always look like she'd tripped over the railing of the Central Park Zoo's croc exhibit.

Getting shot takes something out of you. I still had no idea if whatever that was had any intention of coming back.

My manly chest looked like a used target. There were three fresh scars from three fresh bullets neatly spaced round where I assumed my heart was. By some strange miracle they'd all missed the bulls-eye.

My brain still worked and my lungs still wheezed—that last part probably came from too many smokes and from running around the Philippine island of Luzon breathing the fumes of war. My legs and arms moved when I wanted them too. Everything worked, though I suppose I could say sleeping was a problem—I was doing maybe too much of it.

I could still talk. Not that I'd done much talking since it

happened. Sleeping yes, talking no.

OK, so I was better off than a ton of other guys I'd known coming through an entire world war. Ironic that back then when all those bullets were aimed my way, they missed. Close to four years worth of 'em and not even a hole in my hat. And then, when the world finally settles down to lick its wounds and rebuild itself as an exact copy of pretty much what it was before the war, or maybe worse now we had the A-bomb, what happens to Sam Russo, Private Dick? He takes three rather personal hits from a gun in the hand of one of his oldest friends.

I'd had a lot of time to think things over. Truth was, all I'd done was survive my first real murder case as Sam Russo, Private Eye. I got paid to go through a kind of hellish paradise.

The paradise part was being in Saratoga Springs for the racing season. Getting to know the interesting Mrs. Willingford in a number of interesting ways wasn't too bad either.

Hell was all the rest of it.

I'd come away from Saratoga with two new and important ideas. The first was a life lesson: I liked my enemies better than my friends. It boiled down to this. Enemies were easy. You knew where you stood with 'em. In a nutshell, enemies meant you no good.

But friends? Friends were people you trusted, right? Friends were people you could count on. So was a friend some guy I shared the horrors of the Staten Island Home for Children with? Or dodged Jap artillery with? Or hung around race tracks and drank with? Who knew? I didn't, not any more. A friend tries to kill you—and almost succeeds—a person can lose sight of what friendship means. A person can wind up saying to hell with friends.

Which brought me to the second idea I'd lugged back from Saratoga's racetrack. There remained one person left in the world I knew for sure was a "friend" and that person was a dog named Jane.

Jane came with the case I'd survived. The first guy she'd loved, an up-and-coming jockey named Babe Duffy, had got himself murdered up in Saratoga Springs—and when he did, no one wanted his dog. All those no ones included me. Duffy's dog wasn't one of those cute little mutts women like to lug around and coo to. And she wasn't one of those big useful brutes a lug thinks he looks manly with. Duffy's dog was a Basenji, some sort of African dog. She was also an acute pain in the butt.

Except for three things, name what people didn't like about dogs and that was Jane, the African queen.

The three things were she didn't bark, she didn't slobber, and even when soaking wet, she didn't smell like a dog.

She was mine now, or I was hers. Whichever, I think she was happy with the arrangement. It took a little doing, but I knew I was.


Two long months had dragged themselves by since the end of the Saratoga Spring's horse racing season and with it the job I'd been hired to do—solve the killings of not one, but three young jockeys. Those two long months were spent in Staten Island's impressive downtown Stapleton, still in the same one room where Victory Boulevard bumped into Bay Street lying around on the same Murphy bed.

I'd solved the case but only four people knew it. One was me. One was the killer himself, now also as dead as his three victims, and by the same hand: his own. One was Thomas Clay Jefferson, the walleyed colored guy who shined shoes in a rich white man's hotel called the Grand Union. And the last was Mrs. Willingford.

I guess you could say Jane knew it too. It was Jane who fingered the jockey killer because Jane was there for the murder of one of the three jocks, namely Babe Duffy. So I got shot by one killer and Jane got knifed by another.

Two killers. One case. This all made sense if you'd been there.

Mrs. Willingford phoned from time to time, but as she wasn't the type to set hoof on the isolated Isle of Staten I didn't expect to see her soon. For one thing, there was no racetrack or horse breeding farms. There should of been. We had the room. I'd of really liked to see Mrs. Willingford. Better, I'd of liked to touch Mrs. Willingford, gaze into those hard blue eyes. But the moment she got a load of what I called "home," all I'd get out of it was the last of a trailing silk scarf, the brim of a hat big enough for the guy carrying the world on his back at Rockefeller Center, a whiff of *L'air du Temps*, and that would be that.

I did see her doctor. She'd made the poor sap live in a local hotel so he could visit me daily, then weekly—now we were down to once a month and he was happily back where he belonged: in some snug three story brownstone in Brooklyn Heights tending to a rich kid's sniffles.

Jane saw Mrs. W's personal vet. The vet lasted longer than my doctor. Probably because the vet liked Jane and my guy could do just fine without me.

Once Thomas Clay Jefferson called to see how I was doing. I said I was doing fine. Clay said he was doing fine. Still had the same job, though things were a mite slower without the races in town. He said that was fine by him. I said I was glad it was fine by him. He said he expected me for the 1949 running of the Travers Stakes. I said I'd be there.

Twice I'd gone to the movies over at the Paramount on Bay and both times my snub nosed Colt .38 Detective Special saw the picture with me. Another effect of getting shot. I might stop carrying and I might not. Anyway, the first time was to see *Night Has a Thousand Eyes*. I'd read the book, which was terrific, so even having to leave Jane alone—Jane was a one man dog; she didn't approve of me doing something without her—the movie was a must-see considering Edward G. Robinson was in it. I wasn't all that impressed. More often than not, the book was better. This was one of those oftens. The second time I sat through *The Snake Pit*, sweating out every minute of it. Three mornings in a row now, I'd woken up thinking about the damn thing. But who could resist a title like that? Trouble was, it stirred up a lot of feelings I didn't know I had—like the fear of going nuts.

And that was my life these days. No visitors. No hanging around in bars or coffee shops. No going to the track down in Monmouth or the tracks over in Queens.

No nothing.

But all this was fine by me. Except for Jane, I'd sworn off friends.

Oh crap. Now who was knocking at my door?

## 2

I ignored it. Jane perked up her ears but seeing that I wasn't moving, neither did she. More knocking: louder this time. More ignoring from me and Jane. Enough of that and surely whoever was out there would give up and go away.

Oh, fucking hark. A voice sounded without. "I know you're in there, Russo. I can hear the pages of some crummy book turning."

Goddammit. I should of known that insistent knock. I couldn't ignore Lino. No one could ignore Morelli. For one thing he was the law in these here parts.

I was up and across the room, but very slowly. Who knew? Maybe he'd hurt his knuckles and go away. Instead he started knocking with the butt of his police issue gun.

I opened the door just in time to catch Holly the Hooker leaving for a nice cold evening standing around on the edge of Tompkinsville Park across Bay Street.

Lino pushed his way past me. "Knock 'em dead, kid," I said. This was for Holly, not for Lino. Lino, I didn't say anything to.

Holly fluted, "Don't I always?" Then disappeared in a flurry of Florida pink feathers and the usual eye-watering complete body immersion in *Old Spice* aftershave.

I turned back to find Lino staring out my window. From there all he could see would be my street and the building across my street which looked exactly like my building. I hadn't seen my old pal Lino Morelli since I left for Saratoga in August, which meant not since Babe Ruth died. November and Morelli, a Yankees fan, still had a black band around his arm. For him, Ruth dying was like God dying. I had to feel a little sympathy. And I did. A little.

He said, "What the hell was that?"

"That was an angel."

"Oh yeah? If that was an angel, I'm a—"

"Pest."

Holly must of been making her exit by now, four flights down. I still hadn't figured Holly. He could be a woman. She could be a man. But since she was only a neighbor and not a friend, I didn't worry about it too much. Come to think, I didn't worry about it at all. I liked Holly. Man or woman was OK with me. I said, "Whatever you're here for, forget it, Morelli. You've come at the wrong time. I'm too busy and too rich to do your work for you."

The last part of that got to him. "Too rich?"

"Rent's paid in advance all the way through January. I can afford a paperback book whenever I want one. Only Holly and I share the toilet and tub now the old fart in 4-C croaked."

"Fuck that, Russo. I come bearing gifts. This one is gonna be a— who the hell you sleepin' with?"

"Her name is Jane. She bites."

"Yeah? She bites me, I'll arrest her. We got a big pound in this burg and I got contacts. But if *she* bites, what the fuck bit her?"

"Giant African fleas."

"You kiddin' me? Never mind. Who cares? But no really: what do you mean you're too rich?"

"Somebody paid me."

"For what?"

"To do what you get me to do for free."

"When did this happen?"

"When absolutely nothing was happening here."

"Fuck that too, Russo. Something's always happening here. Which is why I came right on over."

I climbed back into bed. "Even if I wanted to help, Lino, which I don't, I couldn't."

"Why not?"

"I'm still recuperating."

"From what?"

"Getting shot at close range by an old friend of yours and mine, one Paul Jarrett, who, by the way, is now sharing the comforts of Sing Sing with Mister."

Lino found my only chair and sat in it. He was not only speechless, he remained speechless, which made me keep talking. I felt I had to; he looked like he could slide off his seat any minute.

"He's there not so much for almost killing me, but for the cold blooded murder of one of your cops, the dope you kicked out of cop work awhile back. Name of Carroll Goose."

Lino found his dry tongue. "Paul killed Goose?"

"That he did. With his bare hands."

"Where? When? Why?"

"Where? Little town upstate called Saratoga Springs where Goose bumped into a job after you canned him. When? Two months ago, give or take. Why? Because Goose botched drugging a racehorse Paul paid him to get to."

Lino lapsed back into silence. I rubbed Jane's tummy which made her back leg twitch, and I watched Lino. Lino's silence was so rare he was making me nervous. The guy had something to say about everything, even when "Mister" Zawadzki, once master of the Staten Island Home for Children where we'd both grown up with our good friend Paul Jarrett, finally got caught after years of following God's orders that he rid Earth of God's mistakes: namely hopeless helpless young girls. Each one of 'em knocked up for all sorts of reasons and with nowhere to go; so Mister sent 'em off to his God. And he began all this by sending my own mother. But I wasn't going to think about that. If I could help it, I was never going to think about that. I thought about it a lot.

Lighting up another smoke, I read my book some more, I scratched my dog's belly some more. I tried not to, but the truth was I was waiting for Lino to pull himself together. It took him a good three minutes. With Lino Morelli, that was an all time record.

"Okay," he finally said, "when you're ready, you'll tell me. But I get the gist. You got a paid job and part of your pay was gettin' shot and part of it was coming back with what I guess is a dog, but now you're here and you're not getting paid and you're not dead and you're not dying, so you got all the time in the world to come with me."

"Where?"

"Down to the piers. You're not going to believe it."

Where had I heard that before? But he was probably right.

How many times I believed Lino Morelli I could count on half a hand.

## 3

Lino was right yet again. I didn't believe it. But Jane did. It was all I could do to keep her from chewing on it. But I couldn't stop her from growling at it.

"What the fuck?"

"You tell me," said Lino.

What Lino and I and a bunch of Staten Island cops were staring at, and what Jane was first yodeling at, then growling at, was a dead man, a man so dead most of the things that like dead stuff had gone somewhere else for better pickings. But that's not what made him unbelievable. What made him unbelievable was his size. He was huge. There was also some sort of unidentifiable rag which I would of sworn was a huge doily around what was left of his neck, and a ripped black stocking on only one very long, very gnawed leg. He had the other leg, also almost down to bare bone, but it had no stocking. He had both arms, very long arms, but only one very big hand. Where his right hand was, who knew? It looked like it left with a clean cut, not like a long gnaw. And then there was—well, again, his size. Seven feet tall at least. Maybe an inch more.

The body, which I guess by now was on the verge of becoming more a skeleton than a body, was caught up in an assortment of garbage under one of the piers only lately abandoned by the state of New York as a port of embarkation for the U.S. Army. It was sloshing about in said garbage, loose kelp, and tea brown Upper Bay salt water.

I turned to Lino. "Was there a circus while I was gone?"

"Circus? Nah."

"A traveling theatrical troupe come through town?"

"No, not one of them neither."

"How about a carnival?"

"How about it?"

"Any other clothes at all? Anything to get you started?"

"Not another stitch."

"Aside from the hand, any old or new breaks in the bone? Scars? Tattoos? Missing giant report?"

"Autopsy might come up with something—and enough with the wise cracks. Ain't this job hard enough?"

"For some," I said, thinking of not only my childhood friend, namely Lino, but of myself. I didn't exactly shine up in Saratoga Springs no matter how much the rich Mrs. Willingford, horse lover and straight shooter, told her friends I did. You'll see, Sam, she'd said, just as soon as any one of my friends gets bumped off or knows someone who gets bumped off, I'll have them call you. And I'd said: not much of a chance of that considering that every single one of your friends are as rich as Midas, or you or whoever, with bodyguards to match—and now, what with Paul's botched attempt to dope the winner of the Travers, their horses have body guards too. True, she'd said, but one can always hope. I remember looking at her, wondering which of her friends she'd gladly bet on. But I couldn't fault her kindness. After all, she was only thinking of me. Right?

Back to Lino Morelli and his giant floater. "It wasn't a wise crack, Morelli, it was a real question. A guy this big goes for a final swim and it's bound to be noticed. Maybe he even gets missed."

"You're a kick in the pants, Russo. You know that? Making jokes while we're looking at a poor dead slob of a freak."

"This guy alive would make you eat those words."

"Ah, shaddup."

And with that, I turned on my heel. "Come Jane, we're

leaving."

Jane wasn't exactly thrilled, not with a dead giant to yodel and growl at, but she was now mine, or I was hers, and if I was leaving, she was leaving.

"Hey! Where you going?"

"To what I lovingly call home."

"You can't leave. What about this mess?"

"It's yours."

I'd seen sly in my time, but the sly that appeared on Lino's face was world class. I'd been "helping" him solve his cases since he was only knee high to a real cop—that is, I helped until I was sent off to defend America from people who didn't seem to mind getting killed, not so long as they took a lot of us with 'em. As a cop, Lino was exempt from fighting anybody but American criminals, even though he'd lost half of those to the war as well. What he'd done to keep his badge while I was "over there" almost losing my head, he'd never told me. But six months after I got back from the Pacific front, he was made a detective with the Staten Island Police Department over on Richmond Terrace. I'd say that was thanks to me, but why bother? I did it because it taught me how to do it. And I did it because he was a friend in need. Lino Morelli did not possess enough brains to be other than in need at all times. I also did it because he knew he needed me—though he'd get a tooth pulled with pliers, maybe even all of 'em, before he'd admit it—and it was nice to be needed. But it wasn't nice to be both needed and badly treated at the same time. So fuck this and fuck Lino and fuck dead washed-up giants. Gypsy Rose Lee awaited me (my god, if only: OK, she was older than me, OK, she was married and had a kid, and OK she wasn't in love with her hubby but with some other guy—but what does all that matter when a man's been shot and needs a little teasing?) and Jane's between-meal snack awaited her.

But as I said, Lino was looking sly. He got between me

and the street before I could hail a cab. And he did it without getting bit by Jane. That was some fast moving. It also put us both out of earshot of his fellow cops, the ones he was supposed to be in charge of.

"Com'on, Sam. Be a sport. I hurt your feelings? You want an apology? You got an apology. I apologize. But look what we got here. Two murders on my watch since August."

"Murder? For all you know this guy floated in from tripping over a low railing in the Sargasso Sea."

"Nah. He din't."

"And you know this how?"

"The tides and, you know, those rivers that run around in the ocean."

"Like the Gulf Stream?"

"Yeah, like that. One of my guys knows this kind of stuff and about the way the Hudson River works and the way the East River works and he says if the body's an old floater, it came from Manhattan."

He had me. And he knew he had me. My eyes flickered up to look towards the isle of Manhattan. Only five miles away but more like a thousand for all I was ever going to know about it, and it called to me like Circe and every one of her damn pigs.

"Plus there's a hole in his head another of my guys says looks like it was done with an axe."

I lowered my gaze to Stapleton's piers. From where we were standing, what I could see was a lot of cops gathered in a cop clot on one particular pier, all looking down. I said, "You'd have to be up on a ladder to hit that guy's head with an axe. Assuming he was standing at the time."

"You know, that's just what *I* said. So it looks like murder, right?"

"Could be. But one done some time back. And you know what they say about murders— "

"Yeah. I know. They're dead after 48 hours. Or maybe it's 72 hours. Whichever. But I got a feeling about this one. Listen, Sam, I can't work in Manhattan. I'd hafta call 'em in and give 'em what I got and then I'd be out of it. They'd take away my body and my case. But *you* can work in Manhattan."

Jane was looking a little worn out. In Saratoga Springs, I got shot by Jarrett who was trying to avoid being done for the killing of Carroll Goose. In Saratoga Springs, Jane was stabbed eleven times by someone I would never of suspected was a killer in an effort to avoid getting nailed for fatally dropping three young jockeys. Getting stabbed, and with most of the cuts serious, could take as much out of a dog as it could take out of, well, me. I picked her up. She wasn't pleased, but as it was me, she kept her mouth shut. "Guess what happens every week, Morelli."

"What?"

"You get a paycheck."

Lino had the decency to resist taking a swing at me. Even in my shape, he would of missed, not being agile, but even so, he didn't try—and that was good of him. "Money. All you ever talk about is money. OK. I'll tell you what. The department'll pay your expenses."

"You kidding? You'd cough up a whole nickel for the ferry?"

"Whadda funny guy. You're killing me here. I'm talking a hotel for a week. Not one of them fancy ones but one good enough. And some cabs although we both know they gotta great subway system over there. Some food."

"You'd go that far for this one?"

"You bet. This one could maybe put me up a pay grade."

## 4

"It's a ruff."

"A what?"

"A ruff. What Elizabethans used to wear as collars."

The coroner—I was supposed to call him the Medical Examiner, but coroner was more like it in a place like Stapleton—held up the soggy red and yellow mess he'd removed from around the dead man's neck. A dead man, by the way, whose huge dead feet with those huge dead toes stuck out over the edge of the flat table almost halfway up the huge dead calves. "The right hand was chopped off. Without finesse, I might add. And look at this."

He was pulling off what was left of the man's face. I was usually pretty good with this kind of thing, but pulling a face off did something to my knees. He held that up as well. "It's a false beard. Look at this chin. You ever see a chin like this? He could of used it to drive nails."

Morton Hickman and I went pretty far back, as far back as I could remember, which was basically my whole life. As the closest local doc, he used to get called out to attend to us kids, when things for one or another of us got so bad it forced Flo and "Mister" Zawadzki to do something about it. Back then I thought they didn't want one of us dying on 'em, not when the stupid kid could of been saved by a doc: county enquiries, outraged citizenry, that kind of thing. Back then, I had no idea how many were already dead or dying. I just thought they got transferred or adopted or used in secret medical experiments. I read comics with Lino and Paul for that last one. What did I know? (Turns out Lino knew even less and Paul a hell of a lot more. Paul knew us kids were playing on graves. He knew one of those graves contained my mother, Mister's very first gift to "God." Fuck my old playmate Paul Jarrett. I never thought of myself as a vindictive guy, and the people I'd killed were trying to kill me, but if Paul got the chair for Carroll Goose, I'd celebrate at Belmont, make a day of it, bet on anything named Old Sparky.)

I didn't know much more now. It was just that sometimes Flo and the husband she called "Mister"—for reasons entirely their own that I never learned—sent for Morton Hickman.

The best way to describe Morton Hickman was to say he looked like Peter Lorre's dad.

Aside from that, what I knew now was that Mort hadn't seen the inside of the Staten Island Kid's Lockup for longer than me. I was pretty sure his last call was the year Burgoo King won the Kentucky Derby. I'd never forgotten Burgoo King. That year, the colt wasn't considered a real contender so they put a green kid out of Michigan up on his back. For a while there, Eugene James rode like he might turn out to be one of the greats—until he went and accidently drowned in Lake Michigan.

Standing there, watching Mort stick some sort of metal probe through the hole in the giant's giant head, I realized I now knew of three jockey's dead by drowning: Eugene James swimming with friends in a huge lake, Citation's jockey, Al Snider, lost fishing in the Florida Everglades, and Manny Walker, murdered by being first drugged then thrown into a small pond near the Saratoga racetrack.

Horse racing could be dangerous for man and horse. But water's not how you see a jock going.

Burgoo King's year was also the year Mary McEnery died and Mort couldn't do a thing about it. She was seven years old and she'd fallen down an old well in the woods behind the "Home." At the time, we all thought it was an accident. Mort thought it was an accident. Five months ago, Mort and most of New York City's five boroughs learned not much was an accident around the Zawadzkis, wife and man. Turned out poor little Mary had stumbled across Mister burying another of God's "mistakes." So he threw her down the well we were all told to steer clear of.

One thing I knew for sure. Mort and I comforted ourselves that Florence Zawadzki would be forever occupying a small metal room somewhere nowhere near children of any age and that Mister was cooling his heels on Sing Sing's death row.

Mort might not care, but it comforted me to also know Mister had a new neighbor. This kept up, and I might be able to say I was personally acquainted with the whole row.

Now there was a worthy goal.

Jane had taken a seat near the door, not making a sound or a move. I'd already realized it was going to take me some time to know why she did the things she did. I didn't know much about dogs, but what I did know told me Jane was a very odd pooch. How many dogs sat on a hard wooden chair rather than lie around on a nice comfy linoleum floor? I figured she did it to see better. But why she'd want to, beat me. Meanwhile I walked around the table, getting a look from all angles. First thing I noticed—and who wouldn't?— was even in the state this guy's corpse was in: a giant was a giant everywhere. "You're saying he was wearing a ruff?"

"I'm saying that, Sam. Yup."

"Like they did around the time of Queen Elizabeth?"

"Yup."

"He's not *that* dead."

"I know you're kidding, else I'd ask you, nicely, to leave. I hate dopes. No, this is not a three hundred year old dead Elizabethan who fell off some ship of Sir Walter Raleigh's. This is a guy who died from being hit over the head with what I guess was something along the lines of an axe. How long ago he was hit with an axe is hard to say, seeing as he's been washing around between us and Manhattan and maybe even a few visits to Brooklyn and Jersey."

"Not even a guess, Mort?"

"Least amount of time: two months. Most, I'd say six. Maybe eight. But just as a matter of interest, he would of died pretty soon anyway."

I looked closer. "How can you tell?"

"Easy. This guy was at least forty years old. Giants usually don't live that long. Too many complications from being so big. Diabetes. Kidney failure. Tongues so large they can't breathe. All kinds of unpleasant crap."

"Damn. Not to mention someone chopping off his hand and cracking open his head like a coconut."

"Indeed. A very unfortunate fellow bottom to top."

Jane and I went home. But not before stocking up on dog food and Samfood plus a fifth of Seagrams VO, a carton of ciggies, and a new book. I'd finished Gypsy's. Me, I loved the movies, so it had to be time to read the books they'd made 'em out of. I'd read some but not all. There was a good used copy of Hammet's *The Thin Man* and a better copy of *The Dain Curse* in the bargain bin at "Stapleton's Store of a Million Items." Must of been my lucky day since I'd also found a complete collection of James M. Cain. These, and Jane's daily walk, ought to keep me going for a week or so in a life filled with nothing much to do.

But over the next few days, no matter how much I smoked or drank or read or talked to Jane (Jane's health was improving by the hour, while I was learning her language as fast as I could since she already knew mine), the giant in a ruff kept making unwelcome appearances in my thoughts. I'd lose my place, let a ciggie burn down, forget the glass by the bed.

Two reasons for this. First, though Cain was all aces,

Hammett wasn't even a pair of deuces. Well maybe deuces, but they could only win a hand with a bluff like I'd never seen. Hammett was all bluff. The movies, no. They were the real deal. But the books—I'd thrown his *Thin Man* into a corner where it would stay until the butler picked it up. Second, I was thinking about the ruff and the stocking. The rest of the outfit either rotted off or had been washed off. But who wears such things? A guest at a fancy dress ball? An eccentric? An actor? Of course, an actor! Someone in something by Shakespeare. It had to be Shakespeare. All the other playwrights who'd dressed their characters in ruffs had lost their bloom long ago. But not the Bard. On the other hand, the corpse was a giant. Did Willie write a role for a giant?

I couldn't lie still. I had to know. I could of choked Lino. The man was an affliction. Look what he was doing to my leisure time. And to top it off, how could I find out what I needed to know without a lot of legwork? Ah ha, Mrs. Willingford! She'd know, or she'd know someone who would. I had a phone I paid for but seldom used. I'd use it now.

I dialed Mrs. Willingford fully expecting to leave a message with her third footman or her pastry chef. Instead I got Mrs. Willingford.

"Sam! Did you get my invitation?"

"What invitation?"

"A ball in the Hamptons."

"Sure. And did you get mine?"

"You sent me an invitation?"

"No. But if I did, and you said yes, we'd be going to a double feature on Bay Street. Listen, all kidding aside—"

"I wasn't kidding."

"You couldn't pay me to go to a ball, plain or fancy, not if I were starving which I could be, any minute now. Listen, you know your Shakespeare, right?"

"Well, I'm not bad in a pinch."

"More than true." I was thinking of all the pinches we'd shared in Saratoga. Some rather personal. Considering the impact that was having on various parts of me, I pushed it aside. "Then answer me this. Did Shakespeare stick any giants in his plays?"

"You mean like gods?"

"No, I mean like a role that had to be played by someone over seven feet tall?"

"If he did, I never saw the play. But in *Measure for Measure*, which is not my favorite, there is a line that goes something like this: 'O, it's really terrific to be as strong as a giant but it's not so goddamned terrific to use it like a giant.'"

I gave that some noodle, long enough for Mrs. Willingford to wonder where I went. "Sam, you still there?"

"Thinking."

"So was my fabulously wealthy husband, Joker. He's just thought of a line from *Cymbeline*. You'll love it. 'The gates of kings are arched so high that giants can jet through without knocking off their hats'—or something near enough."

"They jet through?"

"That's what he said."

"Without knocking off their hats? Is there something I'm missing about this bard guy? So far, this stuff isn't a patch on what Bogie says on the silver screen."

"Hold on, Joker's got another one although he can't recall which play it's from. He thinks it might be *The Silly Wives of Whimsey*. 'I had rather be a giantess and lie under... ', well, he can't quite remember what she'd rather lie under. Although I can."

"Mrs. Willingford, can Mr. Willingford hear you?"

"Hard to tell, Sam. At his age, his hearing is often attuned more to *Fantasia* than Jack Benny. He says if you really want to know, there's a big musical rehearsing on Broadway as we speak. Tell them he sent you. They have to let you in; Joker's a heavy investor. Hurry up though; they're going to Philly for tryouts. But honestly, Russo, you must come to my ball. I've told one hell of a lot of people about you."

"Hire someone to play me. Then hire a gag writer for my lines. It'll go over better."

Now, like Lino Morelli, I'd made Mrs. Willingford shut up. A banner week. But before I could ask her if she was still there, she yodeled almost as intelligently as Jane. "That's a great idea! I'll do it!"

And with that she hung up and I was left staring at the receiver wondering about friends all over again.

I also didn't get to ask her: what musical?

So I called back. This time I got what was probably a parlor maid. A bit of yelling from parlor to library to ballroom and the answer was something called *Kiss Me, Kate*.

5

I booked myself into the Iroquois Hotel on West 44<sup>th</sup> Street. Lino Morelli would turn a terrific shade of fresh borsht when he presented the bill to whoever had to make good on Lino's deals, but at least I was nice enough to take one of the cheapest rooms on the 9<sup>th</sup> floor and mostly I planned on eating out. But, said I to Jane, the hell with it. Whatever *he* thought I was doing didn't amount to a hill of beans in this world. What I thought I was doing did; I was seeing the town on Lino's dime. He certainly owed me one by now. He owed me enough dimes to buy me a trip to England's Grand National, all expenses paid—which, by the way, was running again now the war was over. The National got won this year by Sheila's Cottage who I did not have a bet on. With a name like that, who would?

If I found out who his enormous body was, and if said enormous body proved to be the subject of foul play, so much cream for Morelli. If I didn't, all the cream was mine.

I was on Manhattan, I was staying in a decent midtown hotel, I was walking its neon streets, smelling its amber colored air, smiling at hot dog, pretzel, and roasted chestnut venders, breaking my neck staring up at the Empire State Building and the Chrysler Building—what a building the Chrysler Building; I'd almost sell my soul to live in it— buying paperbacks I'd have to lug back to Stapleton in a steamer trunk, and just plain gawking. And I was doing all this without a gun. What did I need a gun for? This was basically an in-and-out favor for Lino.

And I had my best friend along. My best friend had

something everywhere to yodel at.

Anyway, now I was sitting with Jane in the back of the New Century Theater on Seventh Avenue between 58th and 59th Streets. I was thinking of something I'd read in one of those *Father Brown* mysteries. Chesterton was as far from my usual kind of thing as the *Ladies Home Journal* was from an old *Black Mask* magazine, but it was all I had the day I was stuck in a dentist's waiting room dogging some client's unfaithful mate while she got her back tooth drilled. Well, anyway, she got something drilled. In the Chesterton story, some "genius" inspector quipped: "The criminal is the creative artist; the detective only the critic."

Not a bad line for such dated stuff.

In any case, it summed up exactly how I felt watching the big brash broad treading the theatrical boards far down in front of me, the one blowing her lines every second sentence. There was a tall fellow pacing the floor in front of the stage, screaming at her. If I was him, I'd be screaming at her. If I was him, I'd of thrown her off and played the part myself. I couldn't do worse. He and I, and for all I knew the entire cast trapped backstage, were fed up to our back molars with her. Stretching a point by assuming none of them were crooks, that meant we were all critics and we'd all say she was murdering her part.

She couldn't be sleeping with the screaming director, a middle-aged man obviously not interested in the opposite sex, so who was she sleeping with? It was for sure not the guy two seats along from me, both of us smoking in the dark. He'd introduced himself as Mr. Porter who'd written this drivel and I said I was Mr. Russo who hadn't. I introduced the lady beside me as Jane, my best friend. He gently shook her paw and she let him. Not only let him, but gave him one of her better low pitched hums. He'd hummed back. If they'd kept it up much longer, he'd have a new song on his hands.

And from that moment on, I knew he was a nice guy and one hell of a talented fairy.

Even in rehearsal, I saw this was a great show, a first rate show—so how come the line-blowing broad?

I got my answer when the director took a break from blowing out his lungs.

Mr. Porter leaned over and said, "I hate to do it, she's related in a thankfully distant way, but I guess I'll have to let her go." I said, "I'll hate watching." He said, "You, sir, are a gentleman. And your companion is a lady. I am, unfortunately, for the moment, a cad." At which point he stood up, wincing in physical pain as he did, and shouted— he had to shout, we were practically in the lobby—"John! A word?"

John, the director, spun on his toe (nicely done), and shouted back, "Yes, Cole?"

"Would you fire her, please?"

"Now?"

"You think we ought to wait until opening night?"

The girl fled the stage in tears which hurt to watch, but it hurt far worse to watch her *on* stage, so I found a way to bear it.

All I'd been doing in the back of the New Century was biding my time so I could ask if John, the one doing all the screaming, had once employed a giant in the cast of *Kiss Me, Kate*, and if so, had his giant gone missing and when? I was also in heaven. I'd been on the Isle of Manhattan a whole day which was as far from being in downtown Stapleton, Staten Island, as a world beating racehorse on the track at Saratoga was from a really fast cockroach in a basement Chinese betting parlor.

It now looked like I didn't need to wait. If anyone knew about giants and Shakespeare it had to be the guy sitting almost next to me.

So I asked Cole Porter instead.

"A giant?" he answered, fitting another gold tipped cigarette into the same ebony cigarette holder. He offered me one—a fancy cigarette, not a holder. I declined in favor of another of my own: humble, but gold wasn't my color. He said, "Not in the strict sense, no. There've been giants in their time, actors of enormous stature, but they're usually short. Not to mention short tempered. Not to mention intolerable."

We both lit up with a lighter he'd slipped out from a vest pocket as shiny and classy as something Mrs. Willingford would produce from any one of her purses. As for the vest, it was as thick as something Mister would wear on winter evenings out digging in the woods.

Me, my first idea about the ruffed and single-stockinged corpse under a Stapleton pier was turning out a bust. Chasing Shakespeare around and I was already lost. But why else would a guy wear a ruff, even a normal sized guy?

A minute went by, two minutes, someone out of the chorus—a long-legged raven haired honey—was being rapidly coached into the newly available part. I watched it all since I couldn't think of anything else to do. Jane fell asleep and so would I if my seat had been bigger and softer and somewhere else. It was a full five minutes before Mr. Porter turned his head to me and said, "I've been pondering your question, Mr. Russo, and I'm sure I can say without fear of contradiction that Shakespeare never wrote a part meant to be played by a giant. He might have thrown a few dwarfs into this or that, but no giants. Perhaps because giants are invariably uncommon. Or perhaps because the idea escaped him. Or perhaps because he had an aversion to giants. Sad, but so many do. In any case, I do recall hearing there'd been a production of *Macbeth* that had a fellow in the cast who was huge. No one ever used the word 'giant,' but huge was certainly bandied about. This was last Spring, around April sometime. I'm sure it was April because I was thinking of throwing myself into the East River but couldn't find a cab. You never can when it's life or death. Of course, waiting for one to materialize out of the gloaming, I also remember wondering what I could do with someone huge."

"You ever figure it out?"

"Yes. But not on stage."

With great elegance and even greater pain—something was wrong with his legs—Cole rose from his seat. "John!" he yelled. "When did I think of jumping in the East River?"

John yelled back, "Right about the time that bitch Hawthorne Smyth claimed I'd pawned your watch."

"Ah yes, Hawthorne. I remember him well."

"Of course you do. But I did not pawn your watch."

"Only because you couldn't get a good enough price. But those of us in the back row would like the benefit of your vast theatrical knowledge—wasn't there a short run of *Macbeth* on Broadway right about then? With Flora Robson and somebody?"

"Indeed there was."

"Where did it play?"

"Beats me. I'd ask someone at the American Academy of Dramatic Arts. They know everything."

"Would they perhaps know where to find my watch?"

"Cole. Have you ever heard of slander?"

"God, yes. I suffer it daily."

## 6

Jane and I found the American Academy of Dramatic Arts right where Cole said it would be—stuck away inside Carnegie Hall.

Carnegie Hall was a big square lumpish rust colored thing taking up a whole block of prime New York City real estate. It was famous. Everyone who was anyone had played there. Mark Twain once gave one of his talks on its stage. Duke Ellington and his entire orchestra, long gone from the Cotton Club, also long gone, were about to play there. It was somewhere I'd always wanted to see, but when I got my wish I wasn't impressed. I thought it'd be round. I thought it'd be white. I thought it'd be covered in carvings of snorting horses pulling naked body builders in chariots or at least a load of naked muses fooling around with musical instruments, or something.

Instead it looked like the box they'd shipped the Staten Island Home for Children to Stapleton in.

I thought about walking in, pushing past whatever they employed for guards by telling 'em Cole Porter sent me, then wandering around looking for the room or smaller theater called the Carnegie Lyceum. Cole said it was underground, so how could I miss it? Since it was where they taught young actors, all I had to do was keep going down and once down, follow the wailing and the declaiming and the tree imitations.

But then I looked down at Jane and knew at once we both needed a drink. After being seriously stabbed eleven times only a few months back, she was exhausted. Fuck

Lino and his very dead very large person. Right across the street was a beckoning hostelry called the Carnegie Bar.

That was for us.

First thing that happened when we'd perched on our barstools, was the bartender staring. And then he said, "All right, buster. Scram. Dogs aren't allowed." And the second thing that happened was Jane drawing back her lips and exposing her teeth while I said, "Yeah? Then what are you doing here?" So the third thing that happened was the bartender reaching under the bar which is never a good thing. And then what happened was a couple of guys sitting at the far end laughing while one of 'em yelled, "For Christ's sake, Norm, wise up. You gonna sap a little dog?"

"This is my place," said Norm the friendly bartender, "an' I don't like dogs."

"Yes, you do," said the second guy, the one who looked short on his barstool so how short he really was had to be short. "I bring dogs in here all the time."

"But they're human."

"Not necessarily. Hey you—" He meant me. "—bring that dog over here. He looks parched."

"She."

"Even better. Jason and I are in need of female company, aren't we, Jason?"

"Constantly," said his friend in a gravely, oddly pleasing, voice.

And so Jane and I spent the next three hours in the Carnegie Bar getting soused with a guy called Jason and a guy called Don. One round and one slender, the slender one morose, the round one chipper, they were both students at the American Academy of Dramatic Arts, but as far as I could tell spent most of their time at Norm's bar.

At some point I got asked what gave with all the fresh scars on my dog, so I told my new friends what happened up in Saratoga Springs. Boy, were they impressed. Telling it, I was impressed. Whadda doggie. By then, an hour of sitting on a bar stool accepting maraschino cherries had given way to Jane's curling up to sleep in an empty red leather booth with one eye closed and one eye open.

I'd learned she did that. What I hadn't yet learned was which eye, the one open or the one closed, was connected to her brain. But I'd decided to assume both were, and take it from there.

Along about sunset, Jason fell off his stool. Before I even tried to haul him back up, his friend Don said, "Leave him be. It's part of the act."

So that left me and Don and a bar filling up with theater students who actually attended classes. Watching 'em come in by twos and threes, now and then a whole clot of 'em, I wondered whether people who wanted to act were born good looking so they could live their dream, or whether good looking people acted to show off how good looking they were. Hard to tell. Jason was good looking. Don wasn't.

Five hours after choosing a bar stool, I finally got round to asking my new friend the question I'd come to ask somebody. "About six months ago, was there something playing on Broadway, off Broadway, near Broadway, written by the great Barber—I mean, Bard? Another friend of mine says there was but he can't 'member where it was. *Mack Bath.*"

Don patted my hand. "*Macbeth*, pard. Brother, if you had a brain before you came in here, it's rolled under a booth by now." He turned on his stool. "Listen up!" He'd yelled so loudly, most of the noise in the bar went silent. "My friend here has lost his mind. We're asking you all to watch where you put your feet." Then he turned back and said, "*Macbeth.* It played for a few weeks at the National Theater. They do that Shakespeare stuff as much as they can get away with it. It was sometime in April. I actually saw it because I was told to see it or quit my class. Watching that thing was when I knew for sure acting wasn't for me. Not if I had to prance around in tights mouthing page long tongue twisters."

"There was a big guy in it? A very big guy?"

"Big? There was a guy in it playing who the hell knew who had to duck making his entrance."

"And the National Theater is where?"

"41ˢᵗ Street. But you don't wanna go there. You wanna go to this strip joint I know where the comics make me sick they're so funny."

About then, Jason had crawled back onto his stool where he hung on for dear life. Jane was back on hers now the place had filled up with Broadway hopefuls. Waving a small dagger, suddenly pulled from one of his boots, Jason said, "Gentlemen and Ladies, especially the lady seated directly to my left, I give you Henry the Sixth: 'Peter, have at thee with a downright blow… '"

In an instant I imagined I was as sober as Jane. Have at thee with a downright blow? What made him say that?

"Not the man's best effort," said Jason, "and not his worst." And then he fell off his stool again, but not before Don seized his dagger and Jane knocked over a huge jar on Norm's bar and swallowed one of the dozens of escaping hard boiled eggs before he could stop her. Or them. The damn things went everywhere.

I think we were both thrown out of the Carnegie Bar. We must of been because there we were, out on the sidewalk, Jane on her feet, and me on my ass.

Ignoring the unhealthy holes in the ground that would take us down to the hissing subway, Jane and I hailed a passing cab. Which took some doing, the shape we were in.

Luckily for both of us, the desk clerk at the Iroquois was off doing whatever desk clerks do when they're not at their desk, so when we staggered on by (well, I staggered; Jane tiptoed) we caught the elevator to our floor without someone shouting: No Dogs Allowed!

We both fell asleep fully clothed. But then Jane always did. It was rarer for me, but not that rare.

## 7

It was true. A really tall actor with a jaw like a snow plow had played one of the three unnamed murderers of some important character called Banquo.

I found this out by finding the National Theater. The marquee said something called *Lend Me an Ear* was currently playing. As kids, this was one of those sayings that got us to thinking about dumber and dumber things to lend each other, so naming a show *Lend Me an Ear* left me gawping. Who dreamed that one up? Whoever it was, if he'd been one of ours, we'd of shoved his head in a toilet once a week.

I got in by dropping Porter's name. And whaddaya know, I learned some straight dope. The name of the tall man who might or might not be stuffed in a drawer at Morton Hickman's morgue was Maurice Oboram. And if that wasn't the tag on his birth certificate, it was for sure the one he used. Oboram had made the entire run of the play, all twenty nine performances. Best of all, Maurice found another job right on Broadway within a week of the closing of "the Scottish play."

My informant, a stringy sort of joe—could of been the janitor, could of been a leading man—said: "Now there was a really fine fella. We were all real glad to hear he was working. OK, sure, no lines, one entrance, but playing the title character, he was like the lead. Not bad in this business. In fact, working at all is a small miracle, especially when you're as tall as Maurice."

Swell. If this Maurice was Lino's giant, he was one of the good guys.

I hate that. Some creep gets his, and it's one less bug on Earth.

I all of a sudden cared about the huge body back in a drawer at Mortie's. If it belonged to Maurice, well hell, the world needed all the good men it could get. As for the show he'd been in, *Harvey*, even I'd heard of *Harvey*. It opened on Broadway the year Pensive won the Kentucky Derby going away by four and a half lengths. The very next week he won the Preakness. In the Belmont Stakes, he was just about to take the Triple Crown when some nag called Bounding Home did just that—by a nose.

Everyone blamed Pensive's jockey, Conn McCreary. I blamed the jockey too. Pensive should of won that Crown.

I was still being constantly shot at in the merry month of May, 1944, so I only found out about Pensive's Derby maybe a month later. I'd got hold of a newspaper some other guy was reading. How he'd got hold of the newspaper I never knew, because about a minute later he was shot dead sitting less than a foot away from me. One second he was jabbing a finger at the paper, some rag from his own hometown, bitching about a local team losing; the next second he was still sitting there with half a head.

Since he wasn't a horse, I didn't cry—men started wars, not horses, and if men got killed, what the hell did they expect?—but I did pull the paper out of his hands before it got too bloody. That's war for ya.

Interesting things like that happened back then. Four years ago, and a newspaper was about all a guy had worth anything. Except his life, and in war, life came cheap.

Anyway, about *Harvey*. It opened in '44 and was this very big hit about a guy and his rabbit. So here it was, late '48, and the thing was still pulling 'em in. It wasn't a musical, it was a play, for which I offered up thanks. Watching the rehearsals for *Kiss Me, Kate* I'd had to hold Jane's mouth shut more than a few times to keep her from singing along. Personally, I thought she was better at warbling *Wunderbar* than whoever it was they had trying to sing it.

Frank Fay, frankly an actor I wasn't too fond of—even if he'd once been married to Barbara Stanwyck who I was *real* fond of—had been starring since its first night as a schnook called Elwood P. Dowd. The part of Harvey was, as I said, a bit part, really nothing more than that. Like the guy said, it was some poor sap stuffed in a giant rabbit suit with one entrance and no lines.

Perfect. Who better to show up as a rabbit towering above the only guy who could see him, namely Elwood, than a seven foot tall nice guy who called himself Maurice Oboram?

Now all I had to do, if Lino got his way, was find out if Maurice was still alive and still gainfully employed as the elusive barely seen character of Harvey. And if he wasn't, then all I had to do was find out why not and when not and whatnot, and also why he was found washed up under a Stapleton pier wearing a ruff and one black stocking—that is, assuming the body once belonged to Maurice. *Macbeth* had closed months ago, at least six or seven of them. And while torn stockings and ruffs might suit Holly—actually they *did* suit Holly, the Stapleton "girl" in the room next to mine—they didn't suit a rabbit at all.

Jane and I were off at a trot from The National on 41st to the 48th Street Theater on, where else? 48th Street, and the entire way—Jane's tail curled over her back, keeping watch for any suspicious moves made my way—I gave my all to Maurice Oboram. If he was alive and playing the part of Harvey, then Lino could cook his head. I was done. But if he *had* been playing Harvey and now he *wasn't* playing Harvey for no good reason, then what the hell kind of case was this? Did I care? I didn't when I got here. I did now. I knew his name, I knew he was an actor and was getting work even as tall as he was, and I knew his last known address was Morgue

Drawer Seven at Morton Hickman's place.

What I didn't know would take up more pages than *Gone With the Wind*.

But it still wasn't my case. It was Lino's. Actually, it should of been some precinct in Manhattan's case, but I knew Lino wouldn't be letting go of a giant killing if he could help it. So me, I'd wind up doing what I said I'd do, take what I knew back to Lino and let him fumble about with the rest of it, whatever that was.

And that would be enough. I'd of done my job for a week's stay in Manhattan.

Jane and I still had a few things to see. She needed to run around in Central Park and leave little droppings for other, lesser, dogs to sniff. I needed to see some movie called *Ruthless* starring Zachary Scott. No matter what part he played, Scott gave me the creeping jeepers but I'd heard that in *Ruthless* this was a good thing. I also needed to eat dinner at Toots Shor's and put the bill on Lino's tab. If Joe DiMaggio could eat there, then so could I. I'd worry about how Jane would dine when the time came.

It was November. The two-year-old races were running, the races where one out of hundreds, maybe thousands, of hopeful owners and trainers would find out if they maybe owned or were training the possible winner of the 1949 Kentucky Derby. So many beautiful dreams flying around tracks all over the country. And the Pimlico Futurity was shaping up into one hell of a race. I had my eye on a well set up dark brown colt called Capot.

I was also itching to keep tabs on the career of an Alfred G. Vanderbilt II owned mare called Conniver, another great female runner by Discovery. Any female by Discovery was something to watch, especially Conniver who was cleaning up in this peaceful year of 1948.

That room of mine back in Stapleton was nothing much. But it was warm, it was my home, it was Jane's home, and it had a radio that reached all the way to Pimlico.

Jane and I were sitting on a bench across from 157 West 48th Street. She seemed impervious but I was freezing.

Mid-November 1948, which wasn't a patch on mid-November 1947—nothing but war had ever been like all of '47: hottest summer in the city's history, snowiest winter; for almost a whole year, New Yorkers thought the sky was falling—but it was still cold enough to sit there shivering. We would of been *inside* the bar that owned the bench, but this time no one was around to protect us from management. I didn't know if we were closer to the West Side or the East Side or smack in the middle of Manhattan. All I knew was we'd spent the whole morning wandering around the theater district, taking it all in: the theaters, the stores, the crowds schooling like fish, the noise of New York City, the smell, the feel, the color—five miles and a world away from Staten Island. It was just me smiling and breathing and the both of us yodeling. I was learning to yodel. I figured the way things were going between us, I'd be speaking African or Egyptian or both in no time. But until then, I was still stuck with English. Or my version of it.

I suddenly said, "What the hell are we doing, kid?"

Jane raised a quick white wrinkled eyebrow in a russet red face. I knew she was listening.

"Would Bogart be wasting his time on something like this? I mean, Jesus, as far as we know, there's no crime, no victim, no villain, no nothing. So Lino's got a dead body? So what? The world is full of dead bodies. What's so special about Lino's? Because it's huge? Because it may or may not have once been a nice rabbit? Because there's a hole in its head looks like an axe hit it? Maybe it's Maurice Oboram and maybe it's not. Maybe he fell off a pier in Manhattan, drunk as a bunny, smacked his head on an iron doodad on the way down, then floated around from piling to piling to piling until he wound up practically naked and wedged under ours?"

Jane said something which I was sure meant: I'm with you, Sam.  Plus, I'm certain I saw another Lassie movie playing around here somewhere.

I was getting a sore throat. I felt a little feverish. The tips of my ears hurt.  And even if Jane was right and yet another Lassie movie, with or without Elizabeth Taylor, had opened, or even if a reincarnation of Rin Tin Tin had just made a movie which was showing in a theater near us, all I wanted to do was lie down on something soft and warm. Barring Mrs. Willingford, that meant the bed in our tiny Iroquois Hotel room on 44$^{th}$.

I nudged Jane. "Should we go home, girl?"

Strangely, I didn't mean the Iroquois Hotel; I meant Room 4-A, Stapleton, Staten Island.

Before it was even out of my mouth, I knew how dumb that sounded. "Scratch that. We're on vacation. We're on the sidewalks of New York City. We have a hotel room. You and me, we'll do one last thing on this wild rabbit chase of Morelli's, then it's enjoy the place until his dime runs out. Like this."

I'd meant at that point to stand up, cross the street to the 48$^{th}$ Street Theater, buttonhole another stringy janitor with answers, ask him a few useless questions, then forget the whole thing. When that was done, Jane and I'd stroll over to Rockefeller Center—we still hadn't watched anyone fall on their ass ice skating yet.

I'd already looked up, checked out traffic, barely noticed who and what was passing by on my sidewalk but captivated by the dandy across the street. The guy was making his way up an alley between the theatre and a delicatessen in a long dark wool coat, a pair of expensive correspondent shoes and a wide brimmed fedora.

An escapee from a Busby Berkeley chorus line, for sure.

I'd finished my speech, stuck one foot out to begin that walk—when Jane gave out with a howl that curled my chest hair (almost grown back after they shaved it all off to crack open my chest and retrieve three bullets which now lived in my distinguished Stapleton room in a Prince Hamlet cigar box with other assorted junk, like my war medals) and was off across 48th Street dodging cabs and delivery trucks and a startled cop on a startled cop horse, all the while scaring the crap out of me. She was headed straight for the 48th Street Theater, a building that had so far interested her about as much as racing greyhounds interested me. Greyhounds chased mechanical rabbits, ran as fast as they could from the get-go, had no jocks hence no tactics, and usually the first dog out was the first dog in. How do you handicap that? Worst of all, they weren't horses.

Last I saw of Jane, she was under a news truck.

## 8

Enough of greyhounds, I was also off the bench and running through the same snarl of traffic, yelling "Dammit, Jane!" What other people, mainly cabbies, were yelling at me wouldn't even make it into an early Mae West flick.

Jane got herself under the truck, barely, had sped by a woman who literally jumped out of her way, then flashed down the same narrow alley the young man in high tone duds had sauntered down a minute earlier—all this while I was still dodging cars. A moment later and I too made it into the alley. No Jane.

Outside the stage door, a cluster of amused faces and pointing fingers told me where she'd gone. I'd already figured that one out—but I could of used someone telling me how she got past the stage door. I was facing a guy with a mouth like a cave-in who was there to tell people like me to shove off. He pushed a finger into my chest. It hurt and I pushed it away. He tried it again, and I pushed *him* away. He had maybe three teeth in his whole head, but I understood what he was saying. I understood because I saw the sap on his desk. "Get that dog outta here or I'll slap it down."

I said, "You sap Jane and you'll be out of body faster than a medium."

Where I got these lines, I'd never know, but this one worked. He put his finger back where it belonged, left the sap where it was, and let me get on with chasing Jane.

I found her by following the sound of a dog fight.

Jane was in a dressing room, and if it wasn't the star's dressing room, it might as well of been. My friend Jane was clamped to the throat of a much bigger dog who, try as he might, couldn't shake her off.

Crouched in the corner was a young woman, or young enough, in a gray sweater big enough and long enough to cover whatever was under it. Anything could be under it: a build like Jack Dempsey's or a neat little package like Lana Turner's. From all I could tell, it could just as well hide tentacles. With no make up, round glasses, that sweater, the hunched shoulders, and a swept up roll of hair the same color as Fleeting Fancy—for a horse, I'd call it chestnut—I didn't know if I was looking at a damp squib or a bombshell.

"Sorry," I said to whoever she was, then I hollered at my best friend. "Jane, stop it!"

My yelling did about as much good as the big dog was doing. Good thing the bigger dog was some sort of St. Bernard mixed with the Abominable Snowman. The hair around its neck was enough to ruin even Jane's attempt at a death grip.

Even so, Jane was holding on to whatever she could find and how I'd get her to stop holding on, beat me. That is, short of whacking her or kicking her, or letting the guy guarding the stage door—a dead ringer, by the way, for Barney Google—sap her, none of which was going to happen.

Not if I had something to say about it.

Right about then, an older lady appeared at my elbow. With a face as crumpled as a handicapper's losing ticket, a build like a bowling pin, and one plump short-fingered hand squeezing the other, I knew who she was immediately. I couldn't quite recall her name, but that face, who could forget it? Nothing but confused concern and unbounded love, she'd been one of Cary Grant's batty old aunties in *Arsenic and Old Lace*. I'd seen it in a tent with a sheet for a screen while outside another world raged around us. Even knowing we could take a fatal hit any second, we all laughed our asses off, including some of the locals who couldn't understand a single word. But they understood the gift we were given: sweet mad respite from a much madder world right over the sand dunes from where we sat watching a world we were trying to save.

I'd liked Grant well enough, perhaps he was a bit over the top at times, but it was the two old dames who got to me. How could you argue that she and her sister, both kindly and co-operatively doing away with sad and lonely homeless old men, then tenderly and carefully having them buried in their cellar with pomp and circumstance, were not sane? From where I sat when I saw it, it made sense—and it still did, even now when I knew what Mister had done to so many sad and homeless girls. My own mother, for one.

This old lady was plucking at my sleeve. "Have you come for the dog?"

"I sure have," I said. "But how I'll get her off the big one's neck is a mystery to me."

"You mean you aren't taking the big one?"

"God no. Just the little one."

Cary Grant's aunt wrung her hands some more. "Did you hear that, Maudie?" Maudie was obviously the dame in the glasses and the sweater. "Oh dear. Oh dear. We've been waiting for someone to take the dog away ever since Maurice disappeared. He's been nothing but trouble."

"That's Maurice Oboram's dog?"

"Oh yes. They both went along home one night, right after a show, but only the dog came back. When was that, Maudie?"

Maudie, who hadn't moved out of her crouch, said, "The next day, Josephine, just when Maurice should have showed up."

Josephine! Right. Now if I could only remember her last name. Nope, wouldn't come.

"That's right! The dog came but not his master. Well, we couldn't shoo it out the door, could we? To wander the streets of this big city, oh no! Especially since he was soaking wet and so muddy."

I felt like Jane. My ears perked up. Soaking wet? Muddy? Now who else had I met, naked and dead, but also soaking wet and muddy?

"But no one knew where Maurice lived—"

Exactly. Maurice.

"— and no one seems to know where he's gone. And aside from Frank—"

I knew she meant Frank Fay who played Elwood P. Dowd so I didn't stop her.

"—who constantly wants to call the pound, and we all know what happens to dogs in pounds, especially a bit of a big sad brute like this dog, the rest of us have just endured and waited for Maurice to come back and get him. Naturally, we all chip in for his food— "

"Mostly Raymond," muttered the small probably plain girl in the big sweater.

I said, "Raymond?"

"Raymond LeGrand," said Josephine, "He was the show's understudy so now he plays Harvey. Raymond cleaned the dog up and made him a bed in my room. I had to take him since no one else would. And Maudie makes sure the poor thing gets served his dog food, don't you dear?— oh for heaven's sake, where are my manners? This is Maudie Rivers. She's my dresser and maid."

Maudie and I exchanged nods.

"But it's young Anders who takes him for a daily walk."

"Young Anders?"

"There are two doctors in *Harvey*. Anders Slydel plays the lesser of them. I mean, of course, the one with the least lines. He's a nice young man from a good family. A bit odd actually."

"Anders is odd?"

Josephine laughed. "I mean it's odd he's an actor. Rich

young men usually content themselves with remaining rich young men—especially when their family isn't thrilled with their choice. I understand Ander's family is less than thrilled. What I meant is that it's odd Anders is serious. He wants to be a star."

"Doesn't everyone?"

Surprisingly, Maudie answered my rhetorical, not Josephine. "Why not? Especially if they've got it."

They used to call Clara Bow "The It Girl." It struck me as cheesy when I was a kid, and it still struck me as cheesy. If Anders was "The It Boy," it kinda got me in the pit of my stomach, but what the hell—good for him. It also struck me that Maudie the dresser was a mite defensive of this Anders character.

I got the conversation back on track. "This Maurice, he never called to say he was sick or that he had a sudden urge to visit Bora Bora?"

"He certainly did not. You can imagine the trouble we had then. I mean, Harvey only appears once in the show, but what a falafel to have him gone. Frank thought we could shove his dog into the rabbit suit, at least he'd be useful, but I said absolutely not. One can never tell if Frank is serious."

"How long's that been? I mean, the waiting for Har… I mean waiting for Maurice to come get his dog."

The sweet old thing closed both her round-as-a-button eyes, scrunched up her button mouth which crinkled her button nose, until she got it. "Three months, two weeks, and two days."

"No hours?"

She slapped my arm. It was like being hit with a feather duster. "Oh you. How did you know? Seven hours and thirty two minutes. We're all counting because there's a pool. I lost long ago. My wager was on less than a week."

"Anyone still got a chance?"

"Funnily enough, considering it's been just about forever

and poor Maurice has long since lost his part, such as it is, yes. Frank for one. And Cliff for another."

"Cliff?"

"Cliff Winker. He's not an actor. He doesn't even work here. But he's married to Glenda who does work here, so we see a lot of him. Judging by Cliff, it's quite nice that other husbands and wives stay home. Anyway, Cliff never comes into my room. He says poor Maurice's dog gives him the heebie-jeebies. I can't imagine why. God knows, there's nothing less scary than Maurice's dog. Especially since he seldom leaves his bed over there."

"Ah."

We'd conducted this conversation all the while a huge hairy dog was crashing about the dressing room with Jane attached to its throat.

"Personally," said Maudie Rivers, "I don't blame him."

I thought: why not? But it was too early for remarks like that.

## 9

It all ended when the big dog, exhausted, finally just sat his butt down near the door to the dressing room and let Jane stay there, swinging in air.

"Jane," I said, "you look ridiculous."

Since she couldn't yodel, her mouth otherwise occupied, she uncurled her tail and wagged it.

"You not only look ridiculous, but you're wasting everyone's time including your own."

Cary Grant's aunt laughed. Maudie seemed to of found something to do in the closet, moving dresses and coats around. "You know," said Josephine, "I think she understands you."

I said, "She knows exactly what I'm saying. Jane, if you don't let go, I'm watching *Lassie Gets Laid* without you."

Josephine'd been slathering cream on her face. She spun away from her mirror to yelp in a voice hot enough to toast bread. "You don't mean it? They wouldn't make a movie like that!"

Maudie Rivers—loved the name; do parents know what they're doing half the time? without any, how would I know?—chuckled. It was a low throaty chuckle, full of juice. For the first time—OK, the second or third time—I really looked at Josephine's dresser. Under that sweater and even with the glasses, she looked like she might be somebody. Like she had a personality inside somewhere. With a body to match.

I said, "Anything's possible."

Whether they would or they wouldn't, it did the trick.

Jane dropped away from the bigger dog, who backed away from her, then she trotted over to me, her eyes winking and blinking.

Josephine gasped. "I'd swear she's trying to say something to you."

"She is. She knows the Morse Code, but I never learned."

"You are one of the strangest men I've ever met, and that is certainly the strangest dog. I've never seen one with a forehead so wrinkled or such odd markings. So interesting."

"They're not markings. They're scars."

"Really? Even more interesting. It makes her look rather exotic. You know, strange things, strange places."

"Oh, I know, Miss, uh, Mrs.... "

"Josephine will do nicely."

"Can I call you Jo?"

"Not if you don't want me calling you Mo."

Mo? Hell no. Everybody I ever knew loved The Three Stooges—except me and maybe Mrs. Willingford. With Mrs. Willingford the topic never came up. But I was the only kid stuck in the Staten Island Home for Children who hated 'em. Correction: the only kid who wasn't a girl. Girls hated them for being coarse and stupid which is exactly why the boys, Paul and Lino included, loved 'em. But then, the male half of the species *were* mostly coarse and stupid. Even me. Who started wars? Old male farts. Who were dumb enough to let the old farts get them to die in those wars? Young male farts. Anyway, about the Stooges. What I hated them most for was they never made me laugh. Cringe, yes. Wince, yes. Groan, yep. But laugh, not once. So her calling me Mo or Larry or Curly was like getting called a dirty word. One *I* wouldn't even use.

"Fine. Now about Maurice, Josephine, what did he look like?"

"If I tell you, will you take his dog?"

Damn. Jane wasn't going to like it. We didn't have one of those open relationships; it was just me and her. Women, when I could get my hands on one, fine. But no dogs. And even if she didn't mind, I'd never be able to sneak this beast in anywhere.

But I was Bogie here. I was detecting. So I lied.

"Sure, you talk and I'll find a good home for the pooch. What's his name?"

"Maurice called him Bluto."

"Uhuh."

"You'll have to excuse me, Mr...."

"Sam Russo, Private Investigator."

"Oh, how thrilling. Are you really? I've never met a real live gumshoe. Have you met a gumshoe, Maudie? No?" Back to me. "Well, you just sit right there and 'rest your dogs'—the language you people speak, so colorful—while I get ready for tonight's performance, and we can just 'jaw away'."

So I asked her again what Maurice Oboram looked like, just to make sure my corpse was her Harvey.

"Well first, all our Harveys are tall, but he was very very tall. When one would meet him anywhere, it never failed to cause a certain amount of, to be kind, discomfort. I rarely saw his face full on. I can't imagine who did. He had a huge jaw that didn't come to a point like most people's jaws, but rather spread out so it was wider than the rest of his face. Everything about him was huge except one thing... "

I knew what that one thing wasn't, but I couldn't imagine what it was, so when I asked: "And that was?" I was eager.

"His voice. He had a beautiful voice. He was forever declaiming Shakespeare's sonnets. A nice change from some of the things one often hears backstage in a theater."

"I'll bet."

"And you'd win."

"How long was he in the show?"

"Oh, um, I do believe he joined us in—— "

"Firsa May. Eggzaktelly."

Josephine, Jane, Bluto, Maudie Rivers, and I all looked up at the door to Josephine's dressing room at the same time. In it stood the great Frank Fay, star of *Harvey* and a bunch of other things I couldn't name and wasn't going to try for. But it was Fay all right, and he, as us gumshoes would say, had had a snootful, was hosed, sozzled, blotto, loaded, sloshed, and generally at least nine over his limit. I couldn't be sure, but I'd make book zero was his limit.

If there'd been no door jamb to lean on, Fay would of had to lean flat out on the floor. As it was, he was slowly sliding down towards it.

"Oh dear. Oh dear," sighed Josephine, "and we go up in an hour."

"I heard that," said Fay, pulling himself back up with the help of the door handle. "The giant replaced whazzzizname on firsa Maaaaay, then fucking walked out fiffy firsa Maaaay. I'd only just got used ta yelling at 'im. But he left that mutt whish he never did do—always took 'is doggie home and brought 'is doggie back. We oughta eat that mutt. Nuff there for th'whole cast."

We were back where we started. Dogs. Maurice Oboram was pretty sure to be Lino Morelli's corpse. Oboram had played Harvey in *Harvey*. Oboram had a dog called Bluto. And then, for reasons unknown, he'd left the show from one performance to the next. But his dog was still here. I had to call that odd. It was a good job for an acting giant like Maurice, so what made him do it? An accident was still pretty likely—after all, the dog came back muddy and wet. So why didn't his dog go home after it happened, wherever home was? Why come back to the theater? Fay'd just said Maurice never left his dog. The real stumper was: why did Jane attack Bluto, Oboram's abandoned pooch? Come to think: how did she even know to bother attacking Oboram's dog? We were across the entire width of 48th Street and I at least was minding my own business, which when I thought about it, wasn't much of a business—maybe I should leave cards in likely places for a crime to occur, or light half the votive candles in St. Patrick's Cathedral for one of Mrs. Willingford's crowd to get "bumped off" or—

Suddenly, and I'm forced to admit happily, these brilliant thoughts were interrupted by a woman's cry—or maybe a man's. Who knew? We were, after all, in a working theater.

Not only Jane, but Bluto, were out the door so fast Fay fell straight over on his back and stayed there.

I think he was out cold. The booze or the dogs. Didn't really matter which.

I held Josephine's hand as she stepped daintily over his body, then, followed by Maudie, we all ran after the dogs, each of us making a beeline for the source of the scream.

Josephine had a few years on me. Plus her legs were twice as thick as well as twice as short. But Maudie was not only fast, she seemed to know where she was going. I was fourth in my group to reach the source of the screams, which had become more than screams, so much more you could describe them as one continuous shriek.

It wasn't coming from backstage; it was coming from *below* the stage. And to get there, we all had to crowd into some sort of prop shop or whatever, then through an open door, then down some rather steep wooden stairs. The only light at the bottom came from one bare 60 watt bulb and the open trap door above our heads. Keeping track as best I could, above our heads was the actual stage.

Jane arrived first, Bluto second (keeping, even in these circumstances, a safe distance from Mad Dog Jane), then a cluster of backstage workers (called stagehands? what they did wherever they did it, I had no idea), then Maudie, and then me. After us came the entire cast of *Harvey*. Cary Grant's auntie was a long way back but she kept on coming; the woman was a trouper. Slight surprise—the shrieker wasn't a woman, but a man. As soon as I saw him I figured whatever part he played in *Harvey* he was ready for it— unlike Fay back up there, out cold and blocking Josephine's doorway. Judging by his robes, the shrieker played a judge.

Josephine pushed herself through to the front of what had become a crowd, dogs included.

"Stop it, Mr. Kirk. You've more than got our attention."

Others were clambering down the dark stairs as she said this, including a dandy little blonde number and a guy maybe a little older than me I'd seen in the movies. Dammit. His name was right on the tip of my tongue. But no, like Josephine's last name, it wouldn't come.

Mr. Kirk stopped making so much noise, but Josephine hadn't finished speaking. "Explain yourself. The curtain goes up in less than an hour. Is Jimmy here? I'm sure we all know by now Mr. Fay won't be playing his part tonight." A hand waved from the sea of theatricals, one that belonged to a slender long-faced fella whose hair looked a lot more durable than he did. Hair seemed to be a motif at the 48th Street Theater. "Oh, thank goodness, Jimmy. I'm sure I speak for us all when I say how grateful—"

Jimmy stopped her. "You know I'd do anything for you, Miss Hull."

Aha. Josephine Hull. It would of come to me eventually.

Josephine flushed. "Oh for heaven's sake. Call me Josephine."

"Broadway can't keep a secret, Miss, ah, Miss... Josephine. Never could. News about Fay was on the street in an hour. I also had the time off."

Me, I didn't know from beans what they were talking about. What I was thinking was that someone on Broadway was keeping a terrific secret about Maurice Oboram. As for this Jimmy, I could see him as Elwood. But I could see him better as the guy who'd played a deputy sheriff who didn't believe in guns in *Destry Rides Again* and as the half cynical, half romantic second fiddle in *The Philadelphia Story* plus a handful of other movies, one of which I'd caught at the Stapleton Paramount just about the time I got that job in Saratoga Springs. The not-so-great movie was *Call Northside 777*. I could see him even better as Colonel James Stewart. My war was on the back of a horse. His was in a cockpit flying bombing missions over Germany. But I managed not to salute. Those days were over. Even so, good thing for me I was no girl. Not that Jimmy was swoon material, but he *was* a war hero and a movie star. I think he'd won one of those Academy Awards for something. But all that was entirely beside the point. A point which Josephine had not forgotten. "Now, Mr. Kirk, whatever *is* the matter?"

Ah ha. I'd just remembered where I'd seen the guy who was trying to push past to see what Mr. Kirk was making such a fuss about. He'd had a bit part in one of my all-time favorite movies: *Kiss of Death*. Much better than Stewart's movies by far. Not that *The Philadelphia Story* was bad, but it had that awkward gawky dame in it, Kate something. Her, I couldn't watch for two minutes. Anyway, not me, not anyone who'd seen *Kiss of Death* would ever forget Richard Widmark as Tommy Udo pushing that old woman in her wheelchair down a long flight of stairs. I would of asked the guy about it, but I got myself under control, pushed him back and moved up next to Josephine.

Mr. Kirk had one hand to his forehead which reminded me of a lousy Garbo flick called *Camille*, and the other pointed with great drama at something huddled on the floor by what I supposed were weights to pull on the trap doors. I leaned forward. The "something" was a body and around the body's neck was an electrical wire.

"Oh my god!" said Josephine. "It's Harvey."

## 10

"Harvey as in rabbit, or Harvey as in that was his name?"

I asked this as I squatted down to the level of the dead guy so I could feel for a pulse. No pulse. But he wasn't cold. He was warm. He couldn't of been dead very long. I was no expert, but solving Lino's cases and hot-footing it through a war told me he'd been alive at least an hour ago.

"Rabbit," sobbed Josephine, who then flung her small cylindrical self against Maudie's mysterious sweater covered chest. "It's Raymond. Why's he down here now?"

Interesting way to put the question. Not: why's he down here? But: why's he down here *now*?

She'd turned on the screamer. "For that matter, Mr. Kirk, what are *you* doing down here?"

Josephine would of made a great PI.

Mr. Kirk pointed straight up. We all looked, and by "all" I mean everyone who was anyone in the 48th Street Theater. That included Barney Google—which meant no one was manning the stage door. And that meant the killer could be strolling out just about now.

Kirk said, "The trap was open which it shouldn't be. So I was closing it. So I looked down into the trap room. So there was what looked like, I don't know—but it didn't look right. So I came down to check. And I... I... I... "

Josephine finished his sentence. "Started screaming. Oh dear oh dear, do we have to cancel tonight? I've never cancelled a performance, not in all my years on the boards."

"Never!" sounded a voice behind us. Frank Fay had made

it down the narrow stairs with the help of the two walls on either side of them. "Any ole rabbit can climb inna Harvey suit. Whaz it take? Shitting liddle roun' pellets?"

He had a point before he reached bottom, where, without walls, he fell over again.

All the while, hands stuffed deep into his jacket pockets, Jimmy had quietly stood looking down at the body. What he finally said was said just as quietly. "The man could have accidently fallen through the open trap, but the wire around his neck is no accident."

Another private dick. Actors were sure a versatile bunch.

"I suppose," said Josephine, "we really ought to call the police."

Just what I'd been thinking. Call the cops and then it was a movie for me and Jane. And then, just for me, maybe a late night club—the one at the top of the Chrysler Building.

"But why do that," continued the delightful Josephine, "when we have our own private detective right here with us?"

And with that she pointed at me as dramatically as Mr. Kirk had pointed at the trap door above our heads. "Ladies and gentlemen. May I introduce to you, Mr. Sam Russo, Private Investigator."

Now they were all looking at me. Even Maudie Rivers. Maudie, standing behind Josephine, looked like she'd never seen me before.

I looked back at all of them. So many faces to remember. So many suspects. One of 'em was probably the killer. I doubted the guy had strolled in off the street. He'd have to get past the goof guarding the stage door. And for that, he'd need Jane.

Did any one of 'em look like they'd just choked the life out of the big guy playing Harvey in *Harvey*? You could say that was a stupid question, but people who do bad things and then stand around trying to look innocent, don't always succeed. The stagehands, for instance, the ones bunched together under the trap door opening; they weren't staring at me or at what most people would stare at, a dead body, but at one of their own. This guy was looking at his shoes. Then he was looking at his fingernails. Then he looked at me. He had a face like Abe Lincoln, all angles and all the angles were the wrong angle. He needed a shave. He needed a haircut. He looked rattled enough to need a chair.

A few feet away from the stage hands were four women, two young, two not so young, all but one in shock, and the one not in shock had chosen hysteria instead. Lurking behind the women was the guy Jane'd followed down the alley and into the theater. From head to foot, he looked like money. You know the kind, gets born with everything going for him: cash in the bank, good teeth in his head, a face he could use to sell vacuum cleaners, a nice taste in clothes, a nice way of wearing them. Now I was closer, he smelled like an actor. That perfect hair sleek with hair oil, the straight nose, those cupid lips—although maybe the chin was weak.

I almost wanted to plant one on him.

He looked scared. But hell, I'd seen my share of crime scenes. Sometimes the cops looked scared.

This was the guy Josephine called odd and Maudie said had "it." There was that air about Anders Slydel—and it didn't come from the hair or the clothes. Maudie said he wanted to be a star. Funny, but I had a feeling that was the one thing he wasn't going to get. Whatever it was Jimmy had, that was what made a star.

"The It Boy" doing his best to keep low, made him all the more noticeable. Guys like Anders, nervous and sneaky, were the kinds of customers Lino was bound to concentrate on. He'd push 'em around, arrest 'em on suspicion, and have to let 'em go in the morning. Sometimes even earlier than that. Lino was always getting his feelings hurt when he'd find out maybe the guy had something to hide, but whatever it was, it was never that he'd done the dastardly deed.

Like the women.  One of the younger ones and one of the older ones were starting to really ham it up.  The hysteric was pretending she was about to faint.  If this was acting, and it was, she wasn't going far in her chosen profession.  The other, now out of "shock," was inching her way back up the stairs.  I noticed.  Josephine noticed.  Jane noticed.  Neither one came off half as nervous as Slydel.  He only got worse when Bluto wormed his way through the crowd so he could sit on the guy's correspondent shoes and lean on his wool coat.

Who did Josephine say walked the dog every day?  Anders Slydel.

I wasn't wrong.  This cream cake was Slydel.

Bluto looked mournful.  He was the only one at the death scene who did.

When my brain finally connected to my mouth, I said, "Sorry, Josephine.  You really do have to call the cops.  For one thing I'm here on another case— "

"You mean Mr. Oboram."

Not a question, a statement.  Maybe I should finally open that office, paint our names on the wire glass window of some door somewhere.  *Russo & Hull*.  Or *Hull & Russo*.  "I mean Maurice Oboram."

The guy whose name wouldn't come back, the one with a half smoked stogie clamped between his teeth, said, "The giant guy?  With the big mutt he brought with 'em every night?  That's him, over there, the one pissing on Noodle's leg.  Name's Bluto, right?"

Noodles?  Who was Noodles?

"Hey!  Fuck off ya fucking mutt!"

So now I knew who Abe Lincoln was.  He was someone called Noodles.  Noodles was a stagehand right out of the Dead End Kids.  The dopey one.  Only a lot older.

Bluto had his leg cocked and was just about to let go. I looked at Bluto. We all looked at Bluto. I'd never liked dogs. I still didn't like dogs. Obviously, Jane wasn't a dog.

"Bluto!" screeched Josephine. "Stop that!"

Bluto lowered his leg.

"Poor dog," said Maudie Rivers, "he's confused. First he lost Maurice, now he's lost Raymond. Raymond was the only person here who liked him."

Josephine patted Maudie's arm. "You like him. I like him."

Maudie smiled. It was a sad smile. "I don't like him, Josephine. I feel sorry for him."

"That's good enough, dear."

The stogie smoker hadn't blinked an eye. "Is that other thing a dog too? What hit it? And why's the giant a 'case'?"

I said, "Let me put it this way. It's none of your business."

The bit part player I'd seen in *Kiss of Death* wasn't buying that. "He never showed up one night. He left his dog here, the big hairy pisser. So Raymond took his role. So now Raymond's dead. And he ain't dead because he wanted to be dead. One missing Harvey and one dead Harvey. So what gives, shamus?"

Actors. Give me a horse any day. I suddenly felt like a greyhound in a pack of greyhounds—all chasing rabbits as fast as we could.

Dammit. I was the real PI here. I had a license and everything. I'd say: Sam Russo, Private Eye, when I answered my phone. That is, I'd say it when I remembered to say it. I'd just solved a case with three—three? it was four—four murders in it. I got shot. My dog got stabbed. I got paid for all this shooting and stabbing and solving things. So the hell with 'em all. I was the fastest dog here.

I said, "Somebody call the cops. It'll look bad if you don't. The cops will close the show; they have to. They'll tell every one of you to stick around. I'd do that if I was you."

"And you, Mr. Russo, what are you going to do?"

"Me, Josephine? I'm gonna take me and my dog to some quiet place—there must be a quiet place around here somewhere—and think."

"Use my dressing room. I'll go with you. Come along, Maudie. The show must go on even if it can't. And you, Jimmy, no having to take Frank's place tonight."

Jimmy said, "I like taking Frank's place, Josephine. But not like this."

Damn. I sure hoped he hadn't killed Raymond. I'd hate to see someone like Jimmy fry. But at least I knew what they'd been talking about a few minutes ago, the chat where he said "News travels fast on Broadway." A show like *Harvey* with a star like Fay needed a stand-in like Stewart.

Once again, only this time more feet belonging to more legs on more people, we all stepped over Fay and went back to where we'd all come from. That included Bluto.

My guess is they were used to Mr. Frank Fay since no one bothered to help him up, or even wake him up. His fellow thespians and the crew of the 48th Street Theater left him there with another dead Harvey.

I figured someone would call the cops.

It wouldn't be me. I was just a visitor here. Just a simple PI over from Staten Island with a friend visiting the big shiny city.

## 11

For years now, I'd been called out to look at Lino's bodies. There weren't all that many, it being Staten Island, but there'd been enough. I'd had my own cases, penny ante stuff for the most part—until Saratoga Springs. There I'd been the first person to see a recently deceased personage: namely that first class goofball, Carroll Goose, who couldn't do the simplest thing right, like drug a racehorse or run for it when things looked bad. But I'd never been Johnny-on-the-spot when someone got murdered.

I suddenly realized what this meant. It meant Jane and me couldn't leave the 48th Street Theater if we'd wanted to. And we wanted to. There were ice skaters to watch, movies to sneak her into—and what about food? I was beginning to get that cocktail feeling.

As the fat half of my favorite comic duo said: Lino'd landed me in another fine mess.

Raymond was definitely murdered. True, he could of accidentally fallen through the open trapdoor, but who opened one of the doors in the floor of the stage? And why? Plus, who wouldn't notice a great big hole and just walk around it? But if he *had* fallen through, who put a wire around his neck once he hit the ground fifteen feet below and who pulled it tight? Was it done because the fall hadn't killed him?

As for suicide, I've heard of a million ways to do yourself in, but self-garroting? Nope. Not once. You pass out too soon and your grip lessens.

There was a glaring conclusion here. One even Lino

would notice. Raymond was murdered and so was Maurice. Raymond wasn't a giant. He was maybe three or four inches over six feet tall. It wasn't some giant killer out there. Raymond and Maurice played Harvey, a rabbit, a pooka. I'd asked Josephine what a pooka was. She'd said it was a spirit. A large invisible spirit. It could be nice. It could be not so nice. It was a shape-shifter. If a pooka wanted to be seen, a pooka could be seen: as a horse, a bird, a cow, even an ass. In *Harvey* he wanted to be seen as a huge rabbit, but only by Elwood P. Dowd, aka Frank Fay, currently keeping company with my latest corpse.

Raymond, last name LeGrand, was an actor. He would be with a name like that. Maurice Oboram and Raymond LeGrand. Two large murdered actors who'd played Harvey. Were there more? I'd already asked Josephine that. She said the Harveys of every Show Past, so far as she knew—and she knew a lot being a mainstay of Broadway—were all still breathing. She said one old Harvey was a few blocks away working in a revue, or something near enough to a revue, called *Make Mine Manhattan*.

I lay back on Josephine's couch, blew smoke rings at Josephine's ceiling and drank vintage port Maudie'd provided from a secret stash. Too sticky, too sweet, too cute, but better than nothing. Should I call Lino, report my findings, then take a powder? He'd sent me here. His department was footing the bill. So? Call Lino?

Not on your nellie. Any time now, Josephine and I, as well as everyone else in the building, were going to get grilled by real New York City cops. Josephine was shining with delighted expectation. I had no idea what Maudie was shining with. It looked a little like fear. But cops scared people. Innocent or guilty, it was a gut reaction. Even Lino scared people. But me, I was beginning to cheer up. Raymond LeGrand wasn't my problem. As soon as they showed up, he was the problem of the New York City Police

Department.

I looked at Bluto and he looked at me. The bright pink skin under his eyes hung like Droopy's. The tip of his pale pink tongue dangled out one side of his mouth. Noticing this, he sucked it in, moved it around in there for a second, then let it hang out the other side. A line of drool made its way down his tongue and plopped onto the worn carpet. I was beginning to wonder if maybe Jane, being African, wasn't really a dog. As for Bluto, who was for sure a dog, he lived in Josephine's dressing room when he wasn't out walking with Anders, an Anders who let him lean on his fine wool coat. I'd never seen one like it. Maybe on Gary Cooper, but on a kid with a supporting role in a play? That coat cost more than his week's salary.

I make book on that.

Now if Raymond *were* my case, I didn't think I'd be getting much out of Oboram's dog. Except maybe I had. Why did Bluto think of taking a piss on Noodles, the stagehand? Was that mutt saying something?

I was doing it again. I couldn't help it. I was thinking of Bogie. Would Bogart lie around on his ass sipping port in an old dame's dressing room with a nice fresh murder to look into? The hell if he would. A whole load of New York City cops were on their way. As soon as they got here, they'd trample all over everything, push everyone around, especially me, because—what the fuck was I doing here? Also because they'd find the license in my wallet and I'd be damned if I was sitting for hours in some bare room in some bare precinct getting the first degree for this mess.

If Raymond was lucky, one, maybe two of 'em, would have more brains than Lino. But probably not. So far, this had not been Raymond LeGrand's lucky day.

I'd spent my time on the couch. Jane had spent hers making sure Bluto knew his place. Josephine, even with her show cancelled for the night, had been dressed for her part by Maudie, but painted her own face. After that Maudie busied herself doing whatever dresser maids did, ironing nylons and polishing curling irons. Josephine'd settled down to read *Photoplay*. Rita Hayworth took up most of the cover. They could of found a better pic. The one they used, Rita practically fell off the edge of the slick paper looking about as wacky as Red Skelton. I didn't know that could be done with Hayworth.

Even with a fellow actor, newly and mysteriously dead—the show must go on. I figured if Josephine couldn't perform, she could at least read about performers.

"Mr. Russo?"

"Yes, Josephine?"

"Has anyone ever told you, you bear a remarkable resemblance to Robert Mitchum?"

Not that again. I might have to grow a beard. "Not really, no. But tell me about Raymond. Just the highlights will do."

"Well... not to speak ill of the dead."

"Go on. It's just us and the dogs."

"Raymond was not liked."

Behind her, Maudie said, "The guy was a crumb."

Josephine sighed, "I'm afraid that's true."

"Why?"

"Well, let's see. If you were to mix into a great big pan all the reasons a man might cause offense to absolutely anyone, and put the pan in an oven, you would have baked our Mr. Raymond LeGrand."

"So you're saying his passing will not cause grief?"

"Oh heavens no, I'm not saying that at all. His passing has closed the show. Think of the cast and crew! My goodness, think about tonight's audience! So very many affected. As for me, I haven't missed a night since we opened."

That did it. Paid or unpaid, was I a PI or wasn't I a PI? Was there a damsel in distress or was there not a damsel in distress? I set down my port and hopped off her couch. "Watch Jane for me, OK?"

"Gladly, dear. Maudie won't let her hurt Bluto. Are you off to solve this?"

"I'm off to have a try."

"Do try hard. One show missed is all I can stand."

With that, I was out her door and back to the prop shop and the door that led to the area beneath the stage.

Seems I wasn't the first to have that idea. Not even close.

Frank was still there, snoring happily just where we'd left him, but the rest of the people under the stage were sober, somber, and each in their own way lurking near the body of Raymond. Perhaps lurk is a little strong, but now I was on the case, everyone was a suspect—if Nick Charles didn't say that, I don't know who did.

And if "everyone" wasn't the entire cast and crew of *Harvey*, it was most of 'em. The hubbub was muted but it was still a hubbub.

Two things I noticed right off the bat was that Anders Slydel seemed to think he was a real doctor. He was gracefully poised in his doctor costume taking the dead man's pulse. Since a dead man doesn't have a pulse, he kept trying to find it up and down Raymond's dead arm. I thought that was pretty damn creepy. The second thing I noticed was the stagehands. They were pushing each other around, calling each other names, and the one who pushed the hardest was Noodles.

One fist raised, the other rising, Noodles said, "Say that again and I'll paste you one."

The guy he was saying that to, a gorilla in a man's suit, said, "Why, I oughta— "

"You oughta what? Who owed the most around here? Com'on. Spit it out. Who owed the most?"

That got 'em all distracted by getting 'em counting on

their fingers.

Three of the four remaining women had become a huddle over a barrel. It was like that scene from Maurice's *Macbeth*, the one about bubbles and cauldrons and trouble. The dame who'd snuck back up the stairs in the first bloom of excited horror, was still gone. Somewhere.

The only one just standing there looking down at the body was Jimmy, and the look on his long slender face was about the saddest I'd ever seen. Sadder than Flo's when they took Mister meekly away in cuffs, or Mister's when they threw a struggling foul-mouthed Flo into the back of a separate paddy wagon.

Aside from Jimmy, there were only two others who weren't yakking away a mile a minute. One was a guy I'd seen in the clot of acting types all come running when Mr. Kirk was doing his screeching number. He wasn't old and he wasn't young, not good-looking, not bad-looking. Normally he'd be somebody you barely noticed—except for the rug. If he'd paid two bits for the thing, he'd been fleeced. Come to think, real fleece slapped on his dome would of looked better. And the other was the classy little bottled blonde I'd noticed before. Very classy and very small. Not small enough to fall on the freak side of the line, but small enough. As for looks, she wasn't Carole Lombard—there'd never be another Lombard—but she was nice enough. Even dressed as a small nurse. Considering all I'd gone through after my last case, another nurse was the last thing I needed. Even a cute little blonde pretending to be a nurse.

These two were sitting together on a large crate, a few feet from all the action, the guy with his arm around the blonde while she did some stage weeping into a huge hanky. Well, maybe it was real weeping. I only assumed it was staged because of what Josephine'd told me. Josephine could be wrong. Maybe this one was Raymond's only friend?

At this point, who cared? The real question was: who was his worst enemy?

## 12

Ignoring the mob, for the second time I crouched down by the very dead body of Raymond LeGrand which made Anders, the dog-walking "Let's Pretend" doctor, get up and move away, embarrassed. Raymond was still warm. Not warm enough to get him going again, but warm enough to remind me he'd been alive a couple hours ago. The wire around his neck was electrical for sure—even Sam Russo knew an electric wire when he saw one. It wasn't long and it wasn't short. Just a bit of wire left lying about like all the other theatrical debris I saw everywhere. And just long enough and thin enough to do the job. Raymond was lying there stage left or stage right—one or the other, these people had their own way of talking about stages—the pressure from the wire strong enough to bite into his skin, deep enough to turn it purple. Whoever did this hadn't done it come all prepared with a nice coil of piano wire. They simply grabbed the closest available wire, meaning the electrical wire, wrapped it around the guy's neck and pulled tight. What this told me was that it wasn't premeditated. It was more like a sudden overwhelming rage. Or a need. Or both stuck together. It also smelled of sudden opportunity.

Judging from the lips pulled back from the long yellow teeth, the unflattering cast to his face, the half opened protruding eyes—still blue, but the color ruined by all the red caused by broken blood vessels—I'd say whoever had done it, did it with everything they had. In other words, they meant business. Maybe Raymond fought. I checked his hands. Neither looked like they'd gotten under the wire before it was too late. It had to be a big surprise for a big man who would of flattened his killer if he'd seen what was coming.

Raymond was not dressed as a rabbit. Considering he didn't show up in the play until near the end, and then only as a suggestion to give the audience a thrill, why get ready with everyone else?

More info from Josephine. Raymond LeGrand, actor, spent most of the play's running time in his usual get-up: slacks, suspenders, shirt, the usual tie, the usual hat, playing poker with the stagehands. Sometimes management joined in the game, sometimes an actor or two. Fay was a regular. So was the guy with a bit part in *Kiss of Death*. So was Doc Anders. And so was one of the younger women, the one who played Josephine's daughter. This was the one who'd made a quick departure my first time down here.

One time only Josephine and Maudie sat in. Josephine lost two dollars and excused herself. Maudie stuck around a little longer and lost a little more.

Seems Raymond did that for hours longer than he ever had to walk around in a rabbit suit. He did it right here where he died. Glancing round, I saw what I hadn't seen before. Up against a wall was a folding table. Along with the table were a lot of folding chairs. So Raymond got bumped off in his own domain, the 48th Street Theater trap room gambling den. It seemed fitting. Not that murder is fitting, not for anyone. Ever.

My mother made an appearance here, filling up my heart, but I pushed her away. Like I always did.

I glanced up at the ceiling which was also the floor of the stage. There were a lot of traps up there, each one numbered. I couldn't see which number was painted on the underside of the open trap but it had to be running along with all the rest, which made it Number 18. Did he really fall through that trap? Is that how he wound up down here this time? If he did, he was either having a severe dizzy spell, or was as drunk as Fay, or someone pushed him. I sniffed. He hadn't been drinking. That left dizzy or pushed. Who could push a guy this big? If someone could, wouldn't he of let out a surprised yell? Until the curious Mr. Kirk, no one, so far, had said they noticed a thing. It'd all been a big surprise to everyone.

Or so they said.

I also took note of where his body was. Not under the trap, but about five feet from the back wall. Again, who could drag someone this big even a foot, much less five feet? Or did he land, and begin to crawl? Hard to tell even though the floor was dirty enough to have marked his trail. Trouble was, so many feet shuffling around for a better view ruined whatever Raymond had, or had not, done.

I felt his legs. If he'd broken a bone, then I'd be pretty sure he'd fallen. Nothing. Maybe an ankle?

"I don't think he fell."

That was Jimmy speaking. I knew it without looking up. It was that voice. I looked up anyway.

"OK. So he didn't fall. What do you think happened here?"

"You know, Mr. Russo, I've been thinking about that."

"Call me Sam."

"Well Sam, I think the trap being opened was so we'd find him."

"Interesting point. The play doesn't use the trap door?"

"No need for it. Ever. If it hadn't been open, we might not notice the fella was here until, well, until… "

"He began to stink?"

By now most of *Harvey* had shut up and were listening intently. On the word "stink," Noodles snorted. He said, "Nah. We play poker here all the time. We'd of found him."

"What I meant to say," said Jimmy, "was not until he didn't appear as Harvey."

Before I could even begin to think what a nice soft-spoken unassuming guy this Jimmy was, up rose such a wailing from the tiny blonde nurse and such a lot of loud tut-tut-tutting from the guy under the cheap rug, all talking stopped like a car hitting a wall, and Jimmy and I both jumped in place.

"Oh poor Ray," wailed the blonde, "poor poor Ray. No one knew him like I did. He wasn't what you all think he was."

My first thought, after getting a load of the cast of *Harvey*, was the cute little blonde had maybe seen a side of Raymond no one else saw because Raymond saw a side of the blonde a lot of guys would of liked to see better. My second thought was the guy who never left her side didn't find her sympathy for Raymond all that wonderful.

But that was cynicism for you. Once cynicism gets a grip—about the time you're in a war with horses against tanks and the admittedly starving guys on your side eat their gallant mounts without a second thought, and about the time you find out your mother was only a knocked-up kid who got murdered by the guy hired to take care of her, and about the time you find out your good old "friend" holding a gun on you tells you he knew about your mother all along, that he thought it was funny you didn't know you'd spent your youth playing on her makeshift grave, and about the time he shoots you, not once, but three times—well, a guy can lose a little faith in the human race.

Turning away from the histrionics, Jimmy and I continued the conversation.

I said, "You think he came down here on his own?"

"I would think so, yes."

"Why come down when the show was about to go on and his usual suckers all busy? Did he do that a lot?"

"I really couldn't say, Sam. But then I'm only here, meaning in this theater, now and again. I played the part last year and this year, two months each time." Jimmy nodded his head towards Frank Fay. Seen through the legs of the crowd under the stage, he looked like he was coming round.

"Unreliable?"

"What do you think?"

We both spared a glance for the mumbling Fay.

"When you're not here, where are you?"

"I'm doing pretty well, getting work again. Kinda worried I wouldn't, being gone so long. You know, the war."

"I know the war. I was in it."

"Thought you would be. Where?"

"Pacific."

"Navy?"

"Nope. Cavalry. Philippines."

It took Jimmy a minute to find his wits. "Horses? You were part of the bunch who rode horses against Japanese artillery?"

"Yeah."

"Damn. I'm humbled. Matching wars with a guy like you."

"I'm no hero, Jimmy. You are."

"Sure. Whatever you say, Sam."

Changing the subject seemed a good idea. "But you're getting work?"

"I just did something for Hitchcock and something with Joan Fontaine, just about to do some other damn thing. This—"

"This" meant Harvey.

"—is a favor to the director and to Josephine. When Fay's on a bender, like now, folks are told he's 'on vacation' and I get to play a great part."

"Some vacation."

Jimmy thought about laughing, but considering the circumstances, decided against it. "Say. I heard you talking about Maurice. Is he dead too?"

"Pretty much."

"Murdered?"

"I think so. Pretty sure."

"My God, now that's a crying shame. I didn't know him well, but we'd talk now and again. The man had a sound mind and a warm heart. He had his dreams like we all do. He would have made a fine actor, a fine actor."

"Except for being typecast?"

"That's it exactly. And there wasn't a damn thing he could do about it. But he bore his lot as bravely as any man I saw under fire." Jimmy was talking to his shoes. I don't think he wanted me to see his eyes. "I always meant to do something for him, and I would have, I surely would have." His head came up, fast, his fists closed. "You'd think, if anyone was going to get themselves murdered, it'd be— "

I finished that one for him. "Fay."

Apparently, this was Frank's cue. He was up off the floor and standing where we were standing almost in a leap. It was done pretty well for a drunk with his hat still on. Snatching it off, he licked his fingers, smoothed down his tousled hair, and slapped the hat back on. No tie to straighten, no shirt buttons to check. His shirt was open at the collar, the better to display a rather large gold crucifix.

"My God, is that a dead body?"

"It is," said I.

More wailing from the nurse, more comforting from the rug.

Fay leaned so far over, Jimmy put out an arm to make sure he didn't fall on the corpse. Fay said, "Hey, that's Ray."

A brilliant deduction. I wanted to say it but I didn't. Jimmy, a generous man, also bit his tongue saying only, "It was."

I liked Jimmy. I liked him a lot. Until I remembered what any shamus knows. Anyone could of done the deed, including a really nice movie star war hero. All it took was a real good reason and the kind of moxie I didn't have. The only people I ever killed were people trying to kill me. And I only did it then, because my own side would of killed me for not killing the enemy. Funny thing about that, not too many years had passed since the world's two biggest bombs exploded over a couple of Jap cities, and here we were looking like friends again.

Oh right, the world was full of friends.

Fay looked at his fellow cast, at his crew, at Jimmy, at me, at the rug and the blonde. "Well, OK, so he's dead. So this means all debts are cancelled which is swell since I practically owed this creep my apartment. OK, Glenda, where are the cops?"

I now knew I was looking at Glenda. Or it was Glenda ever since she'd decided to become an actress and a blonde. For all anyone knew, her name was really Gertie Hashslinger and her hair was the shade of dead rat. Glenda's little head jerked up. "I... where are the cops, Cliff?"

The guy with the ludicrous hairpiece was Cliff, the one Bluto gave the heebie-jeebies to, heebie-jeebies bad enough to keep him out of Josephine's dressing room. "I should know, Glennie? Beats me."

I said, "You guys telling me not one of you people called the cops?"

They all stared at me like I was their director or something, like they'd all forgotten their lines. Even Jimmy.

The guy whose name I couldn't remember spoke up for them all. "What I think is, I think everyone thought someone else had done it. That's for sure what I thought."

"Oh for Christ sakes," I said. "I'll call 'em."

I was getting up from the floor so I could drop a nickel in the closest pay phone, when I noticed something on the corpse's left arm. It'd been hidden by his shirt sleeve but my moving had accidently pushed that up a bit. Not good. First rule of business is Don't Touch Anything. But I had, and having done it, I pushed the sleeve up farther.

In blue ink someone had written *Beware the Tides of March*. Big block letters. Sloppy but easily read. And fresh, very fresh.

They weren't there when the universally admired LeGrand was still alive and kicking. Call it a hunch, but I was sure of that.

## 13

You have to call the cops when a murder is committed. In a lot of cases, especially if you didn't do the dastardly deed, this is a good thing. The police show up, they ask a lot of questions, they take the body away. They solve it or they don't solve it, and life goes on. But if you're a PI and the murder looks like being a case you might or might not be working on, calling the police is a bad thing. They show up, they take the body away, and because you're the one person who isn't supposed to be at the scene, but mostly because cops hate private snoops, you get more attention than a new exhibit at the zoo.

An even worse result of calling the cops was with a case like this case you get every newshound in New York City barking at your heels.

I called the cops anyway.

Before they got there: sirens wailing, night sticks twirling, guns on display, detectives poking people in the chest, and generally scaring everyone, especially the guilty party, as well as taking up a lot of valuable time roughing me up—the only person I knew for a dead cert was innocent—I did what I could.

Glenda was, surprise, an actress. She was twenty two years old, or so she said, and she called herself Glenda Gordon. The real surprise was that Cliff was her legit husband. He wasn't an actor. He wasn't rich. He wasn't good looking. His last name wasn't Gordon, it was Winker. Cliff Winker wasn't much of anything but an average Joe in love with his little blonde wife. Hair concerns ran in their family. Christ, hair concerns ran in the whole show. Glenda wasn't a real blonde. Maudie Rivers covered herself like a prize knitter, yet wore her hair like Betty Grable. From what I could tell, LeGrand had hair thick enough to use as a carpet sweeper.

Most of the crowd had drifted back up the stairs as I made the call, most of which I'd loved to question. Actually, all of which. But Glenda and Cliff stayed put. So I got to ask at least them: where had they been when Raymond was getting his? Cliff said he'd only just got to the theater. Said he came every night and watched the show from the wings, then walked wifey home afterwards. I looked at Glenda when I heard that. How'd she feel about the Constant Hubby? I could sum that one up in one word: confined. Glenda, still whiffling into a hanky, said she was in the dressing room she shared with most of the rest of the cast. Only Frank Fay and Josephine Hull had private dressing rooms.

Neither Mr. nor Mrs. Glenda had seen Raymond before whatever happened to him, happened. Neither had seen the open trap door.

Jimmy, who was now pacing out the distance from the trap door to the body, said he wasn't in the theater at all. Only between roles in a movie, and helping out *Harvey's* director, he'd been spending his time just before the show went on each evening down the street eating dinner at a quiet little French place. No, he hadn't been alone. When he was lucky, he was with a girl called Gloria. Tonight he'd been lucky. Yes, she'd say the same thing. Knowing Frank was on a bender and that he might go on and then again he might not, Jimmy said he always strolled in at the last minute to give Fay a chance to pull a rabbit out of a hat.

I thought that was an interesting way to put it.

Frank, sitting on an unfolded folding chair he'd placed under the open trap, and smoking, listened to Glenda and Cliff and Jimmy with as much attention as he could muster.

When they were done, he spoke as if the chair were something a pope sat on.

"I begin," he pontificated, "not that it's any of your business— " (that part was addressed to me; I ignored it) " —by saying I am *not* on a bender. I've merely had a few drinks." That comment got him a few suppressed laughs from all listening except me. As a "professional," I was supposed to be serious here. "As for Mr. Glenda, I saw him an hour ago hovering around the dressing rooms. I assumed he was keeping an eye on his wife. As usual."

Glenda shot "Mr. Glenda" a glance that could of peeled old show posters off a brick wall. Cliff turned a loud shade of pink.

Fay was still having a good time. "I too had a peek into the communal dressing room. I did not see Glenda."

Glenda had something to say about that. "I was in the can, Frank. Ever think of that?"

Fay nodded at her with a lopsided smile. "I try not to. Now, Jimmy here, I've never heard Jimmy lie, ever. But there's always a first time for everything."

Jimmy took that like I'd seen him take everything that had so far happened, with grace and quiet humor. Busy inspecting the knot in the electric wire around Raymond's neck, he said nothing.

But I did. I said, "And where were you, Mr. Fay?"

Fay stood up and stretched. When he'd finished doing that, he yawned. "Oh, here and there. But to answer your real question, I did not kill Raymond LeGrand. His career was already doing that nicely enough. I mean, wearing a rabbit suit, no lines. Where was that going?"

"Well," I said, "basically, it took two people off to see their maker."

I got a lot of attention with that crack. Two people? They didn't know about Maurice. Unless one did. And then I was up the stairs and gone before anyone could ask what

I meant, and before the cops and newshounds got here and messed with all the people I hoped to question.

The results were pretty much the same results I got when I worked for, with, and around Lino: not one story jibed with any other story. The actor with the unremembered name had been out back in the alley. Why? To get some air. No one had seen him. Most of the cast, male and female, who shared the lesser dressing room said they'd been in it. No one recalled who was also in it with them. Anders was in the Green Room going over his lines. He'd only had his part a year and was still trying for just the right tone. Being alone, he hadn't seen anyone at all. And no one had seen him.

I'd discovered an interesting fact. People in the theater were, to be kind, self-absorbed. A few noticed Fay being "here and there" but as for being anywhere in particular when Raymond died, not one of 'em had a clue. Moving quickly on to the stagehands, things were different. They were paid to pay attention. But not to the actors. They were paid to pay attention to the theater and the shows the theater chose to put on. Not one of 'em said they'd dropped the trap door. Not one of 'em had noticed it open. Especially Noodles. He didn't tell me why he got stuck with a name like that, but he did tell me, maybe three times, he hadn't noticed the trap door, open or closed.

Not one of 'em had a good word for Raymond LeGrand. One of 'em spent a whole lot of time grousing about how much he owed the big dead cheating jerk and how he couldn't prove the jerk cheated, so he'd been thinking of selling everything he had to pay up. If he didn't, Raymond had said he'd get his. In mid-grouse, he suddenly woke up, like Fay before him, to the fact that with Raymond dead, he was off the hook. I never saw a wider grin. That grin could of swallowed a plate sideways. If he was faking it, he was a better actor than most of the real cast. And then there was Noodles again. Noodles said something interesting.

"Check his locker. Betcha he's got markers from everyone here, even those who don't play cards." I was thinking: does that mean what I think it means? when the grouser said, "So what? They ain't worth nothin' no more." So Noodles said, "How true, Eddie, but the names on the markers gotta be interesting to the cops or to some other guy who'd wanna know who needed him dead."

That was exactly what I'd thought it meant. Noodles winked at me. I resisted winking back. It was easy. I didn't like people who wink. I didn't like smart asses. I didn't like Noodles because he'd winked at me. I didn't like anyone but Jane. And Josephine. And maybe Jimmy.

All this, by the way, was done at top speed, and got a lot speedier when the sound of approaching sirens rattled the air.

Three more things. Josephine was right. The cast had no taste for Raymond either, some to the point of downright hatred. To a man, and maybe even a few women, they all owed Raymond money. Like Fay, some of 'em owed him a lot of money. Most were still playing in the vain hope of winning some of their losses back. It didn't happen that way. Raymond LeGrand continued to rack up the markers and laughed while he did it. Eddie wasn't the only one who thought he was a cheat. Seems Raymond didn't give a good goddamn what anyone thought.

Right about then, Jimmy had caught up with me.

In a quiet aside, he said, "Sam, now don't get me wrong, but you're a real private eye, am I correct?"

"You are."

"Did you notice the knot in the wire?"

"Do you mean did I notice that whoever tied it had no idea how to tie a knot?"

"Yes, that's what I mean."

"And did you mean it's the kind of knot a girl or a kid or a man who acted for a living would tie?"

"I meant that too."

"Then yes, I noticed the knot."

## 14

Once upon a time, there was this horse—for me it always came back to horses. Racehorses and war horses. This one was a war horse. It wasn't my horse. It was some other sad chunk of cannon fodder's horse. No offense to the two horses I rode on Luzon, great hearted beauties, both of them, but I spent half my war coveting his horse. His horse was huge, tireless and fearless. Also lucky. Or so it seemed.

Where others fell, man and beast, he was always left standing. Reminded me of the only thing left alive at Custer's arrogant and idiotic Last Stand, the Battle of Little Big Horn—a horse called Comanche. As a reward, Comanche was one of only two horses ever to be buried with full military honors. How they did that for Comanche and also stuff him for a museum exhibit has always puzzled me. Even more puzzling was why they didn't stuff Custer.

There was also a dog who survived, a yellow bulldog, or so they say. Never did hear what became of him.

Anyway, turned out the tireless part about this war horse was true. Turned out the fearless part was also true, even if you chalked it up to the fact the horse was deaf. The horrendous racket going on all around him meant pretty much nothing since he couldn't hear it. But lucky? Not on the day his luck ran out. The big horse wasn't brought down by careening over cannons or racing along a line of constant gunfire. He was brought down by a hole in the ground made by the rooting snout of a Filipino pig. Broke both front legs. I cried when they shot him. But I did it privately. For one of the few times on Luzon the killing was a mercy killing. So I guess he was lucky after all.

Which showed me we're all lucky, but only for as long as it lasts.

For kids like my mother, her luck lasted long enough to survive getting born—if you could call her birth lucky, considering what the rest of her short life was to bring. For guys like Lucky Lindy, luck had lasted a lifetime, except for hiccups like the missing baby business—concerning which I'd always had my own private thoughts, none of which would go down well with his admirers. On second thought, Charles Lindbergh wasn't dead yet. His luck could run out any day. I had my hopes.

So, about this war horse whose name I had not forgotten: Rufus, he was all I could think of as I rushed around backstage asking questions about Raymond. Two dead rabbits. Maurice Oboram and Raymond LeGrand. Both were huge, both survived for ages in the world of the spit 'em out theater, and both seemed unashamed of playing the part of a very large bunny. I'd call that fearless.

Then, like Rufus, their luck ran out.

Questions for Sam Russo: were the deaths of Maurice and Raymond connected? Answer: ask another one, moron. Of course they were connected. Both of 'em were large, in the case of Oboram, enormous, and they both played Harvey in *Harvey*. The big difference between the two big men was that one had a dog, had actual talent, and was likeable, and the other didn't have talent or a dog but did clean out his fellow theatricals as often as he could. Another question: were they killed because something was rotten in the state of Denmark, or because a wild pig had dug a hole for grubs?

Talking to this one and that one, two things happened at once. The police rushed in from the lobby doors, filling the aisles with sound and fury on their way to the stage. And Jane bit my ankle. Just a nip really, meant to remind me she needed food, maybe more of my attention than she was getting, and a walk. The walk most of all.

I barely had time to tell her she'd have to hold it, before the cops were shouting for everyone to remain where they were, not to even think of leaving the building. For all they or I knew, some could already of made their exit—but if they had, there was still one hell of a lot of people left. The actors and stagehands, but also ushers and box office and personnel in offices I didn't know existed.

Lucky for me, being so many and packed so tightly on the stage, they covered my own exit with Jane, stage left or right... anyway, one or the other.

We had a lot of sleuthing to do. Waiting our turn to get our minds, our pride, and our pockets picked by bullies with badges would be no help at all.

Sound is supposed to carry in a theater, and believe me, it does, so I'd decided the best place to hear everything, though not necessarily take all of it in, would be far above the crowded stage. Quietly moving along a catwalk I'd found thanks to Jane, belly to the ground behind me (she was making one helluva personal assistant), we ran right into Maudie Rivers and Bluto.

Fuck.

I knew why I was up there—the better to hear and see things—but I hadn't a clue why she was. With Bluto.

The bulky Bluto was trying his best to hide behind Maudie. I would too if I was facing Jane. She wasn't big, but she was bad. Spotting Bluto, she got worse.

I said, "Fancy meeting you here."

Maudie Rivers said, "Shouldn't you be down there with everybody else?"

I said, "Shouldn't you?"

She said, "Bluto needs his walk and as you can see, Anders is not available to do that."

I looked down on the stage. Who could miss a man with

such shining hair and such a jaunty self-satisfied air? He had a cop in his face, but like all the rest, he was doing fine with the cop in his face. I looked at Maudie. I'd heard how she'd said the name "Anders." There was a caress in it. There was also a hiss. Was she sweet on him? Had he been sweet on her but was now sweet on someone else? Or what?

I said, "Jane needs a piss. Any ideas?"

She said, "I would suggest the men's toilet."

"Good idea. Jane, I swear, soon as I'm able, you're off to the can."

Maudie stared at me. I stared at her. I'd long since learned staring back was the best way to get people to stop staring. This time it didn't work like that. She stared some more. She said, "I heard you talking to Mr. Stewart. You were in the war?"

"Everybody was in the war."

"But you rode a horse? I've heard about you and your horses. You ate them."

Every muscle in my body stiffened at once. I wanted to knock her flat. I wanted to cry on her shoulder. I wanted her to know I didn't do it, I didn't do it.

"You chopped 'em up and boiled 'em in big ol' pots. What's a horse taste like, Mr. Russo?"

And *then* she walked away, taking Bluto for his walk inside since she wasn't allowed outside.

That left me leaning over a low metal railing, my brains spinning, my gut churning, trying not to be sick on the melee far below. Everyone was talking at once; being actors the talking carried all the way to the back of the house reeking of lines learned in other plays, other theaters. Throughout the histrionics, the detective in charge delivered his own histrionics, barking out orders, stomping about the set, his questions spitting out like machine gun bullets. Did the victim notice the open trap? Did he lean over to peer down? Did he hope a rich game was in progress? Did he get pushed?

Did the pusher then rush down the stairs to finish him off? Was there any physical evidence of any of this? And all the while he picked up and put down props—in other words, he messed with most of the possible evidence.

It was a great show.

By then, at least six cops were running for the door to whatever theater people called the space under the stage while everyone else kept their distance from the open trap.

Over all sailed the high pitched, slightly slurred, voice of Frank Fay playing Elwood P. Dowd for the cop trying to question him. If all the rest weren't speaking themselves, they'd of heard him clearly. Jane and I certainly did. He was saying: "And now, I'd like to introduce you to my best friend and closest confidante, Harvey. Say hello Harvey. To whom? This is... I'm sorry, officer, but you haven't given me your name."

I searched for Jimmy. Ah, there he was, relaxing on a sofa, his legs crossed, the top of his head looking as composed as the rest of him always did. And there was Josephine, right beside him. Jimmy was holding her hand as she spoke to the cop who questioned her. He needn't have. I could tell the cop was as charmed by her as I was. I could also tell he was stage struck. Two famous faces right in front of him, both paying him close attention. His wife and kids were going to hear about it forever.

Of course, anyone could of killed Raymond LeGrand. *I* might of killed him if I worked here. It certainly sounded like the notion could get mighty tempting. The place was crawling with suspects. And the motive was a good one. Losing as much as some of 'em had, seemed incentive enough to slip that electrical wire around his neck and then pull like a Percheron. Then there was Maurice Oboram—not that the cops knew anything about Maurice. They probably wouldn't care if they did. But for me, impossible to think the murders of two large Harveys were unconnected.

What was going on here?

At some point someone was bound to mention there was a strange private eye on the premises. How long did I have? With everyone, and I mean everyone, on stage both literally and figuratively, the dressing rooms would be empty.

Getting to them, and fast, was my last best chance.

I shook off what Maudie'd said. I shook off how it made me feel.

"Come on, Jane. The game's afoot."

## 15

I'd assumed everyone and their acting coach was off performing on the stage. I was wrong. Someone was weeping in Josephine's dressing room.

It was Glenda, all alone and sobbing her heart out.

Jane and I stuck our heads through the door.

"Oh," she wailed from Josephine's couch, clasping her hands in what looked like prayer, "Mr. Russo! Thank goodness you've come. This is all just too terrible."

For the first time in hours, Jane yodeled. Jane's yodeling was one hell of a lot more surprising than finding Glenda Gordon running with tears, a Glenda Gordon I'd last seen performing for the police. Jane'd seated herself directly in front of the little nurse. Her red and white ears upright, her red and white head to the side, her red and white tail curled over her back, her scars red but fading to pink—Jane was comforting the woman.

I knew my Jane by now. Jane, who cared for no one but me, was trying to soothe Glenda.

Was I jealous? If not, what was that pang in my heart?

"She's talking, Mr. Russo. I'd swear she's talking."

"She is."

"What's she saying?"

"She's saying things will be fine. She's telling you not to worry. And so am I. Don't you worry. I'll figure this out if I get shot—again—trying."

I got nothing for my bravado. Jane was the big attraction. "Oh my good golly, a talking dog." And then, right in the middle of admiring Jane, the little nurse bust out crying all over again. "Things aren't going to be fine. How can they be fine when Raymond's gone?"

This time I believed her. She really *did* care for Raymond LeGrand. So far, that made a grand total of one in the world—which meant that there was one other person, namely Cliff Winker, who must of felt about LeGrand what I felt about Flo and Mister Zawadzki.

You didn't get taught how to love where I grew up. You got taught how to hate. I'd learned it just fine. I wondered how Cliff's hate was doing.

I sat down next to Glenda, not too close. I wasn't making a play and I wasn't a doctor. "Raymond was your friend," I said. It wasn't a question. "I'm really sorry."

Glenda turned her small sweet silly face towards me. The blue eyes were puddled in tears. "Friend? He was my lover, Mr. Russo. He was the love of my life! We were going to get married."

"But, aren't you already— ?"

"Married to Cliff? That was the easy part." Saying this, she was rummaging in her handbag, coming out with a bus ticket. "See this! This is for Reno. You know, the place way out west in Nevada where they do those quickie divorces."

I was back to staring at someone. This time I could be looking at a champion. Could any woman, anywhere, beat little Glenda Gordon for having the worst taste in men of all time?

"There, there," I said. I was sure it was soothing.

That's when Josephine waddled back into her own dressing room, trailed by Maudie and Bluto. Josephine took one look at a weeping Glenda and she too burst into tears. No one, not even Stan Laurel, could weep with such comedic undertones. Everything about Josephine was slightly aslant. Her nose, her hair, her eyebrows. Hers wasn't a voice or a body built for pathos.

Josephine threw herself on what was left of the couch

what with Glenda and I taking up most of it, wailing, "*Harvey* is a comedy. It's a magical comedy all about pookas and believing lovely things, and now look what someone's gone and done. They spoiled it for all of us. They spoiled it for the world! And just when the world is so in need of magic and laughter after all we've been through. How selfish, how horribly horribly selfish! Why hello, Glenda. I see you've been crying too. Well, I don't blame you. If Maudie could show her feelings, and I know she has deep sensitive feelings, she'd be crying too. Wouldn't you, Maudie?"

We three could see Maudie in the dressing table mirror, settling Bluto onto his blanket. If she had feelings, they were buried deep—except for that one moment on the catwalk when she breathed the name Anders.

"Of course," said Maudie Rivers. And that was all she said.

Josephine took it for more. "And dogs, they have feelings. Look at your dog, Mr. Russo. She's practically crying too. Now poor Bluto, he doesn't say a word. He just lolls around on his blanket and slobbers. Between you and me, he also passes wind. Things can get rather unpleasant in here at times. If it weren't for Anders coming round and taking him for his little strolls as much as he does, and going out with Maudie to buy him food, well I honestly don't know if I could keep him here. But now, your funny little red and white dog—you wouldn't want her to have a good home? I know— "

I was quick off the mark. "She has a good home."

As I said it, I found myself thinking of "home." After Saratoga Springs and the Isle of Manhattan, Stapleton had about as much "hominess" and allure as a parking lot in the Bronx. Basically, I was almost thirty years old and I was still living in a nothing town doing pretty much nothing. Solving Detective Lino Morelli's occasionally serious crimes was getting me nowhere. I'd had only one serious case I could call my own—and that one almost got me killed. It got me Jane, but it also almost got her killed too.

Now what the fuck was I doing? Sitting with two crying dames smack in the middle of a case I had no business being in. But hey, I was getting better at all this. For one thing, I wasn't weeping. I'd found out who Lino's corpse was. I'd also found the corpse's dog. He was just a dog. I wouldn't be taking Bluto home, and that was a dead cert.

Still—think about it. I was seeing Broadway from the inside and that was a big plus.

But did I have an office, a flyblown window with my name painted on it in chipped paint looking out over some flyblown street? Was I Bogart?

I had the hat, the trench coat, the snubby Colt .38 back in my Stapleton room only a ferry ride away, that easy way of thumbing a match without burning the end off my thumbnail, a great way of leaning against any wall. I could, on occasion, crack wise.

But no, I wasn't Bogie.

The real question, the one really getting to me in all kinds of ways, was this question: where was my classy dame to swap wise cracks with? I slid my eye over Glenda. Glenda was about as smart and classy as Bluto. She was also too small. A short movie of her and Raymond played in my mind; the two of 'em together must of been a contortionist's act. I turned my head to look at Josephine. An aging fireplug with bags of talent and a big sappy heart. I fought off the sudden urge to call Mrs. Willingford, to ask her to come help me with the Case of the Two Rabbits. She had a place on Park Avenue. I already knew she was home and not in Kentucky or Paris or Rio or somewhere like that. She'd come like a shot. With that thought, I veered away from Mrs. Willingford. I'd come like a shot too and there'd we be, getting dressed and vying to outrace each other to the finish line. Mrs. Willingford had a taste for detecting.

The sensible thing to do was make a mad dash through Fay's empty dressing room, another mad dash through the bigger dressing room where the rest of the cast got crammed, and if I could find it, which was doubtful, a try for where the stagehands hung out. Noodles mentioned Raymond had a locker. I'd love to get to that locker before the cops did.

An even more sensible thing to do was make a dash for the Staten Island ferry. I looked at my watch. I could make the crossing just before the one that was packed with people who lived on Staten Island but worked in Manhattan. The crowded one scared me. I had a slight, very slight, fear of open water. Well, maybe more than slight.

I could still see Maudie in the mirror. She was teasing Bluto. Offering him a Tootsie Roll, then snatching it back when he tried for it. Why didn't that surprise me? Bluto wasn't a popular pooch. Anyway, what was I thinking? In the official PI handbook I would write one day, Rule Number One would be: PIs do not run away.

It was right about then I noticed the collar around Bluto's neck. Usually you couldn't see Bluto's neck, which was lucky for him with Jane around. But he'd given up on getting a Tootsie Roll, and Maudie had given up offering, so now he was loudly licking his privates—Christ! I sent up fervent thanks that Jane was a female—which made him stretch his neck just far enough to expose the leather collar and something attached to the collar.

I was round the couch and swiftly unbuckling the collar before he lost interest in his balls.

The thing attached to his collar was a small metal barrel. Cute. A St. Bernard mix with a tiny barrel round his neck. If you worked hard enough, the barrel unscrewed leaving a person with sore fingers and two halves of the barrel. Inside one half was a rolled up piece of paper, yellow at the edges, torn on one side. It said: *BLUTO. Maurice Oboram, 24 Commerce Street, Apt. 5.* With Maudie peering over my shoulder, I looked inside the other half. In it was another piece of paper, nice and new and carefully folded. It said: *Beware the Tides of March.* It was signed: *R. LeGrand.*

Jesus pulling a racing sulky! The exact same five words I'd seen on LeGrand's lifeless arm. What did they mean?

Bluto once had someone who loved him, who didn't tease him with Tootsie Rolls, who cared enough to buy him a collar with a barrel attached in case he got lost. Did Oboram put Raymond's cryptic note into Bluto's barrel? Or did LeGrand put it there himself, expecting that at some point Maurice would see it? *Did* Maurice see it? Did he even know about it? Who knew?

I did know this: Maurice had a place in the seediest part of Greenwich Village. OK. Good. But the note didn't mean a damn thing to me. If he did know about it, what did it mean to Maurice?

Most important of all, what did it mean to Raymond LeGrand? Was it a joke? A marker? A warning?

One thing it meant was I wasn't wrong. The two big men who played one big rabbit were connected.

Maurice Oboram ended up in the water. He was washed here and there by the currents and tides. It could of happened in March... or a bit later, since he'd made it through the whole of *Macbeth*. But what if things were already brewing in March?

Beware the Tides of March. What else could "beware" mean other than a warning? Maurice had his warning on a piece of paper. Raymond's "beware" was on his arm. But LeGrand was too dead for it to be a warning. So it wasn't a warning. Was it a reminder?

Forget the 48th Street Theater. For the moment anyway. I had a strong feeling that to understand what happened to Raymond began with what happened to Maurice.

I had to get out of here before the cops saw me.

Good old Josephine. Trust her to know about a back

door leading into a narrow space behind the theater few, if any, used. If I turned right, I'd wind up in the alley with the stage door. But if I turned left, the space was just wide enough between buildings to lead out onto 7th Avenue.

"This has been my home for almost five years," she said, "I know every cranny and nook. You might need a key. You must take mine."

As Jane and I made our escape, she stood in the back door waving a hanky.

You had to love Josephine Hull.

At the nearest phone booth, corner of 47th Street and Seventh Avenue, we stopped. Jane watched cars and shoes and the pretzel man. I watched the phone booth. I was sick of going it alone. Much as I loved Jane, I could use a few first class insults and some good old fashioned bickering about now. I could also use some advice. So I caved. I gave in and gave up and called Mrs. Willingford. No surprise. She'd meet me on Commerce Street within the hour.

I couldn't wait to see what she'd be wearing. But the real truth? I couldn't wait to see Mrs. Willingford.

What a sap I was.

## 16

"Trust Sam Russo to pick the perfect spot."

Trust Mrs. Willingford to get to the village before me. No doubt she'd ridden her best horse, Fleeting Fancy, right down the middle of Manhattan, snarling traffic and hitting cars with her horse whip. Fleeting Fancy was the filly who could of won the Travers Stakes if at least one of us hadn't fingered the wrong killer at the same time.

I couldn't help it. I glanced around. No high class racehorse tethered to a dim lamppost with three toughs guarding her. No nothing but a short dark street with dark red brick buildings and dark curtained windows and the mingled stink of the nearby Hudson River and New York City garbage. We did have company. An orange alley cat was making its way from overflowing garbage can to overflowing garbage can. I caught Jane's collar before the cat could cut her up some more. Jane was more than a match for a dog, but a cat that looked like *that* cat? I wasn't taking chances.

"Hello, Mrs. Willingford. You remember Jane?"

"*You* might get forgotten, Russo, in fact you probably will, but not Jane."

"Thanks."

Truth was, Mrs. Willingford's insults perked me right up. This was what'd been missing. Tasty, if biting, insults.

"So what's the case?"

"Two murdered actors, both tall, one very tall, both in the same big show, and both rabbits."

"You're kidding? Rabbits? Big rabbits? You mean *Harvey*! I saw that. Lucky me: Fay was 'under-the-weather' the night

I went. I hadn't heard of his understudy, but I have now. Jimmy Stewart played Elwood. Is he playing it now? Two rabbits are dead?"

"The last two are."

Mrs. Willingford was dressed like the cover of a Vogue magazine. Her red and black checked shoulder pads would of done fine under a football jersey. As for the hat, the hat could stop traffic. Good thing there wasn't much traffic on Commerce Street.

"Oh look! I forgot the Cherry Lane Theater was on Commerce. So why are we here? Oooh, and how are you, sweet dog? You're looking good. And the scars! Hardly noticeable." Jane allowed Mrs. W to kiss her nose. "You have to admit, the Willingford vet is a peach."

"He's more than a peach. He's a Peach Daiquiri. And we're here because the bigger of the two dead rabbits lived here. Number 24, apartment 5."

"Well, then. What are we waiting for? A locksmith?"

Now here was something I'd kept to myself. Lino Morelli had no idea, no one did—but knowing what I wanted to be, the first thing I did when I landed back in the good old USA was get a job. Not just any job, but a job as an assistant to a locksmith in Bayonne. Without a car, it wasn't easy and it wasn't fun and it took up a lot of time getting back and forth to Bayonne everyday. So I moved into Rudy's back room, about the size of a closet and just as comfy.

Doing Lino's job for him had its good points. One thing it did was make me easy around guns, always a good thing when you get sent off to war (and you miss Shut Out winning the Derby which I will never forgive the Japanese for; some people just don't know what's really important in life), and then when you're back home again, a friend is shooting you with his gun and you're shooting him with yours.

Another good thing working for Lino was learning to keep an ear to the ground. That's how I found out who was the best retired safe cracker in Brooklyn and who was the best lock picker Lino's precinct had ever arrested, twice. The lock picker was Rudy Hiller, an old guy from Bayonne, out of jail for the second time and planning on staying out. I worked for dirt cheap while Rudy taught me all he could teach.

After three months, Rudy told me to go home. I was almost as good as he was. I would only get better with practice.

I was in Bayonne the year Assault won the Kentucky Derby. Right from the moment he opened his eyes on the world, Assault had every kind of problem going. That included getting born a Thoroughbred on a Texas cattle ranch that only cared about racing Quarter horses, accidently stepping on a surveyor's stake, driving it straight through his hoof which left him limping the rest of his life, and starting out a sickly thing, prone to whatever was going round. But none of that stopped him winning. The press called him the Club-footed Comet. He also won the Preakness and the Belmont while I was learning to pick locks.

If a horse who limped into starting gates and ran with ailing kidneys could win the Triple Crown, then maybe a certain PI could win his own kind of derby.

Anyway, that's how I remembered my life. I counted it out not by date but by Derby winners.

I never carried a whole set of picks—that was begging for trouble. But I did carry one: a common beginner's snake rake. Kept it in the lining of my jacket. Rudy'd taught me most locks are cheap locks. Even in a good building. He figured rich people had this idea that with a good doorman, they didn't need good locks. Whatever they thought, a snake rake could open any one of their doors in one second flat. Or in thirty seconds dead drunk or otherwise impaired—like with Jane sitting on your feet and Mrs. Willingford breathing down your neck and ooooohing in your ear.

This had been Oboram's door. A nice normal cheap door with a cheap lock in a half decent building with no doorman. It did have the sound of a ship coming or going somewhere on the Hudson, a low haunting sound that made me hear Bing singing low and mournful of far away places with strange sounding names.

Oboram wasn't normal. Walking the narrow hall lit by the dim light of widely spaced amber glass sconces, he must of felt crowded. To get into his own door with a proper key, he'd have to duck.

I told Mrs. Willingford what I thought about Maurice walking that hall as I picked his lock.

"A real giant? You mean like in a circus?"

"I don't think he saw himself that way. Besides, he wasn't a real giant, just moving up in that direction. He was an actor."

"Holy shit. Who did he play? Goliath?"

"Now, Mrs. Willingford, be nice."

"You're kidding, right?"

Jane squeezed herself in before I got the door opened more than a few inches. And then she was all over the place. It wasn't Oboram's anymore. It hadn't been his for months. Whoever lived there now had it furnished like a monk's cell. One long narrow bed. A dresser. Although I wasn't sure monks were allowed the new radio that took up a lot of room. The place as it was now told me, at a glance, nothing about Maurice, but it told Jane a story as long and as detailed as *The Decline and Fall of the Roman Empire*. She was everywhere, her tail curling and uncurling as it always did when she was "reading" something. She stopped in front of a chest at the foot of the bed, one of those old steamer trunks, the kind some dame would take along four or five of on a long ocean voyage, or maybe like the trunk strapped to the back of a Wild West stagecoach. Whatever it was, it had Jane's full attention. Her rubbery black nose pressed against its lid, what I'd call her eyebrows raised almost to the top of her wrinkled red forehead, she was growling.

What have we here? I said to myself as Mrs. Willingford guarded the door to the room, which was a good idea because who knew? Any minute the new tenant of this palatial rat-hole could come blundering home. I assumed he'd be a "he" since only men were allowed to rent one of these nice rooms, and I assumed he'd blunder since the men were almost all drunks. "Hurry up, Sam," she hissed, "I'm not dressed for all this."

"I'd love to see that outfit."

"If we ever go caving, you will."

By now, Jane was scratching at the trunk at the foot of the bed. It took me nothing more than a pull on the strap for it to swing wide open, but it took me all I had to get Jane out of the trunk once she'd leapt into it, and then what she'd found out of her mouth. It would of been a fight to the finish if I hadn't practically choked her to death getting her out of the trunk.

By the time I got what she'd found away from her, it was shredded, slobbered on, and missing a lot of what made it what it was. But I'd of known what it was with or without Jane's attentions. It was a hairpiece, a toupee, a wig. And if it wasn't one of Cliff Winker's rugs, I'd eat it.

What the hell was Cliff's hair doing in Oboram's trunk?

"Down, Jane," I said, holding it up like a drowned cat, while Jane jumped as high as she could, using me to get even higher. "Dammit, Jane, down!"

Jane dropped to the floor, but never took her eyes off her prize.

Turning, the mess of hair in my hand, I saw Mrs. Willingford had abandoned her post. It figured. Dames loved bathrooms. She was in the bathroom.

"Sam," she said, "look at this."

I looked. I don't know what she saw but what I saw was

that Maurice'd had his own damn bathroom. I didn't have my own damn bathroom.

Maybe this actor's lark wasn't such a bad idea after all.

## 17

What Mrs. Willingford was pointing at was a large bureau next to a sizable claw-footed tub. In it were clothes for an enormous man—and unless the new tenant was also a virtual giant, they once belonged to Oboram. Maurice seemed to have one normal suit, one normal hat, one normal pair of shoes, and two normal ties. Normal for a giant. Aside from these, the bureau was stuffed with ruffs and great big hats with bigger feathers and those short pants that ballooned above the knee. There were things I knew were called doublets, but a lot more things I had no name for at all. There was one codpiece.

After seeing what was left of Maurice on Mortie's slab, I couldn't see what he needed that for.

No modern man would be caught dead—or alive—in any of 'em. But if what all the Hindus said was true, and Maurice got himself born again, he'd be all set for Elizabeth's England.

Next to the bureau was a full length mirror, mottled with age but good enough. Mrs. Willingford had unpinned her ridiculous hat and was trying on one of Oboram's ridiculous hats. Using the mirror as the giant would of used the mirror, but without having to duck, she said: "Oh yes, I want one of these."

"Can't have his."

"I wasn't thinking of his. My hat-maker will make me one. In any case, his are way too big."

I thought about some of her hats and about her hat-maker, but wisely kept my mouth shut. I was getting good at all this. The breaking and entering. The searching and finding. I'd even stopped Jane from shredding Cliff's rug. But I was getting really good at keeping my mouth shut around Mrs. W.

Except for the bathroom all to himself, the single room was much worse than my place in Stapleton. My room had books. And pictures. Of horses. All my favorites had a place on my walls.

Still—funny there was still stuff of Maurice's here. You rent a room and junk from the guy before was still in it, you got rid of his junk. Unless it was good junk, which it never was. But if it was, the landlord beat you to it. Keeping Cliff's toupee was a stumper unless the new guy hadn't bothered with the trunk—which I doubted. But the funniest of all, besides the Shakespearean duds, was the stuff in the bottom drawer of the bureau in the bathroom. Maurice Oboram's real legacy was a collection of programs for the shows he'd either seen or been in. The former far outnumbered the latter. On top of them all was one small clipping from a newspaper review that mentioned his name. It wasn't for *Harvey*. It was for *Macbeth*.

Clad in a black velvet cloak, a black velvet hat, and swashbuckling about with a very real looking sword, Mrs. Willingford said, "What are we looking for, Sam?"

"I have no idea." This wasn't strictly true, but it came out of my mouth anyway. Probably because it felt true. "I haven't had a single idea since Lino got me into this."

"Lino?"

For the first time since we'd met, I told her about Lino Morelli. About being kids together under the loving eyes of Mister and Mrs. Flo Zawadzki, about Lino becoming a cop, about me solving most of his cases for no credit and no money, about dragging me and Jane away from our delightful Stapleton "apartment" to view a dead giant, about how I was dumb enough to think I'd at least get to see Manhattan, about how it had all come down to this.

"Are you serious? You've met Cole Porter! Even with Joker's money backing him, *I* haven't met Cole Porter."

"I have to admit, Mrs. Willingford, that I am surprised. Why, Cole and I are like this." I crossed my eyes.

"And Jimmy Stewart too!"

"Best friends. Never miss his birthday. Knock it off, Mrs. W. I'm drowning here."

"Well, Sam, not like Mr. Oboram drowned—if he managed to live after that nasty cleft in his skull. This calls for seafood. Come on. We're going to Delmonico's. It's not terribly far and Oscar knows me— "

Of course whoever this Oscar guy was knew her. Us poor Yankee Doodles, without royalty of our own, made the rich royal.

"—so Jane will get her own chair and her own bib. We'll solve at least one of the cases over a nice Lobster Newburg."

"Didn't you hear what I said? I have no idea what I'm doing."

"Darling Sam. I admit I haven't known you all that long, but when have you ever known what you were doing?"

I let that one go too.

I thought she'd never notice, but Mrs. Willingford suddenly gave out a squeak over what I'd been holding in my hand all along. "My God, Sam! What the hell is that?"

"In my business, I'd call it a clue."

Mrs. Willingford wrinkled her terrific nose. "In my business, I'd call it dead and have a maid flush it down a toilet."

"It's mine and it's not going down the john; it's going into one of my pockets. Time to leave. First rule of burglary: get in and get out, fast."

Trouble was, when it came time to depart by the door we'd arrived through, Jane wasn't coming with us. While Mrs. Willingford was playing dress up and I was looking through playbills, Jane had nipped back into the one room, opened the trunk all by herself—pulling on the strap with her delicate teeth—and climbed in again, this time covering herself in someone's now demolished sheets. She was in there now, growling and guarding something.

"Whatcha got, girl?" I said.

Jane lifted her head and gave out with a hum like Sherlock Holmes sawing away on a violin.

Mrs. Willingford, back in her own astonishing clothes, and once more holding open the door, said, "Holy mackerel. What was that?"

"Hold on. I'm trying to find out."

I found out all right. It was a hat, one of Maurice's Shakespearean hats, a small one, like an oversized saggy beret, striped in purple and green satin, and coated in long dried river mud. Only about a minute ago, it'd been neatly wrapped in paper—but Jane had seen to that.

My skin was tingling. I was getting somewhere. I was beginning to see things as a real PI would see them. I was making connections, good connections. It felt swell. Now all I had to do was get back into a cop infested theater, grab Bluto without fuss or bother (mostly from Jane)—I was following a train of thought here, one that was picking up speed—and get the hell out again without getting nabbed as a material witness.

"We should leave, Sam. We should get out of here."

"Hold on. Just have to finish this thought."

"Sam, really. I've nothing that goes with a cell."

Right then, I spotted the one item I ought to of seen all along. It showed me what I ought to of known all along. This had been Maurice Oboram's room. That's why some of his stuff was still there. Now it was someone else's room. But I hadn't given enough thought to *whose* room. Or why the new guy hadn't thrown out all of Oboram's stuff like any normal new tenant would do—unless it was worth something.

On the bare wooden floor next to the oddly long, oddly narrow bed, a deck of cards had been splayed out. Next to the cards lay a book with a bookmark placed about halfway through. The title of the book was *Secrets of a Professional Poker Player*.

As someone I once knew said: Blow me out a whale hole.

This was Raymond LeGrand's room now. Or it was until Raymond was rubbed out. I'd known the two dead rabbits were connected but this was getting more than connected. It was getting to be like they were both sewn into the same burial shroud.

When the first big bunny hit the dirt, or the mud as the case might be, the second big bunny burrowed right in.

And I'll bet the slumlord didn't even know it.

Raymond LeGrand took possession of Maurice Oboram's rented room. How did he know it was empty? Gee, I wonder. So what else did he take from Oboram besides, maybe, his life?

Or—a lightbulb! Maybe the second bunny hadn't waited. Maybe he'd thrown the first bunny out. Maybe he'd won the place at cards.

A strange thought got through all these other thoughts: would the killer who'd just garroted Raymond now take the room that was Oboram's before it was LeGrand's?

Forget it, Sam. That thought was too creepy even for Paul Jarrett back when he was eating up stuff like *Frankenstein* and *Dracula* and *Dr. Jekyll and Mr. Hyde*—which he'd read to us after lights out while we all pretended we weren't scared.

Me, I'd always been terrified. It felt great. Mainly because those were books.

This wasn't.

It took me no time to find what I knew had to be there once I knew who lived in the room after Maurice. Under the bed, I found a notebook and in the notebook I found

LeGrand had listed the name of every single person who owed him a dime. I also found out how many dimes they owed. Fay was right. His debt might of made even Mrs. Willingford blink—before she bought another horse.

Of course Noodles was listed, and Eddie the grouser—and where was Eddie going to get the kind of money he'd lost to LeGrand if LeGrand hadn't conveniently died?—and Jesse with the cigars and Cliff Winker and Anders Slydel.

And yep, there he was. Maurice Oboram. Marked PAID.

I think I was right. I think Maurice used his apartment to pay off his debt.

Let's just say that Raymond LeGrand, looking at the sums beside a few of the names—two I figured had to be in the same spot as Maurice and Eddie the grouser had been, namely unable to pay up, and one who could be—was one hell of a poker player, or one hell of a cheater, or everyone else needed emergency room treatment for stupidity.

So now I had a chewed up hairpiece—little doubt it was Cliff Winker's and that little doubt extinguished once I knew whose room we were in—Raymond LeGrand's notebook, and one of Maurice Oboram's mud encrusted hats. All I needed now was a bag to keep them in.

Mrs. Willingford found the perfect thing. Her own huge purse.

Later, in the right time and the right place, they'd all go in their separate paper bags. What I was doing here was tampering with evidence.

Fuck. Before this was all over, I was going to need Detective Lino Morelli postdating me a search warrant.

## 18

"I'm coming with you, Sam."

"No, you're *not*."

"Yes I *am*."

"Do I have to remind you, Mrs. Willingford?"

"Remind me of what, Mr. Russo?"

"You have a ball coming up."

"Do I have to remind you?"

"Of what?"

"Joker pays professionals to do all that. All I have to do is make a fabulous appearance. I'm coming with you because short of a major horse race with a horse of mine in it, you're the most exciting thing I know."

"Thing?"

"You heard me."

So off we all went, man, woman and dog. No racehorse tethered and waiting, the three of us climbed into Mrs. Willingford's chauffeured town car with its well stocked backseat bar. From where I sat, I couldn't tell a thing about her driver except that he was young and clean shaven. He also had shoulders on him like the kind of guys Knute Rockne used to shout at. Did I expect anything else from Mrs. Willingford? After all, she *was* Mrs. Willingford.

The only thing that worried me was Jane. How was I going to get Bluto out of the 48th Street Theater without bloodshed?

Around about Times Square, with the cherry in my Old Fashioned slopping around in my glass as we wove through traffic too fast, I said, "Jane?"

From her place by my side, her eyebrows went up and her ears came forward.

"I need you to do something for me. I need you to leave Bluto alone. Do you hear me? No biting, no snarling, not even any growling. If you can't do that, you get to stay in the car. That clear?"

Listening, Jane looked into my eyes. Hers were dog's eyes. Egyptian eyes. Round and amber brown, outlined in black like a woman's, or a cheetah's, her forehead a mass of hairy copper colored wrinkles. If I knew anything, I knew she understood me. What I didn't know was if she'd obey me.

Well, guess we were going to find out.

The stage door guard had seen a lot of class acts pass in and out of his side alley stage door—including Tallulah Bankhead. I don't know how he felt about Tallulah. I was no big fan except for the one great review she'd gotten for her portrayal of Cleopatra: "Tallulah Bankhead barged down the Nile last night and promptly sank." And the one great thing I'd heard she'd said: "My father warned me about men and booze, but he never mentioned a word about women and cocaine." But I could tell what he felt about Mrs. Willingford. Most men felt what that old fart was feeling about Mrs. Willingford and as far I could tell, a lot of those men got to express their feelings. Me included. Why my nose wasn't bent out of joint, I couldn't say, but it wasn't. Maybe it was the way Mrs. Willingford had of not taking anything seriously, anything, that is, but horseflesh. Or maybe it was because I didn't expect anything of Mrs. Willingford. Good thing too, since I wasn't likely to get it. But the thing I think it was, was this: we'd become pals, Mrs. Willingford and I. And I liked that just fine.

Plus, Jane liked her.

I've said friends were no longer on my menu and I wish I'd

been kidding, but I wasn't. Even so, Mrs. Joker Willingford, until she proved otherwise (and these days I was ready for anything), was still a meal I couldn't resist. OK, so maybe one night I'd get a bad case of food poisoning, but until that night I was more than happy to get a little nibble whenever it was offered.

Before she went to work on the poor guy, I made her leave her hat and that precious purse in her town car. It was parked on 7$^{th}$ Avenue around the corner from 48$^{th}$ Street; the gum chewing, linebacker of a chauffer settled in to wait with a comic book. I got a look at the cover. *Tarzan*. Hell, why not? I read Tarzan. Of course when I read Tarzan, I read the actual books and I was twelve years old. Anyway, a hat like Mrs. Willingford's could get her not only noticed, but remembered. A hat like that could get her a job in Ziegfeld's Follies. If there were any Ziegfeld Follies anymore.

I needed her to razzle-dazzle the stage door guard and any possible cop guarding the side door along with him, while Jane and I got back into the theater through Josephine's seldom used back door. No lock picking needed. I had Josephine's key.

It worked like a charm. Mrs. Willingford was not only an eyeful, she could talk the hind legs off a mule. I'd heard that expression somewhere and still wondered what it meant.

Jane and I got all the way to Josephine's dressing room without incident, although we could hear plenty of incidents going on all around us. Since every actor, stagehand, and whoever else was as innocent as a babe, every one of them was bawling like a baby. The loudest was Frank Fay. He sounded completely sober and profoundly insulted.

For the first time in my life I pitied the cops. Trying to make sense of people who lied for a living—or to be kinder, people who could be anybody for a living—had to be half impossible.

Right now the denizens of the 48$^{th}$ Street Theater were, to a man and woman, playing the unjustly accused innocent.

There was only one person in Josephine's dressing room, and one dog. Bluto was the dog. Jimmy was the person. Bluto was loudly snoring on his latest blanket. Jimmy was lightly snoring on Josephine's couch.

The hair on her back standing up like a Mohawk Indian with a great barber, Jane sidled over to Bluto. No talking, no growling, no teeth showing. While she was doing this I was stepping away from the door the better to go unnoticed by the cop and actor infected theater.

All I wanted was Bluto to go quietly. I had no idea if Bluto could do anything quietly. Or Jane for that matter. I knew Jimmy could, but I wasn't there for Jimmy.

I'd brought an old leash I'd found in the bureau back in what was once Oboram's place on Commerce Street hoping Bluto would find it comforting. The idea was Mrs. Willingford's. Something from home, she said.

Tiptoeing across the carpet in my "sneaking around shoes"—a good idea I'd learned from Mrs. Willingford back in Saratoga Springs: always bring sneaky clothes and unsqueaky footwear—I held the leash up to Bluto's nose. He was smelling it long before he woke up, and smelling it, he woke up happy. Which made me sad. It meant Bluto'd liked Maurice Oboram. It meant he missed the fellow and was only waiting to see him again. Instead, the first thing he saw when he opened his red rimmed eyes was Jane. He wasn't happy anymore and that made me sadder. But a PI I was and a PI I remained. Cowed by Jane, Bluto allowed me to clip the leash to his collar, and then dragged himself up off his blanket to come when I pulled.

I had one foot out the door when Jimmy said: "Good luck, pard. Raymond may not be missed, but Maurice was a treasure, a first rate, very tall, fellow."

"I'm doing my best, Jimmy."

"That's the best you can do."

Without Jimmy the Bluto plan would of gone bust. Jane saw the cop first, but Jimmy got to him first. An arm around his shoulder, talking like *Mr. Smith Goes to Washington*, Jimmy steered the cop away while we slipped out the deserted back door towards 7$^{th}$ Avenue. Woody, Mrs. Willingford's driver—no one told me his name was Woody; I had to catch it in passing—drove us all round to 48$^{th}$ Street. I could see Mrs. Willingford practically fan dancing at the end of the alley. Even when she saw us, me and Jane and Bluto and Woody had to wait a good five minutes before she was finished with the cops and with the guy I would always think of as Barney Google.

Mrs. Willingford never shortchanged those who admired her.

I stood and waited and admired her.

## 19

When Bluto'd returned alone to the 48$^{th}$ Street Theater, Josephine, backed up by Maudie Rivers, said he was soaking wet and muddy. They said he stank. This had to mean he'd been there when Maurice went into the drink. Just like Jane'd been there when the Saratoga Springs killer had quickly and slyly rendered her owner, Babe Duffy, senseless, then stuffed a ham sandwich down the jockey's groggy throat until he choked to death. Jane hadn't let that go unpunished. She'd fought for Duffy's life, and later came very close to dying for it.

What had Bluto done for Oboram?

I had no idea. Mrs. Willingford had no idea. But whatever he did, the least he could do now was show us where his master was killed.

Mortie Hickman said Maurice Oboram was hit over the head by something like an ax. After that, he was thrown or pushed or stumbled, dying, into the East River or the Hudson River. I bought both Mortie's conclusions. The hole in Oboram's skull suggested an axe. Where Lino's men found the body suggested he died near water. Bluto's stinking mud suggested a dirty river. Where else was there river mud in New York City except by the East River or the Hudson River? It would of been good to know which, so we'd know where to start looking. Since we didn't know which, I decided to begin on the side of Manhattan where Oboram lived—the Hudson side.

Mud told us we could ignore piers and the like. It said we were looking for a bit of actual riverbank.

I'd seen enough movies, read enough books, solved enough of Lino's crimes. One step led to another step. Enough steps and one day you'd arrive somewhere.

Usually.

Anyway, that was the idea. One murder at a time. The cops were working on Raymond. Lino may have pushed me into it, but once pushed, I was hooked. Sam Russo, gumshoe, was working on Maurice and just Maurice. Without Lino. If I was hooked, at least there was no Lino calling the shots, and missing. There was no me telling him what to do and where to go and how to think when no one was looking. I wasn't getting paid, as usual, but it was still my case. It was my case now. I was gonna do what I could do to solve it. I didn't believe in murder. Not even when it came to Raymond LeGrand.

But like George Orwell could of said in *Animal Farm: All murders are equal, but some are more equal than others.* Maurice Oboram was worth a lot more to me than Raymond LeGrand. As Doc Hickman said, being almost a giant meant he didn't have long to live anyway, but that didn't wash no matter how I looked at it. It was like killing someone old. The killer was taking away the last few years, months, days of their life. Who knew if those last days would prove to be the best they'd ever have? Or the worst? Either way, who had the right to stop that happening?

Me, a born snoop, curious enough to irritate people, I wanted to know what happened to the guy. I wanted to know why someone would do away with what Jimmy and Josephine said was a gentle word loving Shakespearean giant. I wanted whoever that someone was to pay for it. Maybe I wasn't a good guy myself—hell, who could be good with all their examples getting set by the Zawadzkis?—but there was good in me.

I'd learned that in the war. The war showed a man who he really was. My war was a grim lesson in what my own species could do. It was a proving ground for real heroes. It was the downfall of phonies. Me and a lot of my buddies learned who a lot of public heroes really were. Like Dugout Doug, known to millions as General Douglas MacArthur. They hadn't seen him in the Philippines. They didn't know that their hero ran for it when things got tough, leaving Skinny Wainwright to surrender us to the Japanese. If not for sheer luck, I'd of made point man on the Bataan Death March while the great American hero was "sweating it out" in Australia bloviating about how he was "going to return." I wanted to be one of those unsung people: able to act quickly and with honor, able to see the other side of things, able to share whatever they had, able to keep caring and keep fighting when the odds said they were dead men. Truth was, I would never be as good or as fine as those men, but no reason why I couldn't keep trying.

So I kept trying.

Once more Lino lucked out. I was up to my teeth in his case. And when, and if, I solved it, Lino, like a small-time MacArthur, would take all the glory.

Who really cared as long as the job got done?

It took a lot of looking and a lot of time, but between us, me and Jane and Mrs. Willingford and Woody, we found a stretch of real riverbank with real mud near the end of Cortlandt Street. There was a nice stretch of reek between Piers 9 and 10 of the United Fruit Company not too far from Commerce Street.

We'd left the town car, with Woody inside, parked in a small lot on the edge of West Street. This was an order from Mrs. W. Me? I'd rather he'd come along; he looked pretty handy for a chauffeur. The dogs and Woody and I stood around in the cold while Mrs. Willingford changed into a more suitable outfit; obviously she had a clothes closet in the back as well as a booze cabinet.

Then we were off, hoping Bluto would wake up.

If I thought Bluto was a dog like Jane was a dog, boy was I wrong. The moment he got a whiff of the docks and the water and the mud, Bluto was backing up fast, whining with his huge hairy tail stuck between his huge hairy back legs. Jane's contempt was worse than mine. So was Mrs. Willingford's.

"What a mutt. A big stupid hulk like that and he's chicken."

I felt kind of sorry for him. If this is where his master got his, you had to think it wasn't a place Bluto wanted to see again.

Not Jane. She was up to her hocks in blue, black and brown river mud, lalloping back and forth snorkeling up more mud with her red and white nose. Mrs. Willingford was right behind her, leaping about in galoshes and a pair of baggy denim blue jeans—men's blue jeans with a zipper in the front. For about a second, I stood there with Bluto wishing she wouldn't do things like that. But since everything she did was delectable, I gave up wishing for impossible things, and plunged into the mud dragging Bluto with me.

"Look," she shouted from twenty feet away, holding up a large mud filled shoe.

"Forget it," I shouted back, "that wouldn't fit Maurice, age ten."

"Damn. He was big."

"Yes, Mrs. Willingford, he was a very big man."

Suddenly my right arm was almost yanked from its socket.

Considering my recent Saratoga experience with the wrong end of a gun, it was worse than if I hadn't had that experience, much worse. I yelped with pain as Bluto began plowing through the mud, me keeping a death grip on his leash no matter what. We were headed straight for a pier or a dock or whatever the difference was. As we went, the mud got deeper, deep enough to slow Bluto down, deep enough for cool clammy mud to caress my personal regions.

Bluto stopped. I wish I'd stopped. I ran right over him, fell flat on my face in muck. Bluto'd plunged his massive head into the stuff, all four legs digging at once.

I was up and dripping by the time Jane caught up with us, Mrs. Willingford puffing along behind her. Mrs. Willingford had a lot of Mrs. Willingford left for even deeper mud, but Jane had to keep her nose straight up to keep breathing air.

Mrs. Willingford said, "What's he doing?"

We were both watching Bluto.

"Beats me, but if he doesn't stop doing it soon, he'll die by mud."

With that, up came Bluto's filthy head and in Bluto's filthy mouth hung the mud dripping hand of... someone. No someone attached, just the hand—very little flesh left attached and no thumb at all. Whose could it be? Gosh, who else? It had to be Maurice Oboram's and he probably once used it to scratch behind Bluto's ears and to hold Bluto's leash.

"Oh my god," said Mrs. Willingford.

"Yeeeooooollll!" said Jane.

I would of sat right down in shock, but thought better of it.

Bluto dropped the hand—which meant I had to grab for it fast before it sank back into the mud—and plunged his great head yet again into riverbank mud. Not in the same place, maybe ten or so feet towards the pier. I still had hold of his leash in one of my own hands and the skeleton hand of Maurice Oboram in the other and I was still getting painfully yanked along behind him.

For all the unusual things I'd done in my life, this about took the biscuit.

Bluto's second search was shorter. In about the time it took a fast horse to run six furlongs, his streaming doggy mouth came back up with a stick. Only it wasn't a stick;

it was a handle. A handle with an ornate double headed ax blade attached to one end.

Either blade was the perfect size to make a nice big hole in a giant's huge head.

"Where's Jane?" said Mrs. Willingford.

The alarm in her voice jerked me away from Bluto and severed hands and ax blades in heads. Mrs. Willingford's voice filled my mind with mud.

There was Mrs. Willingford, mud to her knees, there was Bluto, mud to his chin, there was me, mud pretty much everywhere, and then there was mud. Calm blue-brown mud stinking of spilled oil, rotten garbage, and your basic mud smell. There was no Jane.

"Jane!"

Thrusting the hand with its missing thumb into Mrs. Willingford's shocked grip, I struggled back to where I'd last seen my dog and threw myself into the muck, thrashed about in it, submerged myself in it, almost drowned in it. No Jane.

I called her name, over and over. And over.

## 20

I was about to have a heart attack when I heard, "Wooooooooo!"

From a face buried in stinking sticky urk, I was off and trying to run towards Jane. Damn dog was standing on the riverbank, all four feet on solid ground, no longer red or white but a thick nasty brown.

I was thirty feet away, still trying to run in river sludge.

"Dammit, Jane!" I'd yelled loud enough to hurt my throat which reminded me my throat already hurt. "You scared us!"

"Hooooowoooo."

The "hoooowoooo" was muffled but it was still a "hoooowooooo." That capped it. Now I knew I was learning her language fast. That was either Egyptian for "why are you idiots still messing around?" or my name was mud.

Bluto and Mrs. Willingford, who I'd relieved of the hand, were already halfway back to Jane and I was right behind, pulling each foot out of the muck with a huge sucking sound. Mrs. Willingford had Bluto. I had a double-headed ax in one hand and Oboram's huge thumbless skeletal hand in the other. The long sad finger bones trailed along in the mud beside me until I got close enough to the bank to put both me and the hand out of mud's way.

The whole distance back I was thinking: who chopped off Maurice Oboram's hand and who slammed an axe into Maurice Oboram's head? And why? Did whoever it was chop off his thumb first and was Maurice still alive when he did it—first the thumb and then the hand? Mister was also going round and round in my head. Thinking of his twenty-eight-or-so year long god-blessed kid-killing career, I wondered if there were more bodies out there under the mud than the part we'd found of Maurice. There might be. It was the perfect place to get rid of someone you'd bumped off. Perfect if the person you'd killed didn't have a big dumb dog who maybe, after you left, and you feeling pretty good about how you got away with it, pulled your prey out of the mud as far as he could. But it didn't really make any difference because what the dog was trying to save had this great big horrible crack in its skull, and being in or out of the mud couldn't change that too much.

We'd found a thumbless right hand and an axe. But someone else found a hat—and that someone was Raymond LeGrand. Another piece slotted into my puzzle.

I also thought: was it time to call some more cops? By "cops," I meant was it time to call Lino? I decided to decide that last one on the Staten Island Ferry. No time to change clothes or hose down Jane. Time enough to do both once we were back in my luxurious Stapleton apartment with its kitchen tub-table.

Gaining the bank, I noticed what was in Jane's mouth. A big bony thumb.

Perfect. Just perfect. Me and the hand and the thumb and the axe had a date with Morton Hickman, Stapleton's coroner.

Mrs. Willingford had her own grand ball to attend, one she didn't want to bother with, but balls will be balls. So off she and Woody went uptown, a spare blanket covering the back seat and Bluto covered in mud covering the blanket. Mrs. W. was taking Bluto in through the servant's entrance to have someone clean him up before Woody drove him back to the 48th Street Theater. She herself was off to a bath in what was bound to be a sunken tub big enough for Ali Baba and his Forty Thieves. Funny how we think of thieves whenever we think of wealth. Or at least funny how I do.

Anyway, I was in Hickman's inner sanctum in Stapleton as fast as the Staten Island Ferry could get Jane and me there, which was damn fast.

"Hell, Russo, you ever hear of soap and water?"

I didn't bother with that one. Instead I unwrapped what I'd wrapped up in the classified section of the New York Daily Mirror. Found the paper covering a sleeping bum on a bench near the aquarium in Battery Park. I didn't think he'd mind me taking a coupla pages. As for the ax, that was covered with an old torn shirt someone'd left on a stoop. I kept the ax wrapped and waiting. It felt like being a lawyer with a surprise courtroom exhibit.

Mortie peered inside the Daily Mail wrapping with more delicacy than I'd seen him use inspecting a human heart. Or maybe it was just suspicion, me being a graduate of the Staten Island Home for Little Rascals and all. "What the hell is this?"

"That's what I was gonna ask you."

"Where'd you get it? It stinks as much as you and that mutt do."

I didn't mind the insult to me, but calling Jane a "mutt" bothered me a little. "Morton, are you in a bad mood or are you trying to put me in a bad mood?"

By then, he was moving the fingers, looking at the long nails, fitting the thumb onto the hand. He looked at me. "Surprise me. Tell me this belongs to the big fella in one of my drawers."

"OK, Mortie. I think it belongs to the big fella in one of your drawers."

"Clever you. It must have taken some doing, finding these."

I once said Mortie Hickman looked like Peter Lorre's dad and I wasn't taking it back now. "You have no idea."

He said, "From the smell of you and your dog, I think I do. Now you get to tell me what *you* know about this."

So I told him what I knew. But I didn't tell him what I suspected. What I suspected was that where there was a part of one body, there were probably more bodies. The mud between the United Fruit piers was ideal for getting rid of 'em. The idea wasn't a long shot, not by a long shot. Not that that was any of my business. There could be hundreds of bodies sunk in the mud, it could be where Murder Inc. once got rid of most of their problems, or the dumping ground for every murderer in Manhattan. For me, all it really came down to was Maurice Oboram. It was where he was killed.

When I was finished telling Mortie what I felt like telling him which included Bluto but did not include the recently deceased Raymond LeGrand or what I'd found in Oboram's room, the same room recently occupied by my latest stiff, he said, "That explains the mud. And I can presume since you're here and that dog's here and the hand and the thumb are here, you haven't yet called the cops."

"You presume as beautifully as Astaire dances."

"But you will?"

"Have to. Unless I'm planning on mounting this over my mantle. If I had a mantle."

"Right then. Sit down and shut up. Keep that dog quiet too. Those noises she makes? They make my nerves ring."

I thought about that. Made his nerves ring? A guy who peeled the faces off dead people? A guy who stuck his arms up to his elbows in dead guts and gore? Well there you go, to each his own. I sat down, I shut up, I picked up the classifieds I'd brought the human hand and thumb in. Without a sound out of her, Jane lay at my feet and watched Morton Hickman go to work.

We both got to see Maurice Oboram again. After a few days and once out of his drawer and back on the table, he wasn't any prettier this time than the last time we met. But

I felt different. He was a man now, someone Jimmy'd liked, someone who loved his dog and lived with dignity, who still had dreams in spite of his size. This time I felt bad. So I read the paper.

By the time Mortie spoke to me again, I'd found an apartment in the Village near where Maurice had lived I thought I could afford. With my own body sitting in a small gray room with a little gray man doing horrid gray things, my mind had me and Jane living in Manhattan, getting crazy cases from Chinatown to Bellevue Hospital to the George Washington Bridge, had rented me an office with my name on the window somewhere in some building you'd expect to find a PI, and I never had to see Lino Morelli or Stapleton again.

The voice of Morton Hickman jerked me out of that sweet dream as fast as a fire alarm two inches from my ear. He'd placed the hand at the end of Oboram's arm and the thumb where a thumb usually goes.

"This," he said, "is the right hand of a large human male, approximately thirty five years of age. The hand has been forcibly removed from the wrist with a sharp instrument, a single clean cut or chop made by what I imagine is the same instrument that made the wound in the top of this particular skull. As noted before, the wound in the top of the skull is deep enough to have exposed the brain. The brain was, perhaps, even extruded."

I winced. If he noticed, he ignored me.

"The thumb belongs to the hand and the hand without doubt belongs to the very large body recently discovered under a Stapleton pier. The skin, flesh, and tendons of both hand and thumb have been eaten by the kind of organisms that live in mud. The list of these is endless. I've already assumed this is also true of the rest of the body kept in Drawer Seven. And even though the nails on both hands are filthy and clotted with river mud, there are traces of blood under all but the two smallest. The nails also show violent use, as if the victim tried to dig with them or climb something rough. Like shale. Stone, anyway."

I squirmed in my chair. I said, "Which means he was still alive after his head was split open. Jesus."

"Speaking as a Jew, my sentiments exactly. Although only barely alive. What happened to this poor fellow?"

"Not sure yet, but I'm working on it. Maurice Oboram was by all accounts one of the good guys."

"Maurice?"

"Oh, right. I forgot to tell you. I know who the giant is. I know where he lived and what he did to get by. And no, I haven't told Lino yet. It's getting too complicated and I wouldn't want to strain his brain. Not until I can explain things nice and easy so he can explain things nice and easy to the press."

I got the first smile out of Mortie since I couldn't remember when.

"About Bluto, the dog I told you found the hand?"

"Yes?"

"Bluto belonged to Maurice Oboram. He must of seen what happened to the poor guy. He may not of defended his master—after some acquaintance, I'd say the dog was a weak sister—but I think once the killer had gone, he at least tried helping his master out of the mud. Trouble is, as you say, the poor sap was more than half dead and too heavy even for a dog as big as Bluto is. I think Bluto hung around the body until the tide took it away. And when that happened, sometime on the night our giant was killed, Oboram's dog did the only thing he knew how to do. Maurice always took him to work with him. So off he went to work. Bluto made his way back through the streets of Manhattan to the theater, and when he got there, he was not only alone, he was still wet and muddy."

"Theater?"

"Maurice was an actor. He had a good part in a good play."

"That explains the ruff and the tights."

"As big as he was, Maurice was a gifted Shakespearean actor. Or so I'm told. Had a trunk full of tights and ruffs. Anyway, me and Jane found the hand and the thumb thanks to Bluto taking us to the right bit of riverbank." Best to leave out Mrs. Willingford. Mrs. Willingford was hard to explain under any circumstances. "Never would of found 'em otherwise." I began unwrapping my second parcel. "We also found something else. Bluto retrieved the murder weapon."

Mortie's eyes lit up like a follow spot at any theater in New York. Follow spot. I was learning the lingo. He said, "That's what you have with you?"

"That's what I have."

"Hand it over!" Mortie snatched the axe out of my grip—its handle still in its old shirt wrapping to protect any possible prints that could of lived through months of submersion in mud—and danced to the end of the table, the end Maurice Oboram's poor dead head was. "Now we'll see if it fits the wound in the skull."

It took him less than a second to be sure that it did.

I watched as either blade slipped in perfectly. "I knew it. But as soon as I call Lino, him and his cops'll trample all over this mess like hippos in a Disney cartoon. Or like other cops are doing right now back at the 48$^{th}$ Street Theater."

Mortie handed me back the axe with its wrapping. "I won't bother asking you what's playing at this theater you're talking about. I'm not going to bother asking why cops are making a mess of a crime scene over there. I won't even bother asking about the crime. I don't suppose it's much ado about the murdered giant I keep in one of my drawers since according to you he didn't die in the theater, and we both know he didn't die recently. So, when all's said and done,

what's it got to do with me?  But you, what if you don't tell
the cops about the axe that killed my victim?"

"They'll trample all over me."

Mortie was washing his hands. "Never a truer word. You
have a plan?" he said.

"Working on one.  One that needs you."

"Uhuh?"

"When you put Oboram back in his drawer, if you'd pop
his hand and his thumb in there with him—give me a little
more time?  And the axe, throw that in the drawer too?"

He thought about it.  He thought about it long enough
for me to try working out alternate plans 2, 3 and even 4,
each one more useless than the one before.

He said, "OK. What have I got to lose? You don't call the
cops, they'll never know a thing. You do call the cops, you
take all these things away first. They were never here."

"Deal."

"It's for the kids, Russo. The young girls.  I missed so
many of 'em at that place you grew up in, I need some
absolution.  I'm counting on you giving me a little bit."

"So no talking to Lino, right?"

"That was meant to be funny, right?"

"Right."

## 21

Jane and I were back at the good old homestead over the good old Rexall on the corner of Victory Boulevard and Bay Street. The park was still across the street, Holly and her friends were still walking its paths after dark. In my place the dust was deeper, looked like the cockroaches'd had a party, the clock'd run down to nothing, but otherwise all was as we'd left it.

Our room with the private bath was still waiting for us at the Iroquois Hotel but I wasn't going back until we were both scrubbed and polished.

Stapleton was much closer to Mortie's house of the dead than Manhattan, so Stapleton it was.

There were five messages slipped under my door when we got there. Two were from Lino. I didn't read 'em. Why bother? They'd both say the same thing. *Where are you? How's it going? When can I close this case?* The third was from Holly. I always read Holly's notes. Sometimes they were as droll as Dorothy Parker's once were. Sometimes they were drunken ramblings like Dorothy Parker's once were. Half the time, Holly was in trouble for just being Holly. When they rambled or were troubled, I'd go over to her or his place to see if everything was all right.

"*Darling Sam,*" it began—Holly always began with Darling Sam. "*Darling Sam, I'm in a bit of a jam and could use some help. Where are you?*" No wit there. No rambling either. It was the usual letter: trouble—just when I was up to my hocks in trouble galore. I read the fourth note with my mouth dry, also from Holly. "*Darling Sam, ignore my last note. All is unjammed. Are you coming to see me sing at the Green Garter tonight? You promised."*

Shit. "Tonight" was last night. I'd forgotten all about it. I'd write her a quick note, slip it under her door as I left. Tell her I was sorry I'd missed her show. But what a relief that whatever Holly trouble was brewing had settled down.

The fifth note was interesting. What was most interesting about it was how it found its way here in the first place. How did she know where I lived? How did she know I'd be here to get it?

The whole thing had me stumped. I hated the feeling. Was Bogie ever stumped? I mean, completely at a loss? If he was, you never saw it in his movies. He'd give his earlobe a pull and you could almost see a light bulb go on over his head. I tried pulling my earlobe. Nothing. I was as stumped as ever. But then, big surprise, looking for a clean pair of socks, I had a light bulb moment. She knew because Sam Russo, PI, was in the phone book, with address. How would I ever get any business if I didn't list my good old Saint George 7 prefix number in the yellow pages under "Private Investigators"?

There was probably another message just like it waiting for me at the Iroquois Hotel.

In a thin envelope, almost thin enough to read through, I read:

*Mr. Russo,*

*Please meet me at 11 p.m. at the Merrie Maide. It's a little place on 49th around the corner from Lindy's. I'm sorry about the hour but I don't think I can get away from the theater before then.*

*Love,*

*Maudie Rivers*

Love? Maudie Rivers? Oh well. Like most people, I could do with all the love I could get.

I glanced at the big brass Big Ben clock on what I thought of as my bureau. Now rewound and ticking along, it was a few minutes after 8 in the evening. The first of Mrs. Willingford's Park Avenue guests must be arriving right about now. The police must be winding down over at the theater on 48th Street. I was supposed to be, but I wasn't, there. Did they know that? If so, were they looking for me?

I shrugged. For all I knew, they'd solved it in record time and without me. But I wouldn't of placed a bet on it, not even for a measly nickel, not even if I got a hot tip, one of those "straight from the horse's mouth" tips. I knew my police. Unless the murderer was caught standing over his victim with a knife dripping blood, they'd be at it for days, weeks, longer. More times than not, other crimes, bigger crimes, flashier murders, would come along and Raymond would be just another forgotten case, a file gathering dust in some Manhattan precinct's back room filing cabinet.

No one liked Raymond LeGrand. He wasn't the star of *Harvey*. He was just a big guy who played a serious game of poker and wore a rabbit suit when he had to. Who was really going to spend the city's money and a lot of time to follow it down? Especially since no one but me and Mrs. Willingford and Morton Hickman knew about the hand and the thumb and the axe dug out of the Hudson River's mud. No one but me and Mrs. Willingford knew that LeGrand had "won" Oboram's room. Only me and Mrs. W and Jimmy knew about a second murdered Harvey.

So who cared?

I cared. Sam Russo cared. Not about Raymond LeGrand, but about Maurice Oboram. I'd known in my muddy gut the two big men were connected. How I knew that, I couldn't say. But that was part of the job—pure instinct. Bogie didn't tell me that. Nick Charles didn't tell me that. No crime movie I'd ever seen told me that. I knew it because I knew it. Discovering that LeGrand took over Oboram's room made that gut hunch a sure bet. I also knew that if I solved Raymond's murder, I'd also solve the murder of Maurice.

Like him or not, I had to solve the murder of Raymond LeGrand—even as I already knew, or was pretty sure I knew, who killed Oboram.

I thought of the nasty little hairpiece Jane'd found in the trunk at the foot of LeGrand's modest bed. If it didn't belong to Glenda's homely hubby, Mr. Glenda, aka Cliff Winker, I'd wear it myself. I'd already let Jane smell it. Jane smelling something was like watching someone inhale a reefer. She gave it the best her nose could give before I'd put it back in Mrs. Willingford's purse. Any other place, and the cops'd find it once I let them find me. But sure as shootin', there was going to come a moment when it'd play the lead in some scene that was all mine and Cliff's. And probably Jane's.

I decided I'd carry my gun. Off to Manhattan the first time round, I didn't think I'd be needing a belly gun. This time I did. From now on, me and my gun would be constant companions. Ready for anything, that gun.

For two months, my days had been spent eating too little, smoking too much, and reading as much as I could find worth reading. But on this one day alone, I'd done more than I'd done since Saratoga Springs.

The day was far from over.

My room came with a shared bath, but I did get my very own closet where I kept my spurs and my cavalry boots. After the war, we were allowed to keep those as well as any medals they felt like handing out; I had a Victory Medal and a Medal of Honor in my Prince Hamlet cigar box. I also had a tin table-tub that held up my kitchen table.

I washed Jane in my table tub.

Holly was rather fastidious for a man unless he was a woman. I liked Holly enough to use the tub under my table and not mess up "her" shared tub with our grime. I also used it because I didn't have the time to clean up the nasty mess we were making.

Jane hated it. You'd think she wanted her caked coat of

mud, the way she squirmed and yodeled and made a terrific fuss. After rubbing her dry—she shut up for that—I washed me as I sang *Singin' in the Bathtub* (great song I learned from Tweety, an all round great bird), changed into what I could find, all my other clothes being at the Iroquois. Then we both grabbed a mouthful of food, not much to choose from, but better than nothing. And, as said, I stuck my gun into one of my coat pockets, a Colt .38 Detective Special, the very piece that put one shot into Paul while he pumped three shots into me.

Last thing I did was slip a note under Holly's door.

*Glad you're alive and well. Sorry I missed your act. Be back soon. I'll take you somewhere swanky for dinner. Wear your best boa.*

*Your pal, Sam.*

Back on the isle of Manhattan, me and Jane hit the Rockefeller Skating Rink before moving on to the Merrie Maide. I'd promised her we'd see the place, and who knew when we'd get the chance again. Turned out to be a bunch of people going round and round and round, some of 'em going round backwards. Forwards, backwards, compared to a horse race, it stunk. Which was exactly Jane's opinion. She was off talking a guy out of a hotdog with all the fixings over at the hotdog stand before I'd finished admiring a cute kid in a short green skirt, a tight green top, and curls like Shirley Temple. Only she was a lot older than Shirley, old enough to be someone I ought to get to know. Only I never would because curly top was skating with a guy who looked like George Raft.

Sure enough, there was the exact same message in the exact same thin envelope waiting in a slot at the Iroquois Hotel. I had to hand it to Maudie. She was resourceful and determined.

I had one more message waiting in my room slot at the

desk of the Iroquois. I knew who it was from right off the bat. Who else perfumed a note?

> *Sam,*
>
> *Why do I do these things? If it weren't for the horses, money is the bunk. Be glad you didn't come to this "ball." I must know 300 of Mrs. Astor's Four Hundred. They're all here now, as dead as your average mummy only in more colorful wrappings. And much better hats. I'll be tracking you down as soon as I bust out of here. Or you could help a rich lady out and call her.*
>
> *Mrs. W.*

I stuffed this note in a pocket with the other two from Maudie Rivers, and Jane and I began our walk to the Merrie Maide.

## 22

It was all coming to me now, what this whole thing reminded me of. It reminded me of the third race at Monmouth Park awhile back. I had a lot riding on a mare named Zip Me Up who was going off at 5 to 1. Zip Me Up was coming to the end of her racing days, but she'd won a lot of good ones in her time, nothing eye catching, just nice solid wins in nice solid races. I didn't have a tip. I didn't believe in tips. I believed in knowing if the jock fit the horse, if the race fit the horse *and* the jock, and who they were both up against. Zip Me Up was good every which way and I was already counting my money. But after I'd bought and paid for the five dollar ticket, Zip Me Up's original jockey fell off his mount in the second race—horse was too young and too rank—so now the replacement jock didn't fit. Then, coming out of the gate, the number 4 horse slammed into my mare, driving her so wide it would of taken every other horse coming to a dead stop to get her back in contention. At that seemingly hopeless point, and before I could rip up my ticket, Zip Me Up proved her worth. She found something inside that took her sailing past the pack, something that kept her up there and driving until she was only a few lengths from home—flying for the wire until that something killed her. It drove her to her knees, flipped the wrong jock over her head and broke both their necks.

That's how I was feeling about all this. The wrong jock, the wrong race, the wrong compulsion driving me to work on something that no one was paying me for, that no one but me and Jimmy really cared about, and was something that in the end, I was going to wish I'd never seen.

About a block from the Merrie Maide, Jane walked calmly over to the gutter, threw up her hotdog, licked her lips, and walked calmly back to my side.

"That bad, eh gorgeous?"

Jane said... well, I don't know what Jane said because before I could hear it, I got my arm grabbed and was jerked into an alley I hadn't even noticed was there. The grab hurt. It hurt a lot. It was followed by a knife in the ribs.

The guy doing the grabbing and the knife play was bigger than me—seemed lately everyone was bigger than me in one way or another—but he wasn't bigger than Jane. Not even a running start, she made a spectacular leap that took her scarred action-packed body all the way up to his throat. If he hadn't been turning his head in surprise, she would of got him in just the right place for a death grip. As it was, she was hanging off the side of his neck just as she'd hung off Bluto's neck. Problem for the guy was he didn't have Bluto's fur. What he had was a bare neck with a sharp-toothed dog clamped on and blood flying out of her mouth, *his* blood, as he let go of me and the knife, so he could make a grab for her. But now I was free, and I had a gun in my pocket. Or I did, until it wasn't in my pocket. It was in my hand and the muzzle was pressed against his belly. I kicked the knife under about twenty nearby banged-up garage cans. The noise scared the hell out of the rats, scattered 'em in all directions. If Jane hadn't been busy—

"Let go of my dog. Now."

If the guy could of, he no doubt would of asked me to get the dog to let go of him, so I asked her. After all, having both gun and dog didn't seem fair odds to me.

Jane dropped back down to the alley where she sat and licked the blood off her lips with the same snort of disgust she'd shown when she saw the hotdog again. Then she waited, her teeth bared, a long low rumble in her throat, and her back legs ready for anything. Jane hadn't taken her eyes off the man with the bleeding holes in his neck. Both she and I could of seen 'em better if he hadn't had his hand clamped over 'em and if we didn't have to listen to him whine about how much they hurt and how much I was going to have to pay to get 'em sewed up. Once, that is, we all stopped wasting time and got him to a doctor.

"You expect me to pay for a doctor?"

"You expect *me* to pay? It's your dog." He took a long look at her and while looking, something happened to his voice. His register went up almost an octave. "Jesus. What's wrong with it? Is that a skin disease? I mean, is it catching?"

"She's fine. And it was your play."

"I didn't bring a dog."

"I didn't bring a knife."

"So who's got the gun?"

"I do. So stop crying and start talking, Noodles. Why'd you grab me in the first place?"

At the sound of his name, Noodles turned an unattractive shade of gray.

"What makes you think— ?"

"Who could forget a guy who let people call him Noodles? You're a stagehand. You owed Raymond LeGrand a lotta green; you think he cheated you; but you weren't the worst grouser, Eddie was."

Even if he wasn't called Noodles, I would of remembered him. Who could forget the stand up hair, the stretched mouth, the enormous nose, and the chin that needed only a few weeks growth to make him look like the sixteenth president of the United States? He was the grouser I remembered most of all the grousers, the one that told me too many times he hadn't seen anything. Right now I was looking at a guy with bulk, mostly in the middle, a face full of resentment, and a thick neck with holes in it. Noodles also had an accent from somewhere I'd never been. It wasn't New York and it wasn't

New Jersey. Maybe from up near Boston somewhere? Or maybe even farther north, like in Canada.

I said, "This your idea of a stick-up?"

"Jeez, no. All I wanted was your attention for a minute."

"With a knife?"

"Well, you know, I didn't know, it's New York City, and... you know."

"Sure, I know. So you got my attention. What now?"

It was pushing eleven at night. Speaking of time and New York City, you wouldn't know what hour it was just by looking around. When someone said it was the city that never sleeps, they weren't just being poetic—it was the truth. 49th Street was as lit up and as busy as Stapleton on the only day Stapleton was ever really busy, Christmas Eve. Stapleton took Christmas seriously. It had to. It was the one day it did a lot of business.

Now, one thing Sam Russo didn't do was, he didn't stand up a lady. Maudie Rivers could be one of those early types, the ones that would already have chosen us a nice table in the back of the Merrie Maide and was waiting while she sipped coffee and nibbled a very late night Cheese Danish. In about five minutes, she'd be checking her watch.

But I was still standing in an alley with Jane crouched and ready to leap, a gun in my hand, and a guy called Noodles who was looking at all the blood on his hand and winding up to whine again about us getting him to a doctor.

"Look fella," I said, "I'm kinda busy right now. So if you'd get to the point, any point, I'd appreciate it." I was trying to be nice and patient with him. After all, he may of had a knife, but it was his blood he was looking at.

"I saw ya at the theater."

"And I saw you. In a pack of stagehands, any one of which could of killed Raymond LeGrand. There wasn't one of you didn't make it clear what you thought of the guy."

"What! You think I coulda killed LeGrand?"

"Sure. You or any one of your friends."

That relaxed him a little. "Nah. I didn't kill nobody. I never have. Don't suppose I ever will. Unless maybe if a guy did something bad to a kid. Or if a guy did something I didn't like to a skirt I *did* like. Or if a guy cheated but I couldn't prove he cheated, so— "

"Noodles? Shut up."

"You don't have to be rude, buddy. So anyway, I heard ya was a peeper."

"A peeper?"

"A shamus."

"OK. So?"

"Well, it's like this. There's this thing I know— "

"Which you'd like me to know."

"You said it."

"For the small sum of—how much is this small sum?"

"Say, I don't know about it bein' so small. I got some wounds here need lookin' at."

"If it's not small, it's not at all." With that, I began walking away. Maudie's coffee could be getting cold. And where I went, Jane went.

"OK. OK. I'll tell ya."

I stopped. I took out my wallet. I wondered if I had enough time to get an expense receipt for Lino.

"I saw who opened trap 18."

"And you haven't told the cops?"

"Nah. Just like if you was to kill a guy who owes you, where's the profit in that?"

Still thinking of Detective Lino Morelli, I said, "You have a point. So who opened the trap?"

"That woman who works for Miss Hull."

"Maudie Rivers?"

"That's the one."

I said, "Well, hot damn."

## 23

Jane at my heels, I walked out of Noodle's cozy alley into a steady stream of New Yorkers going here and there along the sidewalk. I got bumped into a couple of times, sworn at once, someone tried to pet Jane which was a mistake, and got bumped into hard by a small guy in a thick winter overcoat and a dark hat pulled down past his ears. Not a bad idea. The season was turning as fast as the cars zipping past on 49th Street.

She was there. But not in the back. The Merrie Maide was too small to have a back. It was almost too small to have a front. It was about the smallest soda fountain I'd ever seen. But it had all the right stuff. A counter, stools, a guy in a white paper hat making her an ice cream soda. As I said, it was November, it was cold inside and out. Maybe she grew up in Alaska and the city's chill was as a zephyr to her. Or maybe she just liked cold things.

Before I had even a foot in the door, the soda jerk said, "No dogs."

"Oh Hector," said Maudie, adjusting her glasses, "knock it off."

Hector knocked it off and went back to sitting on his own stool near the cash register. He picked up the book he'd been reading: *Tropic of Cancer*.

I thought about that for at least a second before taking the stool next to Maudie's. I'd heard of Miller. The stuff he wrote was banned in the U.S. The only kind of copy Hector could be holding was a smuggled copy. I almost dropped the whole case so I could get to know Hector and borrow his book.

Then I remembered who I was. I was Bogart and I'd been invited to a soda fountain by a woman who might turn out to be, who knew? Anyone at all. Miss Rivers might even turn out to be my killer. I couldn't pass that up for a little welcome obscenity.

That was when I noticed what I should of seen straight off. Maudie had a shiner. Left eye. A beaut.

I pointed at it, I opened my mouth to ask, I got shut down before I said a word. "Don't ask," she said, and by the way she said it, I had no doubt she meant it. So I didn't ask. Instead I ordered a coffee. Even a soda fountain had coffee. Weak but drinkable.

When it came and I was lifting the cup to my lips, Maudie took her own lips off her straw. They'd been stuck there, sucking at sloppy ice cream, since she'd had that word with me about her eye. All along, she'd been staring through her shiner and her glasses out the Merrie Maide window.

I was about to get the conversation started when, suddenly, she slammed her ice cream soda down, hard enough to clang on the marble counter. "I've changed my mind. I've got nothing to say to you."

I said, "Now wait a minute—"

But Maudie Rivers was off her stool and out the door before even Jane could turn her head.

I would of been out the door right after her, but Hector stopped me. This was a serious Hector, one with the paper hat, the contraband book, and steel in his bulbous blue eye. "Hey! Who's paying for the soda and the coffee? Pay up, buster, and then you can chase the dame."

"But— "

"Pay up, bub, or I'm calling the cops. I don't even need a phone."

He was right. A beat cop was that minute passing the window of the Merrie Maide. I threw all the coins in my pocket on his counter, more than he needed, and Jane and I were out the door. What this taught me was, I needed to teach Jane to follow people—but that would have to take a rain check. It was too late now. Maudie was gone in the hustle and bustle of New York City at night.

Why I did what I did next still stumps me. But I did it and I did it almost as fast as Maudie had disappeared. There was a phone booth half a block back from the alley where Jane and I had met the interesting Mr. Noodles, the man who thought getting a guy's attention required a knife. The man who called me a peeper. A peeper. Now, there was a term to make me quit the game if ever there was one.

The Willingford butler answered. I guess it was the butler; it could of been a masseuse or the head gardener. Whoever it was, it didn't sound like Woody. Woody, when he had something to say, which was seldom, sounded like he could go a few rounds with Dempsey. This guy sounded like something was stuck in his teeth. "Good evening. You are speaking to the Willingford residence. How may I help you?"

In the background I could hear a live dance band, a pretty good one, playing the pretty awful *Sabre Dance*.

"I'd like to speak to Mrs. Willingford please."

"I'm afraid Mrs.—"

"—will want to speak to me. She asked me to call."

"And your name?"

"Russo, Sam."

"Rusto?"

"That'll do."

The receiver on the other end was set down so carefully I didn't hear it land, but it could of been slammed against the wall and I'd still be treated to *Sabre Dance*. I wasn't worried. Most of America was getting the same treatment, and most of us had so far survived. Jane sat at my feet, her ears cocked up and humming along. She had her eyes closed. Almost four months, and I was only now beginning to wonder if she was maybe something besides a dog. Bogie didn't have a dog hanging around, puking up hot dogs and hanging off necks. Nick Charles had a dog, but Asta wasn't a patch on Jane. Asta was cute. Jane was not and never would be cute.

"Sam!"

The sound of Mrs. Willingford's voice came out of the phone as excited and as welcome as a race caller's. I said, "You still want out of there?"

"More than ever."

"Meet me at Lindy's as soon as you can."

"I might make it before you."

"I doubt that."

"Never doubt a Willingford."

She was right. How the hell she got to Lindy's before me I didn't bother to ask. With her money, she probably owned a Tesla patent on some sort of time machine. She also owned more than one sneaking-around outfit. This one was as black as the last one, but it came with a black hat that covered her expensive hair and short black boots with soft soles that protected her expensive feet. Her expensive hands were bare, the long red nails tap tapping on one of Lindy's checkered tablecloths. But I was sure she had a sneaky pair of expensive black gloves with extra long fingers on her somewhere, and a black mask by Chanel.

I knew a few designer names now. Chanel. Dior. Somebody else.

Anyway, we were both in a booth and I'd told her everything that had happened since we'd last seen each other, which wasn't that long ago. Not more than a few hours back, we'd been dripping with Hudson River mud, herding two muddy dogs, when she went her way with Woody and one dog and I went my way with Jane. Now we were all squeaky clean again and going the same way.

The last person I sat around with and spilled my guts to

was Jimmy. The one before that shot me. Here I was, doing it again, blabbing about Mortie and Maurice and Noodles and Maudie Rivers. Obviously, I hadn't learned a damned thing. But Mrs. Willingford probably wouldn't shoot me. At least not with a gun.

"OK," she said, "here's what we'll do."

"We?"

"You called me. Of course *we*. The police have no doubt sealed up the crime scene. And unless they have a suspect, which I doubt or the gentleman you met in the alley would have said so, everyone's gone home for now including the police. They've all been warned, of course, not to disappear. If I were the killer, I'd take that advice. Running off would be a dead giveaway. Meanwhile, there's probably a guard left at the theater. Maybe two. But all the rest will be back in the morning. It's their job to be back. The show must go on. Police as well as *Harvey*. So what we'll do is sneak in."

I'd been patient as I listened to all this. Was she kidding? Telling Sam Russo, an old pal of Detective Lino Morelli, what cops did. But that last sentence surprised me. "We'll what?"

"Sneak in. We have to find what I'll bet the cops didn't find. We have to find out what your mysterious Maudie Rivers was going to tell you, but didn't. And we have to find out when and why this Maudie Rivers—heavens, how I love that name—opened the stage trap. Oh, and who gave her the black eye. And Sam?"

I'd been listening. I'd been hearing every husky word. But I'd also been watching the little movie behind my eyes. Me and Jane and Mrs. Willingford getting caught sneaking around inside the 48th Street Theater, which by the way, was huge, trying to find something the cops had either already found, or had already destroyed, or was so well hidden it might as well not be there. Or was never there in the first place.

"Sam!"

Not only me, but Jane, jumped in our seats.

"What?"

"We have to do all this without getting seen by the cops left to guard the place. What are we waiting for? It's past midnight. Time to get moving."

## 24

Normally, Mrs. Willingford could walk into anywhere anytime. From the New York City Center (which looked like a cut-rate mosque without the usual robed and bearded crowd salaaming around) right in the middle of a performance of *Madame Butterfly*, to crashing one of Mayor O'Dwyer's dinners at Gracie Mansion. It helped with the ancient hubby Joker Willingford tagging along, but Joker wasn't really necessary. What was appealing about Joker was his money. What was appealing about Mrs. Willingford was Mrs. Willingford.

My Mrs. Willingford was the third Mrs. Willingford, and considering Joker's age, probably the last Mrs. Willingford. Although you could never tell with these really old, really rich, guys. They traded wives like horseflesh—not that I could see him swapping my Mrs. Willingford for anything less than Gene Tierney. Or, in a pinch, Veronica Lake. Joker owned one of Kentucky's biggest distilleries (*Joker's Special Blend*) as well as the virtually legendary Beeswing Farm, breeder of some of Kentucky's legendary horses. Not only did the leading stud, Joker's Wild, stand there, but both Joker Willingford and the present Mrs. Willingford were the proud parents of one of the country's greatest fillies: Fleeting Fancy.

That was basically gate-crashing. This was breaking and entering. It wasn't anything like making a grand entrance where you weren't invited. Especially breaking and entering a crime scene. Here's where I'd earned a few stripes. The years spent doing Lino Morelli's job taught me about cops. First off, I knew how many were probably stuck inside the

theater. As Mrs. Willingford correctly guessed: two at the
most. Second, forget that old saw about criminals returning
to the scene of the crime. Pyros maybe. Most of those guys
didn't go anywhere in the first place. They usually stuck
around at a safe distance and watched their fire burn. For
firestarters, watching it burn was the whole point. But
not killers. If they didn't have to, they rarely came back to
admire their kill. Especially since the body and/or bodies,
once discovered, were removed. I also knew what the cops
who pulled an all-nighter did with their lonely, usually
useless, all night watch. They played cards. When that got
boring or one of 'em ran out of cash, they went to sleep. It
was supposed to be one at a time, leaving the other on duty,
but once one slipped away into slumberland, the other was
almost always bound to follow—although that one would
try to do it sitting up. Anyway, at some point they'd both
sleep and pretend they hadn't. I also knew about Josephine's
back door which they didn't, so they wouldn't be hiding aces
or snoring anywhere near it.

What I had was knowing how they worked, plus having
access to a secret back door. What they had were badges and
Bluto. But Bluto was most likely doing his own twelve hour
shift snoring on his makeshift bed in Josephine's dressing
room. The more I knew about Bluto, the more I knew there
were dogs and there were dogs. Some were Lassie. Some
were Bluto. I'd never seen one like Jane.

Off to the back door Jane and Mrs. Willingford and I
snuck.

It was like I thought. They were playing cards in the
Green Room, which is where I would of played cards. There
was a couch, a table, a floor lamp. There was even a radio.
They had it on low. Dinah Shore was singing *Buttons and
Bows*. I figured they were both too tired to turn the stupid
thing off. If they hadn't heard *Button and Bows* over a thousand
times by now, they'd be two of America's luckiest listeners.

It was twelve thirty in the morning; they were already yawning.

Obvious neither of 'em took the job seriously. If it were Lino's watch, one would of long since snuck out for burgers and a bottle. It wasn't Lino's watch, but it might as well be. These two already had a bottle and plenty of smokes. There was also a box of doughnuts on the table. As far as I could see, they were set for the night. I'd bet they'd already tossed a coin for who got the couch.

Jane sat by my feet staring at them. The only light in the whole place was their light so they were easy to see. We weren't. Especially Mrs. Willingford. I now completely understood why all the black.

"Sam," said Mrs. Willingford in a whisper I barely heard but was probably clear as day to Jane, "maybe there are some things we ought to do alone."

"Mrs. Willingford," I said, "now's not the time."

She should of pinched me, but she refrained. Who knew how much noise I would of made? "I meant Jane and you know I meant Jane. What if Bluto wakes up? You told me what happened last time."

"Jane," I said.

She looked straight up, her eyes wide, her ears wider.

"Leave Bluto alone."

Her reply was barely audible, but I heard it. She said: *Fine with me—the big fat-head.*

"The trouble with all this, Mrs. Willingford, is we don't know what we're looking for."

"Ah," said she, "no one does but the killer. But perhaps you're not asking yourself a crucial question."

"Oh yeah? And what's that?"

"Aside from why Maudie Rivers, nothing more it seems than a dresser for Josephine, would open the stage trap at all, what did she know and why make an appointment with you, keep it, and then leave in such an almighty hurry before she told you whatever she meant to tell you?"

"Someone scared her off."

"Exactly. First she gets biffed in the eye, but she still kept the appointment, so the really scary part didn't come until she was waiting in the Merrie Maide. That means the scary person was nearby at the very moment you sat down. She must have seen him through the window."

"Good thinking, Mrs. W."

"Of course, Mr. R. I didn't get where I am today without a good hustle."

"I love your hustle."

"Knock it off. We're pros here, so act like one."

What could I say to that? If I reminded her who between us had a license, she'd remind me that only made it worse. Even without a license, she was doing better than me. So I knocked it off and put my Bogie face on.

She said, "So we know the scary person works here at the theater."

"Because he— "

"I hate prejudice, Sam. Or she."

"I was thinking of Noodles. On the spot with a knife."

"Oh. Of course. True."

Having won that one, I could now be generous. "Because he *or* she was the one Maudie saw when she opened the trap door."

"Exactly. So we either find Maudie or we find out what she knew. Which is why we're here. Where does Maudie spend all her time? Answer. In Josephine's dressing room. So that's where we're going."

"That's where *you're* going. I'll meet you there as soon as I can."

"Excuse me?"

"I said— "

"I heard what you said. What did you mean?"

"I mean you search Josephine's. Me and Jane, we'll search

the communal dressing room. You could be right about Josephine's dressing room but you could also be wrong."

Mrs. Willingford never stopped scaring me. The look I got scared me. On the other hand, what she was doing— sneaking around the theater even when it was guarded by New York City cops—I would of been doing myself, because believe it or not, I would of thought of this caper on my own. I just wished she hadn't thought of it first. Or said it first. Or did it first.

Oh, what the hell.

## 25

I never heard a sound she made moving past the Green Room and towards the dressing rooms—and me, I was right next to her carrying Jane so her claws wouldn't click on the floor.

Bluto was right where I expected him to be. On his blanket, asleep. Even sleeping he smelled her. One sight of Jane, now on her own four legs in the middle of Josephine's carpeted floor, he didn't move a hair as she dared him to move a muscle. I didn't want him moving anything. Him moving would alert the guards.

Maybe.

I said, "Good dog," and ruffled one of Jane's ears. In return, I got exactly nothing. Her attention was on Bluto and nothing but Bluto.

At that point, Mrs. Willingford and I went to work, her in one room, me and Jane in another.

For the next half hour or so, if she was doing what I was doing, and she was, we each rifled every drawer, every closet, every hat box, every shoe in every shoe rack, stuck our fingers in every jar of cream or make-up container, shook every book left lying about, peeked behind pictures and mirrors and screens, snooped in every possible place anything—even a scrap of paper—could be hidden in. Like me, she must of found all sorts of interesting things. Only mine belonged to a lot more people than hers did.

What I didn't find was anything that told me a thing about Glenda Gordon's hubby, Cliff Winker. I was looking for something to explain how or why LeGrand had one of

Mr. Glenda's rugs. What was it doing in the apartment of Maurice Oboram? Or was it Raymond's place at the time? If it was Raymond's place, had Cliff paid a call on his rival and come away, the poor sap, second best?

Over in Josephine's dressing room, things went pretty much the same for Mrs. Willingford—except for that one thing that changes all things. If there were rules to what makes a good PI, I was still working 'em out for that book I'd never write. But if there were, the first one had to be: Luck is Everything.

My luck was walking into Josephine's dressing room the moment Mrs. Willingford tripped over Jane who just happened to be taking her shot at Bluto, and when Mrs. Willingford tripped, she made a grab at the dressing table for balance. The table held her up the best it could, but not being stable, it couldn't do much. So she sat down fast and hard on the floor at the same time as Josephine's dressing table hopped up into the air, flinging off an address book. The stuff on that table could fill Macy's cosmetics department.

It was a nice black leather address book that should of been in Josephine's purse, but wasn't—probably due to the day's excitement.

All along, it'd been sitting in full view while Mrs. Willingford searched the place, but I couldn't blame her. I might not of noticed it either.

I opened it up, flipped through to the Rs and lo and behold! I discovered it wasn't Josephine's book, it was Maudie Rivers' book. Flipping back to the inside front cover, there was the proof, Maudie's address and phone number.

Mrs. Willingford had the book out of my hand faster than Citation out of a starting gate. Out dropped a piece of folded paper.

I looked at her and she looked at me. Stooping neatly, Mrs. W picked it up from the floor.

Embossed on top of some nice quality stuff was Anders

Slydel's name in a curly fussy font. There wasn't much left of the note since there wasn't much left of the paper but what there was, was interesting. In a sloping hand, it was dated a little over two months back: September 7. Under that was written in the same sloping hand: "*You know I can't have this getting out. So you'll keep quiet, won't you, darling? If you don't, they'll...* "

Bingo.

Anders Slydel was writing to Maudie Rivers. He was calling her "darling." Add that to how I'd heard her inhale his name as well as hiss it, and we were cooking here. Although you could look at it another way. Our pot might boil over. This was getting to be one rich stew. Mr. & Mrs. Glenda. Slydel & the missing Rivers. Two large dead rabbits. Noodles. And a whole host of theatrical characters who'd gain by the loss of LeGrand.

Anyhow, we now knew where Miss Rivers lived—I assumed she was a Miss, but I could of been dead wrong; after a war, the world was awash with widows. She lived near where Maurice Oboram had lived which was where Raymond LeGrand also lived—once Maurice vacated the premises. The address, 92 Barrow Street, was almost right around the corner from Commerce, even closer to the Hudson River.

I said, "Did I ever mention how I found Oboram's place?"

"No, you never did, Sam."

"It was written on a rolled up piece of paper in a doohickey hanging from Bluto's collar. It still is."

"Well, that makes sense. People like to know that if their dogs get lost, some kind soul will bring them back. It helps to know where to bring them to."

"I know that."

"But I'll bet you don't know what Anders Slydel doesn't want getting out or what *they'll* do if it does or why his note was torn or even if it was written to Josephine Hull's personal dresser."

"No. I don't. And neither do you. But for the moment, it doesn't matter. What matters is now we can find Maudie Rivers. Where's Jane?"

"Oh shoot."

We both turned around just in time to stop another terrific hullabaloo caused by Jane. If not, even the cops in the Green Room would of come running.

"Dammit, Jane. What did I tell you?"

Jane surprised me. For the first time since we met I got to see what she looked like feeling guilty.

"Never thought I'd see that," said Mrs. Willingford.

I said, "Me neither. You two up to paying Maudie Rivers a visit at this hour?"

The hour was past two on a November night in New York City. It was cold out there. But half the lights were still on and all the cabs were running and millions of people were doing a million different things, most of which I would never know or care about. But I cared about Maudie Rivers. She'd been scared. Scared people scared me. It meant something, and what it meant was almost always bad.

"On Barrow Street?"

"When they're scared and don't know what else to do, most people run home."

Mrs. Willingford was opening a box on Josephine's dressing room table. "When was the last time Jane, or you for that matter, ate anything?"

"Can't remember. I think Maudie knew, or almost knew, something really important and she was going to tell me. I think— "

"In this box, Sam, is Josephine's collection of Tootsie Rolls. There's also some crackers, and God help us, Velveeta cheese. Fresh."

Jane wolfed down half the cheese while Mrs. Willingford

placed the other half near Bluto. The drool was a dead giveaway: he wanted it, but he wasn't going to try for it with Jane around. So I picked up Jane. Me, I pocketed a lot of Tootsie Rolls.

"I think—" I continued, chewing on a Tootsie Roll, "—that if Maudie's not home, then—"

Mrs. Willingford dug her claws into my arm. Ouch. The woman was lethal. "If she isn't, Sam, is she dead? Do you think someone killed her?"

"Only way to find out is go and look. If she's not there, then she has to be—"

From behind us came the sound of an animal chewing off its own paw. Or near enough. All three of us turned to look at Bluto who was having some trouble opening or closing his mouth thanks to Josephine's Velveeta cheese.

"Good lord," said Mrs. Willingford, "the only thing dumber than that dog is one of my sous chefs."

"He cooks with Velveeta?"

"Shut up, Sam."

I shut up. It wasn't hard. Worrying about Maudie had dried up my mouth. It also wasn't hard getting past the two New York City cops guarding the scene of a murder.

We could of roller skated by the Green Room carrying on in ancient Egyptian for all the two cops could care. Any noise we made was smothered by both of 'em snoring like overtime at a saw mill. I would of stopped in awe, but Mrs. Willingford kicked the back of my leg.

"Ouch!"

"Sam, sometimes I think I'm working with Elmer Fudd."

"*You're* working—?"

"Just keep moving, will you?"

## 26

I'd never met anyone like Mrs. Willingford.

It wasn't because she was rich. For one thing, she hadn't been born any richer than I'd been. From bits and pieces dropped here and there, I'd say she was a Midwest transplant, maybe Iowa, maybe Indiana. I wasn't great at recognizing accents, so truth was she could of hailed from the coal fields of West Virginia for all I knew. But I did know this. Wherever she'd begun, she'd got out on her own and nothing was taking her back.

And it wasn't because she'd been to places I'd probably never see or knew people I knew I'd never know. It was more than that. Or less. I think the problem I had was I couldn't pin her down. I couldn't predict what she'd do or say. It made me uneasy. It made her something I'd never known in a woman before. She was her own man.

I liked it—and I didn't like it.

Some people remind me of horses. The moment I first saw her, Mrs. Willingford brought to mind the most cantankerous horse ever bred: a stallion called Boston. Boston lived his life furious and he died furious, kicking his stall to pieces. They found him like that, drenched in his own blood. I still saw Boston in Mrs. W. But more and more she reminded me of a great mare with that rare thing: true grit. The mare's name was Pan Zareta but everyone called her Panzy. Panzy wasn't born in a Kentucky horse barn that most folks would say was a mansion. I don't think she was even born in a barn. She arrived on some spread in Sweetwater, Texas, and her breeding was so suspect they wouldn't list her in the American Stud Book.

Panzy raced from Mexico to Canada, trained by anyone available, ridden by anyone handy, was entered into any race she qualified for. Her largest purse was less than a thousand bucks, but over and over she put her life on the line for a hundred. Panzy raced more than any mare in U.S. history, and she won more. Carrying more weight than any other runner, male or female, she took first in anything and everything, running the legs off male and female. She set world records, she beat Old Rosebud, winner of the 1914 Kentucky Derby. In time, even with her non-stop two-bit races, major sportswriters called her the "Queen of the Turf."

In Saratoga Springs, I gained Jane but I lost my feeling for people. Most people. But long before Saratoga, the two-bit bozos who thought they owned Panzy sickened me. To them, she meant nothing but money.

They raced her too much.

Pan Zareta, the Queen of the Turf, died of pneumonia, untreated and alone on Christmas Day in a crummy stall in New Orleans. She was only eight years old.

The track she raced on most often knew who she was. The New Orleans Fair Grounds buried her whole, in the infield right next to Black Gold. I was four when Black Gold won the Kentucky Derby—I missed that one. But not one single Derby since. Of course, I only heard them. I didn't see them except on newsreels.

I wished I met Panzy. I wished she'd been mine. I'd get myself down there one day. I'd pay my respects to Black Gold and to Pan Zareta, two of the greatest of them all.

I was beginning to see that Panzy, without a saddle and bit, was Mrs. Willingford.

As I said, I didn't know her breeding and I didn't know her background—I probably never would. I just knew, like Panzy, she could run the legs off anything.

Nothing like Panzy's end would ever happen to Mrs. Willingford. When Mrs. Willingford died, they'd lower the flags at every race track in the country. And me, if I were still around, would go on a jag for months in her memory.

We grabbed a cab to her place on Park Avenue so we could take one of Joker's cars all the way down to 92 Barrow Street. No Woody. Just us and Jane. I was unhappy about that. I liked having Woody around for a couple of obvious reasons. Mrs. Willingford said he was too busy with driving her drunk guests home.

92 Barrow wasn't anywhere like I'd imagined Maudie Rivers hanging her hat. Too shabby, too many rough looking characters lining the street, too many bars making too much noise, too much dogshit on the sidewalks. Once out of the car, Jane, high stepped through it all, nose in the air. So did Mrs. Willingford.

I didn't know whether to go first or last. If some nasty character out of Dick Tracy came along, which was best? I chose last.

Looking back at where we'd parked the big long classy car, I started to say something about it not being there when we got back, but she got in first. "Joker has two more of them."

"I figured that one out all on my own. And Woody isn't your only driver."

"No. But he's my favorite."

What could I say to that? Nothing. So I shut my mouth.

There were three apartments on the three floors of number 92. *M. Rivers* was neatly typed on a nice white card taped beside the first floor bell. Not one light was lit in a single window—which wasn't surprising when you took into account it was 3 a.m. on the isle of Manhattan.

I've said New York City never sleeps. It doesn't. But

some of its working people do.

"Now what?" said Mrs. Willingford.

"Now we pick the lock."

There were two of 'em on the shared door, both smooth as cream. Things went a lot faster without Mrs. W breathing down my neck.

Once both were unlocked, I said, "Wait here with Jane. I'll be back as soon as I can."

Mrs. Willingford slammed me in the back, in that sweet spot right where it took out most of my wind—we were all inside before I could catch my breath again.

"I forgot to tell you," she said, pointing at the locks, "but you're teaching me that. Just as soon as we have a few free moments. Right now, though, time to open Maudie's door."

I gave her my best evil eye. "I never break in before knocking."

"How polite, Sam. My respect for you grows by the hour. So knock."

I knocked. Nothing. I knocked again. Nothing. I gave the woman some time to wake up before she answered a coupla knocks on her door in the middle of the night. I didn't expect her to open up. I wouldn't. No one with half a brain would. What I expected was for her to check her peephole. Nothing.

One last knock.

"For pete's sake, Sam, you keep this up and you'll wake the whole building. Pick the damn lock."

Seated primly on the bottom step of a curving stairway, Jane agreed with a low yodel. Like a cat, she was cleaning her left paw, then her right paw. I wasn't sure I'd ever get used to that.

As for Mrs. Willingford, I'd finally had it. I was up to here with Mrs. Joker Willingford. She might be Pan Zareta, but she was also Boston. If Boston hadn't sired Lexington—

the sire of every good horse America saw for one hell of a lot of years—someone would of shot him.

"Listen, you. Keep talking to me like you're talking to me and you're out of the picture. Not even an extra. You understand?"

"You mean I'm fired?"

"In a word, yeah."

"You're serious?"

"Dead serious."

"You can't fire me."

"I can go home with Jane right this fucking minute. I can forget about giants and trap doors and mud and women with secret information who disappear in the night."

Mrs. Willingford put her face right up to mine—damn, but she smelled good—and studied every angle in my face. After some of that, she made her decision. "I'll be better."

"In that case—start the fuck now and shut up."

I picked the lock. And before my wondering eyes, Mrs. Willingford turned into a good little rich girl; she kept her lovely red mouth shut and her big blue eyes open for late night tenants, or other night owl types who might also arrive to pick a few locks.

Maudie's lock was as easy as the two front door locks. Easier.

Why most of America wasn't robbed blind nightly, beat me. All us would-be burglars had to do was take a course from Rudy Hiller back in Bayonne, New Jersey. Look what he'd done for me.

Mrs. Willingford and Jane were right behind me.

Unlike Josephine's dressing room, this time we didn't have to ransack Maudie's apartment. Someone had already done it for us.

This was a real apartment, with a kitchen, a proper bath, and *two* bedrooms. The furniture was tasteful and new; there was a brand new television set and a brand new record player and a lot of brand new records. And all of it—living room, bedrooms, kitchen, and bathroom—was kicked in or smashed on the floor or dumped willy nilly. I picked up a record. Guy Lombardo. I picked up another and another. Mario Lanza. Rudy Vallée. I shivered and left the rest alone. I didn't think they were catching, but I didn't want to take the chance.

Two things were going on here. The first was that someone had really gone to town on Maudie's apartment, enough to make me very nervous. Maudie, wherever she was, could be looking as bad as her pad. The other was that Maudie Rivers wasn't hurting for cash. On a theatrical dresser's salary, I had to wonder why, although the why was obvious. Pinned to a wall by her phone was a name I knew. The name had a phone number beside it. An uptown number. It was the same exchange as Mrs. Willingford's: PL 5. The PL was for Plaza. Anders Slydel would have a Plaza prefix.

To Mrs. Willingford, the place probably looked pretty ordinary, but to me it looked like a man's castle. OK, a woman's castle. A sacked castle, but a castle nonetheless. Of course, if it were mine, I'd get rid of the ruffled pale yellow curtains and the daisyed dinner set. As for the collection of Hummel figurines, each one of 'em smashed where they stood in what Mrs. Willingford informed me was a display cabinet—and a tasty one to boot, said she—those things: pink cheeked milk maids and kiddy angels and chubby knee'd kids in lederhosen—even in pieces, they set my teeth on edge.

We'd just fought a war against the people who made this mawkish crap, and we won. Who needed reminding?

But otherwise, the whole place, plus its location, would suit me just fine. Once it was cleaned up.

So, who was Maudie Rivers? What did she want to tell me? Why'd she change her mind? Or... who changed it for her? And where was she now?

With all this running through my head, I'd neglected Jane. Jane had been darting from room to room, sniffing and humming and curling and uncurling her tail. Finally, she'd run straight for the front door and yodeled.

"Dammit, Jane. You'll wake the neighbors."

Jane yodeled louder than ever, rose on her hind legs, caught the doorknob in her mouth, and turned it.

I looked at Mrs. Willingford and she looked at me. Neither of us had a clue.

Nothing for it but to open Maudie's door and then the one to the street, where both Mrs. Willingford and I were hard pressed to keep up with Jane flattened out, running—straight down Barrow Street towards the Hudson River.

Towards the river. This time, in the dark.

Hell's bells. Not again.

## 27

Back at the old Staten Island Home for Children, whenever "Mister" Zawadzki felt flummoxed or surprised or pissed off, or anything foreign to his limited "Mister" Zawadzki feelings, he'd yell: "God's great nuts!" For this, he'd earn a terrific wallop round the ear from Flo Zawadzki, but he couldn't help it—he'd get that feeling and out it would come, wallop or no wallop.

For us kiddie captives, aside from running away and staying away, or listening to his radio while we hung off the outside of his personal shed by our fingertips, that wallop made our day.

God's great nuts, but Mrs. Willingford could run. I knew she was in good shape, but this was a shape I'd never suspected. The woman was a born sprinter. Maybe she couldn't beat Fanny Blankers-Koen who'd taken four gold medals at the London Olympics, but she could sure give Fanny a run for her money.

In seconds, she was behind the wheel of her town car— unstolen and undamaged: amazing—and was pulling up next to me with a screech of brakes before I was even half way there.

A man's thoughts, maybe even a woman's, are a zillion times faster than Fanny Blankers-Koen or Seabiscuit racing War Admiral or Mrs. Willingford's filly Fleeting Fancy. But watching her swerve the long lean car into Barrow Street, I remembered up in Saratoga Springs when I gave chase to Carroll Goose who'd tried and failed drugging Ace Admiral to stop him winning the Travers. If we'd switched so Mrs.

Willingford'd done the chasing and I'd stayed behind to soothe the horse and harass the track management, Carroll Goose would be alive today.

Mrs. Willingford could of tackled him in half a shed row.

I was wearing socks at the time (it's a long story) and in socks I'd stepped on something that hurt, not as bad as Assault with the surveyor's stake, but bad enough—which made this particular story less shaming. Even so, enter Mrs. Willingford in the Kentucky Oaks and I'd bet her at least across the board.

"In," she said, leaning over to open the passenger side door. "Now. Before we lose sight of Jane."

We hadn't lost sight of Jane. She was pelting right down the middle of Barrow Street. By the time we got to where she'd just been, she'd veered south and was now doing good time down one side of West Street.

Mrs. Willingford knew where Jane was headed. So did I. Back to the mud between Piers 9 and 10 of the United Fruit Company.

Just great. And in the pitch dark.

We caught up with her at the New York Telephone Company building. Fat lot of good it did us. This was the exact moment when Jane, yodeling like a berserk Heidi, leapt into the goddamn mud.

Once again, Mrs. Willingford stunned me. Without hestitation, she was right behind. All I could do was thank whoever or whatever that the telephone company, like most of New York City, never slept. We could see just enough by the lights in its thirty two floors of windows to tell we were in for it—again.

With Jane plunging about and digging, it didn't take long to find something.

For a second there, I thought we'd found the body of poor Maudie Rivers. It wasn't, but it was close enough.

Too light to sink into Hudson river mud, Maudie's glasses were glinting in the moonlight about twenty feet from solid ground.  Some dark part of me, something crimson and childish and cruel left over from growing up the way I did, wanted to make a joke about it, her name, the river, the mud; it took all I had to keep that ugly little darkness as sealed up and as secret as J. Edgar Hoover's sex life.  Not even a crack about what a free mud pack could do for a fresh black eye.

Instead I said, "Fuck."

The only reason I knew about the head of the Federal Bureau of Investigation's sex life was because of California's Del Mar racetrack.  Everybody who cared about horse racing knew Del Mar had a special section of private boxes owned by fairies and used by fairies.  A whole lot of people knew that whenever Hoover went to the races, that's where he sat—in one of those boxes.  We all knew who sat with him, some fellow named Clyde something or other.

I didn't care—as long as they didn't scare the horses.

Mrs. Willingford said, "I'm not sure I like your life, Sam."

I said, "I'm not sure I like it anymore either.  I think Bogie would hate it.  I don't recall him ever wading around in mud."

"Bogie?  You mean Humphrey Bogart?  What's he got to do with it?"

Someday I was going to have to tell her about Bogart and me.  For now I contented myself with a one word answer. "Everything."

We were up to our hocks in sludge again.  We could barely breathe for the stink again.  We were mucking about in mud again.  The rest of Maudie had to be around here somewhere.  Jane was still working at it, harder than we were.  There was no way Maudie's round rimmed glasses were here and she wasn't.  Someone had pushed Maudie Rivers far down under the river mud, dead or alive at the time, I wouldn't know.

The medical examiner would—as soon as we hauled out the body.

If she didn't get found, she'd stay right where she was, in whatever shape she was in—her body doing what various types of human tissue did in mud—for years. Probably too many years to count. Maybe so many years we'd all be dead too, and it wouldn't matter a tit about a woman with the unfortunate name of Maudie Rivers.

It took a lot of struggling and slipping about and grabbing each other and pushing away Jane or something disgusting as well as unidentifiable for us to give up.

"Maybe the river took her," I said, "like it took Maurice Oboram."

Mrs. Willingford shuddered. "What a way to go, Sam. Drowning in mud. It's hard to even think about."

"Then think about this. Judging by the state of her apartment, she was probably already dead and didn't feel a thing."

Mrs. Willingford started to put a muddy hand to her mouth before she thought better of it. "So she died some other horrid way. She was alive and then she wasn't. It must have been awful." Mrs. Willingford looked as close to unhinged as I was ever likely to see her. "We have to call the police, Sam."

"And say what? We don't have a body. I'd have to explain why I left the scene of the crime—I refer to the murder of Raymond LeGrand. I'd have to tell them Maudie Rivers was going to tell me something, and they'd want to know why me, and not them? If we call 'em, we're both going off somewhere with a load of angry New York City cops where at least one of us, namely me, will spend the rest of the night, wasting everyone's time and probably winding up with a dislocated nose and a sprained knee, and I'll never find out what happened to her. So no, I'm not calling the cops."

"You mean we just give up? We leave her here in the mud?"

"Is she still here?"

"She must be, Sam. If she's drifted off, she can't have got far."

My knees buckled with the sudden sound of one of Jane's better yodels. Ten feet to my left she was struggling over something. I struggled to get to her before whatever it was she had hold of got ripped to pieces.

It wasn't Maudie's body. It was Maudie's sweater. The long one, the one that covered what I was now sure was a great body. Anders Slydel couldn't be that dumb. Maudie Rivers did her best to hide it, but I'd known from the first she was a dame with a lot of charms. Or she *was* a dame with a lot of charms. Right now, all that charm was lost to mud and the river.

"What now, Mr. Russo?"

"Now we get the hell out of here, and *then* you call the cops— "

"Me? Why me?"

"They'll like your voice better. Phone in an anonymous tip. Right after that, we're all cleaning up."

"Where?"

"Where would you like to clean up?"

"Well, Sam, I can't show up like this at my own home. Not again. This time there must be a dozen snozzled socialites lying about on the Chippendale."

"A public bath then?"

"Droll. You must have a hotel. We'll go there."

I was standing in mud, a dead woman's slop of a sweater in one hand, and Mrs. Willingford and I were acting cute. I was disgusted with both of us. I was also elated in the usual way Mrs. Willingford elated me. People. They made me sick. And to think, I was one of them. No better, perhaps a little worse.

So was Mrs. Willingford. Or maybe she wasn't. To be fair, I hadn't known her that long to judge.

But I'd known me long enough.

I said, "Fine. We'll go to my place. But as soon as the 48th Street Theater opens its doors tomorrow, I'm going back. Somebody killed Raymond LeGrand. Somebody killed Maurice Oboram. And somebody killed Maudie Rivers right where Maurice was killed. It's obviously a popular place not only to do people in, but also to get rid of the bodies."

Mrs. Willingford pulled one of her legs out of the mud with a loud liquid glop. It got her moving towards the river bank with all we'd found of Maudie, her glasses and her sweater.

"I don't doubt that," she said, "not for a second."

"Neither do I."

With my free arm, I'd picked up Jane. As usual, she wasn't pleased, but it kept me from worrying she'd disappear under the mud.

I dragged the sweater up the shale of the sloping bank. I handed the glasses to Mrs. Willingford. "These go with all our other stuff."

"Right." She took Maudie's specs like she'd take a lit fuse.

I now had a thin rug, a muddy hat, a notebook, a sodden sweater that weighed as much as Bluto, and a pair of round glasses. One, or all, of these was going to tell me something. Eventually. They were already telling me things. But I needed the whole story, not just a few pieces.

Walking back to her town car, dripping as much as we'd dripped the first time, Mrs. Willingford said, "It doesn't make sense, Russo. Two very tall actors died who played the same role in the same play. Josephine's dresser, also working in that very same play, with what seems too much money for a dresser, sees something or knows something, and now she's dead as well, dreadfully horribly dead. She's where we found a hand and a thumb along with that double axe thing that probably killed one of the Harveys, and that's where the killer leaves Josephine's dresser. Why?"

"Beats me. But I'll be damned if it beats me much longer. I'm supposed to be a PI. I'm supposed to figure these things out."

"I'm going along too."

"Why you? You just said you didn't like my life anymore."

"I don't have to like it. I just want to be part of it."

"You're not part of it."

"Oh yeah? Who called who?"

She had me there.

Jane, bathed, toweled off and fed, spent the night on my comfy hotel couch under the window overlooking 44th Street. A clean Mrs. Willingford spent the night in my comfy bed.

I was learning to like caviar. I was learning to like champagne. I was trying not to learn to like Mrs. Willingford more than I already did. That way lay, if not heartbreak, then heart burn. But if Mrs. Willingford wanted to sleep in my bed instead of hers, there was no way I wanted to stop her.

That night, I was a very tired, very clean, very happy man.

As for Jane, on the couch and not on the bed—I'd make it up to her. Somehow.

No stars, no moon, only Manhattan streaming through the window, my head wouldn't stop working. I saw Raymond LeGrand's huge body lying on the trap room floor far from the open stage trap. I saw the electrical wire twisted tight and tied around his neck, his eyes bulging and his tongue swollen. He'd pissed himself. Funny I didn't see that then, but I saw it now—so I must of seen it then but blocked it out. I saw Jimmy standing over him. Most of all I saw sweet little Glenda weeping and sniffling while her pathetic little husband Cliff held her—his rug as cheap and obvious as Reggie the Ringer (no one, in the entire history of the sport, was as bad as Reggie when it came to trying to run a good horse as a poor horse; fuck, in one race, the black mare he'd entered finished white at the wire). Cliff wouldn't have only one toupee. Bald men liked owning a few. One for every day, or maybe if one blew off—like into a river.

No matter how I saw it working out between Cliff who clearly adored his wife, Glenda, and Glenda, who was clearly heart broken that Raymond LeGrand, that great actor and even greater poker player, was dead at her feet, I couldn't figure how Cliff's toupee got left in a trunk at the foot of the bed of Raymond LeGrand. So maybe it was someone else's toupee? Yeah, right, and maybe I could box like Joe Louis, paint like Van Gogh, and ride like George Woolf.

I don't remember falling asleep, but during what was left of the night, I dreamed of stinking oil-slicked mud. I dreamed of Maudie Rivers' mud filled mouth and her once shapely body floating around with the rest of New York City's garbage.

I dreamed of one huge hand, once plump with flesh but now only fragile bones sticking out of Hudson River mud, waving bye bye, bye bye.

## 28

We slept until noon.

First thing she did when she woke up, after fooling around which was a great way to greet the day, Mrs. Willingford called Woody to come get her car. Then she also ordered the best room service had to offer.

Jane got steak tartar.

If dogs weren't allowed in the Iroquois Hotel, no one dared telling Mrs. Willingford that.

The first thing I did all by myself, after eating Eggs Benedict and buttered toast cut into long thin pieces and smelling my red red rose in its crystal vase, was read the headline in the New York Times newspaper left outside our door—"ACTOR MURDERED IN 'HARVEY' THEATER." Then I walked Jane. She behaved like a perfect dog. No talking to strangers, no begging food off the hot dog or pretzel men, no darting into traffic. But I was learning. She could turn on a dime so no falling asleep at the leash. I checked the other papers at a newsstand. No mention of a body found near the fruit company piers.

Mrs. Willingford's tip-off hadn't borne fruit.

It was still a mystery to me why Jane streaked across 48th Street, burst past the outraged schlub guarding the stage door, found Josephine Hull's dressing room, all so she could attack Bluto. I had no idea then and I had no idea now. I spent the walk thinking about it. How'd she know Bluto was over there, a full street and both sidewalks, plus half a theater away, lolling around in the dressing room of a dumpling shaped actress who was never out of work?

How did my sharp witted, red and white, barkless, odorless warrior sense he was there?  Strangest of all: why bother? Jane had a temper.  But why mess with a big dumb cowardly dog she'd never met?

Watching her now as we strolled along 44th Street—my Jane, as clean as Loretta Young pretended to be, guarded but not fierce—a little niggle told me I ought to know.

The niggle said: Russo, if you knew that one thing, you might actually know something.

Jane took two quick steps to every one of mine.  Keeping up, what I thought was: I'd better learn ancient Egyptian faster.

Two hours later: fed, watered, walked, washed, perfumed and as well dressed as a Fred Astaire movie, two humans and Jane made their way to the theater.

I suspected we might be on our way to one of the wildest events on Broadway.

The truth? I was pretending I suspected anything.  Unlike Bogie working it all out in *The Big Sleep*, I had no idea what we were on our way to.  I just knew there was nowhere else to go.

I didn't tell Mrs. Willingford that, but I'd be willing to bet she knew.

To keep us all occupied on our cold crowded afternoon stroll from 44th to 48th Streets, I told them about the sweetest thing I saw Magpie ever do.  Telling it felt like that story Hammett told somewhere in the pages of *The Thin Man*. Something about a guy who turned out to be a cannibal once he was prospecting with a bunch of other guys.  Hammett's last book was already too short so I'd figured he'd stuck it in as a filler.  It sure didn't have anything to do with the mystery Nick Charles was supposed to be solving.  I felt like Hammett making a few bucks for a few more drinks, but I kept on talking.

My story went like this: The 26th Cavalry Regiment was

ordered to defend some town in northern Luzon, began with a B is as close as I could come then or now to remembering its name. It looked Spanish. I remember everything looked Spanish. If you couldn't see the people, you'd swear you weren't in the Philippines, you were in Spain. Anyway, in the middle of that B mess, we got cut off from the rest of our unit so there were only a few of us left, and among those few of us was Magpie and me. But even as few as we were, starving and exhausted and low on ammo, our regimental motto was *Our Strength is in Loyalty*. By then I had no strength left and very little loyalty. All I wanted to do was survive. As for Magpie, she had all the loyalty in the world, and all of it was given to me. What did she care who won what war? Anyway, good thing one of us had something left, because we were told to raid an airfield. A big one. This name I do recall. I don't know why, but I do: Tuguegarao airfield.

Tuguegarao airfield was full of what it was meant for: airplanes. Planes taking off, planes landing, planes getting repaired. Trouble was they were Jap planes because our enemy, swarming all over the island, had built the field.

Those of us left on horseback, maybe twenty in all, were told to cause a diversion for foot troops sneaking in on a moonless night and the best diversion command could think of was an all out charge by horses towards the control center. Brilliant. It would get the Jap's attention all right, but it would also get us and our horses killed. No matter. Those were our orders. Half way across the airfield, I fell out of my saddle. Anyone, even the best rider in the world can fall off a horse, and that's exactly what I did when Magpie took a bad step. Magpie, under fire, came to a dead halt. She could of run off, back the way she came and left me there, but she didn't. She nudged me with her muzzle, pushed me around a bit to see if I was still alive, which I damn well was. I'd only had the wind knocked out of me. Magpie waited until I got it back, me lying there and desperately trying for air. She waited until I crawled up into the saddle, and then waited for me to urge her forward into a nonstop barrage of bullets. By then, what was left of our small band, very few, came racing back. They'd achieved what they'd set out to do, at a huge loss to man and horse, and I whirled Magpie round and raced off with them.

"She didn't have to stay there," said Mrs. Willingford in a voice as low as I'd ever heard her use.

"No, she didn't."

"But she did."

"Yes, she did."

Mrs. Willingford sighed. I sighed. But I did not cry in front of Mrs. Willingford. I did all my crying in front of Jane. When I cried, Jane would sit directly in front of me and stare. When I finished, she'd lick my hand. It's all I wanted and all I needed. I didn't need, or want, Mrs. Willingford licking my hand.

By now we were standing across the street from the 48th Street Theater, pretty much where Jane and I had been sitting the day before. Mrs. Willingford called it reconnaissance— and I guess it was. We were wondering how to cross police lines. There was also a brace of New York City traffic to face, honking, shouting, swearing, no one giving an inch. In the middle of that mess, there were two horse-drawn wagons, one a milk delivery van pulled by a horse looking well cared for, and the other, the one that could of been a prairie schooner, pulled by a horse not as well off. He didn't look starved or beaten. Good thing too or I'd be off on a quest I cared more about than who killed a couple of big rabbits.

I was still gawking at the prairie schooner when a brown mid-Thirties Nash snuck up at the curb in front of us and with a little huffing and puffing, out popped Josephine Hull, as plump as her car. No chauffer, only Josephine lucking out on a great parking spot.

"Mr. Russo!" she said, holding out her hand, which I took

and kissed—like Maurice Chevalier. "And Jane!" Josephine
fluffed Jane's ears. If I hadn't seen it, I wouldn't of believed
it. Jane hated her ears fluffed. She hummed a tune to Jane,
who wagging her curved over-the-back tail, hummed back.
It was in harmony.

Only then did Josephine turn to Mrs. Willingford. "And
you are, my dear?"

Me, I was thinking: God's nuts. Here was our ticket.
Josephine was how we'd get back into the theater.

"Well," said Josephine, now introduced to Mrs. W, "Of
course we've all heard of Joker Willingford. My goodness.
He's backed Cole when the rest of those, those, those...
moneychangers thought he was done. The poor man
accidentally getting his legs crushed when his own horse
rolled over on him, so for years now he's in constant pain."

Thinking back—how long ago was it? it seemed days,
weeks?—I now knew why Porter could barely stand in the
back of the Schubert Theater.

"But done? Cole Porter finished? Oh my, no. Of
course you've seen *Kiss Me, Kate*—well, we all knew it was
a hit as soon as we heard the first few bars of *Too Darn Hot*.
Gosharoonie, everyone on Broadway knows its one of those
shows that come along once in a lifetime. So you're his wife?
Well, someone like you would be." Josephine clapped her
fat little hand to her fat little mouth. "Oh gosh, oh golly, I
don't mean to insult you. I just meant—"

By now, we were weaving through stalled traffic. Mrs.
Willingford never paused in her stride. "That I'm not a fool
and know which side to butter well baked bread."

Josephine laughed. "My dear, if I'd ever been as good
looking as you, I might very well have done what you did.
But look at me. You think a rich man would fall over himself
to get at me? Never in a million years. But the stage called.
Of all the people on this earth, it called to me. It said:
Josephine, you get your funny little butt to Broadway—and I

came running. And now look at me. I still don't understand why I get work and so many lovely things don't."

"In a word," said Mrs. Willingford, "talent."

"Why thank you, dear."

"If I had your talent, Josephine— "

"You do, Mrs. Willingford," I said, "you just haven't brought it to a stage."

Mrs. Willingford gifted me with one of her looks as all four of us were sauntering past the police line—well, I was sauntering, every one else was acting like a normal human being. Or like a dog, as the case might be.

Josephine, as a Broadway star, stopped to speak breathlessly to one reporter or another, all shouting at her about the murder of someone called LeGrand, popping flash bulbs in her face, but mostly she chattered away to Mrs. Willingford. Mrs. Willingford got recognized and had her picture taken too. I brought up the rear with Jane humming by my side. To the tune she sang—and I swear by my mother's short sad life there was a tune—I sent off a little prayer to Epona, Celtic Goddess of horses. At least I thought she was a Celtic goddess, but a formal education was not my strong suit.

I sang, under my breath, but it was me singing as loud as I could: *Let me win this one. Let me solve it and say I solved it. Let me, for just this once, cross the finish line first.*

## 29

*Harvey* was going up that very evening. Raymond LeGrand getting himself dead only turned off the lights for one night. A new *Harvey* was already in place, another big fellow whose name I'd yet to learn. *Harvey* always sold its seats, but now it was more than a sell-out. They could of bartered for chandelier space if they'd wanted to. Staff at the door and on phones were turning people away.

It didn't mean the place was free of New York City cops. They were everywhere. Knowing cops as I knew cops, this was a case most of 'em had fought to be part of. Standing around watching a load of theater people was one hell of a lot better than standing around the usual murder. The usual murder was messy, it was ugly, it took place somewhere sordid, and everyone starring in it was either pathetic or stupid or lowlifes or all three.

Here, it was more like a movie. Everybody loved the movies. But I'd bet anything they wished it was a different movie. Josephine'd said it: she wasn't a sight for cop eyes. But Glenda was—which made her hubby Cliff act like a scrawny rooster with one sweet hen to protect against a world of wolves. It was a losing battle. Glenda lay back on the prop couch, showing off her legs and talking cute to every cop who came by. They all found a reason to come by. Cliff was losing his hair shooing 'em away.

Jimmy was at my side, arriving as quietly and as smoothly as he seemed to do most things.

"Sam? Have you seen Fay?"

"No. But since you've asked, I presume you're going on

tonight."

"I am. Unless he shows up. No one's seen Frank."

"Crap. Don't tell me he's covered in mud."

"Excuse me?"

"Private joke. Anyone else missing?"

"Not that I know of."

Jimmy had this little hitch in his voice, like a permanent frog. On top of that, he drawled. There was something about Jimmy Stewart that made me turn and look at him long enough to make him check his sleeves, his shoes, his teeth.

"You need an ear, Sam?"

Before I could stop myself, I said, "I do."

"I'm your man."

I wanted to talk to him, I *needed* to talk to him, I needed to talk to somebody and, for once, Jane wouldn't do. My Egyptian wasn't good enough. I couldn't talk to Mrs. Willingford. She'd know how badly I was doing. I couldn't talk to Josephine. Josephine believed in me.

Had she noticed Maudie wasn't there yet? She would, and when she did, more hell would descend on *Harvey*.

Who knew what about Stewart? All I knew was what I read in the papers and I'd seen on the silver screen. All I knew was what he was like in the 48th Street Theater. A nice quiet faraway fella. What if all this was his doing? I couldn't imagine it. A war hero. A movie star. But then I never saw it coming with the guy I thought I knew up in Saratoga until it smacked me in the back of the neck like a wet sandbag. Who knew a fellow like that could kill three jockeys in cold blood, then try and kill my dog? People. Did anyone really know anyone?

Back I went to my recent thoughts about friends.

Standing downstage or upstage or wherever the hell we were, listening to the cast and crew of *Harvey* play bits of every part they'd ever played, I came to my senses.

I said, "I made a mistake. Forget it, Jimmy."

Jimmy looked long and hard at me. "You need to talk to someone. You're a private eye so you have to think anyone could do it. And that includes me, so you can't talk to me. I understand. I'd be thinking the same thing."

"In a nutshell, Mr. Stewart."

"What if I told you I didn't do it?"

"I'd believe you. For a shamus, I'm a bit of a schmuck."

"For an actor, so am I. Let's you and me and your chewed up dog—"

"Stabbed. Those are scars."

"Sorry, Sam. They look serious."

"They were."

"Well, let's you and me and your serious dog go sit around in Fay's dressing room—I know for a fact he's not there, unless he's sleeping another one off under the sofa—and see where it gets us."

I amazed myself. I followed him through the mayhem that was now the 48th Street Theater getting ready to perform *Harvey* in the middle of what seemed an entire precinct of performing police and right to Fay's private dressing room. I looked. Fay wasn't under the sofa and he wasn't hanging in the closet.

I sat on one end of Frank Fay's sofa and Jimmy sat on the other. Between us, Jane sat as primly as only Jane could sit, head up straight, tail tightly curled, tongue neatly in her closed mouth, front paws as nicely placed as Flo insisted us kids kept our hands in our laps as we sat at the table waiting for another wholesome meal. In the Staten Island Home for Children, wholesome meant whatever the Zawadzkis could get away with without actually starving anyone. They ate separately. Separate room, separate time, separate food. No one, not even the resourceful Paul Jarrett, ever discovered what they served themselves. What I discovered was I'd never eat another bean as long as I lived.

Frank had been using this room, off and on, for almost exactly four years. It looked like you'd think it'd look considering who he was. I figured when *Harvey* had its run or Frank's Elwood P. Dowd had his, the people who ran the theater would not only get the cleaners in, but the carpenters, the plumbers, the painters, and the fumigators.

Not one of the three of us wasted our time talking about Fay's taste in decor.

I told Stewart everything. I told him more than I'd told Mrs. Willingford. I wasn't Bogie. I'd never be Bogie. And I'd never be a Private Investigator if I couldn't learn to shut up. But I needed to work this out. I needed someone who could listen. I'd be lying if I claimed Mrs. Willingford couldn't listen. I'd be telling the truth if I added: but only for about one and a half minutes. That was her limit. After that, I'd be listening to her, and for a lot longer than she'd been listening to me. I needed a lot more from someone than one and a half minutes.

Jimmy listened like a priest. Not that I knew much about priests. The Zawadzkis had a god but whatever it was and wherever it hunkered down, drooling, it was no kind of god I'd ever want to follow around. All I knew about priests I learned from Pat O'Brien.

That's how Jimmy was. Like Pat O'Brien. Attentive. A quiet question here and there in that quiet voice of his. Careful in his wording. And kind. For the first time since Saratoga Springs I felt I had a friend. At least I felt I had a friend for an hour or so.

As I spoke, Jane put her head down on my knee. She stayed that way, her eyes looking up into mine, as attentively as Jimmy on his end of the sofa.

I felt as if I talked for hours but the clock on Fay's dressing table said only fifteen minutes had passed.

And then Jimmy began talking and when he did, he leaned forward, his long interesting face absorbed first in

my story and now in his response. Unless he was acting. He
was, after all, an actor. He'd even won an award for it.

He said, "So Miss Rivers is dead too?"

"Looks like it."

"Oh my... three gone now, you say. I don't understand
it. Nothing makes sense. Tides of March... is that someone's
idea of a joke? I'd think it was Raymond's if it weren't on
his arm and he was smart enough. Does Anders know about
poor Maudie?"

"You know about Anders and Maudie then?"

"The poor rich kid has no one to talk to, so yes, I know.
Although I've never really known Maudie herself."

At precisely that moment we heard Anders' foolish laugh
all the way back in Fay's.

"No," said Jimmy, "I don't think Anders knows."

So far as I knew, Jimmy was a quiet man, calm and
controlled. He slammed his fist down on the arm of
Frank's couch. "I knew Maurice Oboram. He was a fine
Shakespearean actor trapped in a huge body. Who knows
what he might have achieved if he'd been, and I hate to say
this, a normal size. I don't know where he was born or how
he was raised, but that voice. And that accent. As if he'd
been trained in the best school in England. I liked the man.
The man liked his dog, sort of like you like yours." Before
I could say anything, Jimmy held up his hand. "Granted,
they are very different dogs, that much is obvious. Even so,
Maurice liked that dog. And the dog liked him. But then
one day he just up and disappeared. It surprised me. All
he wanted was to act. And there wasn't much for him. So
why give up on *Harvey*? If he'd had a good reason, why give
no notice? And then there was this: why did his dog come
back when Maurice didn't? No one else seemed to care,
except for our lovely Josephine. But, me, I always thought
something was wrong. I knew Maurice wouldn't just leave.
He was concerned about something here."

"Concerned about what?"

Jimmy shrugged. "I don't know. But when a man gets concerned about something, sometimes he isn't allowed to walk away."

"What are you saying?"

"All I know is that the last time I was in town, which is about the last time anyone saw Maurice, he was a different man. He'd been a close friend of Anders Slydel, and then he wasn't. Sorry. I can't tell you why. I don't know."

"But Anders would."

"One would assume. Then Maurice was simply gone. Right away Raymond LeGrand stepped into the role. Nothing wrong with that since LeGrand was an understudy. That was his job—to step in for any male part except Fay's. But I'll tell you, Sam, I learned a few things over there—"

I knew what he meant by "over there." He meant the war, the one he fought in Europe.

"—and I guess the most important thing was how to judge a man. Maurice was a lovely fella, but Raymond had little to recommend him. He was mean. He was crude. He was a cheat. He lied. He thought it was funny to snatch Cliff's toupee off his head in front of Glenda and hide it."

There went my rug clue. Nothing more than a prank. It must of made Cliff, already not too happy with Raymond, a lot unhappier.

"I'm sorry to say," Jimmy was saying, "that it's no surprise that someone had it in for him enough to kill him. Worse, it's no surprise that he could kill someone himself. For any sort of reason. To clear a debt. To take another man's woman. To save his own skin. There's not too many people I can say that about."

I thought of the people I could say that about. Mister Zawadzki. Flo Zawadzki. Paul Jarrett. Two different guys I'd served with. At least half the mugs Lino'd put away for acts that made me sick to my stomach.

My guess was Jimmy had higher standards than me. Or knew a much better class of people.

"But I can't think who'd want to kill Maurice. Except for Raymond."

I thought that was clever of him. It was something I'd already chewed on. The only reason I could imagine for getting rid of Maurice Oboram was for something he knew, something he could prove.

Actors who succeed have everything: fame, money, women—assuming we're talking about males here, although Tallulah and Garbo and Dietrich and a few others would fit just as well. But actors who succeeded out of the number who tried were only a tiny handful. That meant Oboram's job was worth more than the guy on the street might think.

And that meant Maurice would never quit *Harvey*.

What I'd come to was he knew a little too much about a certain someone for his own good.

"Basically," Jimmy was saying, "it's possible Raymond killed Maurice because Maurice knew he cheated at cards. Maurice as good as told me that."

I said, "Maurice gave his apartment to Raymond to pay off his debt."

Jimmy shook his head. "I didn't know that. Poor Maurice. I wish he'd told me. I might have been able to help. A lot of the men here thought LeGrand cheated, they've all said so, many times. But unless they knew for sure, it was all sour grapes. The way Maurice talked, he knew for sure. So perhaps LeGrand killed Oboram to shut him up. But now, who killed LeGrand? True, his death is a boon to so many— yet I can't help but feel it was because someone knew what he'd done and they didn't like it."

Another thought I'd thought myself. Funny how great actors think alike. I'd begun thinking of myself more an actor than a PI, mainly because the PI thing was looking more and more like acting.

Jimmy said, "Maurice disappeared months ago. Why wait so long to avenge him? Because that someone only just found out? Yes, that could be why. And poor Maudie saw it. She'd peered into the open trap because she heard something strange under the stage, and when she did, she saw Raymond's killer, who probably saw her. Did she know she was seen? I mean, of course, did she know she was seen by more than just the stagehand you said was called Noodles?"

"Ah," said I, "the charmer who peached on her in the alley near the Merrie Maide."

Me, I figured she must of known she'd been seen by the killer. But for some reason she wasn't scared enough about it. I thought about how much thought I'd given that one. Why wasn't she scared enough? She should of been scared. If she had been, she could still be scared today, just like the rest of us. One thing I knew for sure in this world: most people are scared and what they're scared of is life itself.

"So," said Jimmy, "she was going to meet up and tell you because you're a PI. She knew you were looking into the killing of Maurice. But someone got to her first. Who else could that someone be but Raymond's killer?"

"Jimmy, I'll tell you what. I'll be an actor and you be the private eye."

"Don't kid me, Sam. You've already figured this stuff out."

I didn't respond to that.

"What neither one of us knows," he said, "is what other thing besides Raymond cheating at cards Maurice was worried about. I never learned why he and Anders were no longer friends. What we also don't know is who the second killer is. Or why."

"What neither of us really knows could fill Madison Square Garden."

"With that one, Sam, you'd make Socrates proud."

I let that go too. What I was wondering was this. I knew

why Noodles peached on Maudie. For some dough. Or so he said. What I couldn't figure was why Maudie took so long to peach on who killed LeGrand.

It all came down to one simple question. Why wasn't she scared? Was it because it was only Noodles? Even with a knife, Noodles looked about as scary as Bluto. And I should know. Alone in an alley with Noodles and his knife, I felt irritated.

Had Maudie felt like that? Until she didn't?

## 30

Jane's head rose from my knee, her hackles lifting. The door to Fay's dressing room was opening and opening fast. In stepped Mrs. Willingford, her face flushed, her eyes shining. Behind her, the door got closed just as fast. Jane's head and hackles went down.

Mrs. Willingford was almost out of breath. Breathlessly, she said, "I know why."

Both Jimmy and I asked the same thing at the same time. "Why what?"

"All right I don't know why. But I'm close. I even know who."

"Who?" That was me.

"I can answer that when I get the why for certain. Hello! You're Jimmy Stewart. I'm Mrs. Willingford since Russo here has forgotten his manners."

Jimmy stood for a lady. I was going to have to learn to do that. The standing as well as the introducing the lady part. I was also going to have to learn to wedge in introductions in less than a second. Mrs. Willingford arrived talking and she hadn't stopped since.

Jimmy said, "He's spoken highly of you."

"Highly, eh? I wouldn't go that far for him, but he's not bad. I suppose he's blabbed his head off?"

"He's filled me in."

"I get filled in too. But not quite in the same way."

Jimmy laughed. It was one of those real laughs, right from the heart, and it made Jane yodel and it made Mrs. Willingford crack a small satisfied smile as she lit a cigarette.

But the worst thing it did, it did to me. The idea of friends came rushing through my heart like Pan Zareta winning another race.

Exhaling smoke, Mrs. W. looked at me. "You'll be sharing all this 'filling in'?"

Bogie didn't have friends. He didn't spill his guts about a case to a "friend" and then when the love interest (although the idea of Mrs. Willingford being the love interest was too strange to allow room in all this) walks in, they're all friends together, including the dog, and they laugh.

I might have to find another job. But all I knew how to do was fiddle around with locks and shoot guns. Sam Russo: lockpick and sharp shooter.

The way things were going it was back to my first love, Jimmy Cagney.

I would become a public enemy.

Mrs. Willingford pushed me off the sofa. I went and sat on a chair. Jane exchanged my knee for her knee.

"Normally," she said, "I wouldn't speak in front of a stranger— "

Jimmy gulped and began to stand. "Of course not. I should have realized. I'll go."

"Sit down, Stewart. You've been filled in. We're all in this now."

Jimmy sat. I sat. Jane gazed up at Mrs. Willingford with eyes as keen as ours.

Mrs. Willingford crossed her legs, perhaps not as daringly as Glenda had done, but it was done well enough. It caught my attention and it caught Jimmy's.

She said, "Do we want to solve these murders or not?"

This pulled my eyes away from Mrs. Willingford's legs. "Excuse me," said I, "Who's the PI here?"

This was when Mrs. Willingford looked me straight in the face and said what was true since the moment I met her—up in Saratoga Springs holding the halter of the beautiful filly,

Fleeting Fancy. "You are, Sam darling. But I read murder mysteries. Sleuths always have a sidekick."

"And that's you?"

"See, Jimmy! I knew he was good. Look how quickly he catches on."

The droll little grin I got from Jimmy boiled my blood. For one thing, Mrs. Willingford was right. She didn't call me; I called her in on this one. For another, sleuths *did* have sidekicks. Nick had Nora. Sherlock had Watson. Hercule had Hastings. Nero Wolfe had Archie. Actual cops had whole police departments. Hold on. Did Bogie have a sidekick? Didn't matter if he was Philip Marlowe or Sam Spade, he did not.

"So here's what I learned while you two were in here having a tea party."

I said, "We weren't— "

"Just an expression, Russo. So listen. I'm watching this woman named Glenda— "

Jimmy said, "She plays a nurse."

"Indeed she does. But for the past half hour she's been playing Theda Bara. I noticed that there's a very silly fellow also watching her—this is aside from virtually every cop in the joint, naturally—and this silly fellow has a rug on his head." On the word "rug," Mrs. Willingford gave me a knowing look. The explanation for Cliff's rug was going to be part of my filling her in. "Something he must have found at a five & dime. In his younger days, Joker would have shot it. He was a crack shot back in the Spanish-American War."

Jimmy said, "The 'silly fellow' is Cliff. To most, he's Mr. Glenda."

Mrs. Willingford nodded her hatless head. Her hair shone in the lamplight like—Jesus, Russo, who cared about Mrs. Willingford's hair? She said, "I kind of figured that out for myself. So at some point while Glenda is almost showing us the crotch of her panties—pink, by the way, with pinker lace trimming, and she is *not* a natural blonde—this Cliff sneaks away. And I mean sneaks. He looks this way and he looks that way, and when he thinks he's not being watched, off he tiptoes. Have you ever seen someone tiptoe? On him, it was funnier than Fanny Brice. So I followed him. And where do you think he went?"

I answered her. "To the shared dressing room. My guess is that once there, he poked around in his wife's private footlocker. Everyone has a small private footlocker."

"How did you know that?"

"I searched Raymond's footlocker yesterday, before the cops and the newshounds got here. I figured he might keep his 'They Owe Me' book there, the one we found on Commerce Street. While I was at it, I also tried Glenda's footlocker. But it was locked and I didn't have the time to get it open. I would also guess that Cliff has a key."

"He does, and he used it."

"And you're going to make Jimmy and Jane and I ask what he found."

"Of course not. I'm playing fair and I'll expect it of you. He reached right in, ignoring a red velvet box I would have gone for in a second if I'd never opened the footlocker before, rummaged around a bit, and pulled out another box. This one was pink velvet."

"He opened it?"

"He did. It was hard to see exactly what he saw in it since I had to hang back peeking round the door. But it was easy to see what he removed from his coat pocket. His pocket was full of letters. You know, the kind that get tied up with a pretty ribbon."

I knew the kind. The movies were full of them. Though I'd never seen any in real life. What burned me is the idea that Raymond not only wrote love letters—letters to Glenda had to be from the man she'd planned to run off with—but that he could write at all. Just goes to show, people always have a surprise or two up their sleeves. Not to mention an ace.

At that, I recalled his dead arm and what was written on it.

Mrs. Willingford was still talking. "So Glenda's hubby stuffed the letters into the pink velvet box, then he put the box back where he got it from and locked the footlocker. And then I had to run for it because he was coming back."

I sat there for a moment, expecting Jimmy or Mrs. Willingford or Jane to have something to say. Instead they all waited for me. When they waited long enough, I said, "Jimmy thinks Raymond killed Maurice. He thinks he did it because Maurice could prove he cheated at cards. If Maurice could prove that, Raymond was not only out of a job, but out of a lot of cash, as well as becoming a target for a lot of interesting things happening in dark alleys, with the kicker being his loss of Mrs. Glenda."

Mrs. Willingford almost choked on her smoke. "Raymond wrote the letters?"

"Yes. Perhaps LeGrand, who already had Oboram's room and most of his stuff, got Maurice into that room one last time. Maurice was a really nice guy, so if he did, it had to be easy drawing him in. Raymond jollied Maurice along, got him to dress up in one of his outfits and take a walk along the piers. He probably dressed up too. They were both actors. Only Maurice was playing Shakespeare and Raymond was playing Maurice, as in 'stringing him along'. Raymond also must of known by the time he took his chance, Bluto was nothing to worry about. He was right. Bluto did nothing but come back here, which gives us a date for when Maurice was killed. And then there's what Josephine said about a pool on when Maurice himself would be coming back."

Mrs. Willingford said, "There's a pool? Isn't that a trifle tacky?"

I said, "Apparently not when you're innocent and you

don't know the man is dead. Only the killer knew he wasn't coming back. Josephine said Bluto showed up alone three and a half months ago. Anyway, LeGrand gets what he wants. Silence. But before all of that might of happened, Jimmy says Maurice was worried about something else. Right about now, maybe we should guess what that could of been."

Jimmy said, "It wasn't about Raymond or cards or losing his room. It was something else. I'm sure of that."

Mrs. Willingford said, "Then what? If he was worried, Maurice must have seen something or known something. I think it was something here, at the theater. My god, it must have had something to do with the two Glendas."

I said, "Why the two Glendas?"

"Because neither of them are on the up and up. I'd be willing to bet if Maurice was concerned, Glenda was also concerned and Mr. Glenda was twice as concerned. He just now put her letters back. How long has he had them, and having them, you can bet he's read them. More than once. I'll just bet Maurice was concerned something was going to happen to Glenda. He just never got a chance to do anything about it because something happened to him. And then something happened to Raymond."

Jimmy hadn't taken his eyes off Mrs. Willingford. It was a hard thing to do under any circumstances. He said, "So you're saying that Mr. Glenda killed Raymond?"

"Yes, I think so."

I said, "Raymond LeGrand killed Maurice to cover up his cheating and Cliff Winker killed Raymond LeGrand because LeGrand and his wife were lovers? It's a bit over the top, wouldn't you both say? Two guys in the same theater who think that killing is an answer? And one of these two guys killing twice, Raymond then Maudie?"

"You have a point, Sam Russo," said Mrs. Willingford, standing and moving towards the door. "One which I now ponder."

I'd been doing some pondering of my own ever since I'd leaned over the body of Raymond LeGrand—how many hours ago now? Time was getting muddled. But whoever killed who, I knew this, and I'd known it ever since Glenda cried out: "Oh poor Ray, poor poor Ray. No one knew him like I did. He wasn't what you all think he was." I knew it wasn't true. Raymond *was* what everyone thought he was. What they didn't think, because they didn't know, was that Glenda had a ticket to Reno in her purse. But Cliff must of known. As Mrs. W said, he'd read her letters.

I meant it when I said it was over the top. Jimmy thought Raymond killed Maurice. Bluto was the only witness and no protection at all, not like Jane, who tried to protect Babe Duffy. There was no connection to Raymond killing Maurice and Cliff killing Raymond. Mrs. Willingford thought Cliff did away with Raymond, a killer himself, because he was insane with jealousy. Somebody, presumably also Cliff, killed Maudie Rivers because she witnessed one of these murders—Raymond's by Cliff. Maudie tried to tell me about it but was scared off by... the killer. A killer she walked out of the Merrie Maide to meet? So Cliff, who didn't kill Maurice but did kill Raymond under The 48th Street Theater stage with a show getting ready to go up, got to silence Maudie by killing her exactly where Maurice got killed. Which he knew about—how? Oh right, and he also ransacks Maudie's locked apartment. Which he knew about—how?

There've been long shots in my life, a hundred of 'em. But not one of 'em ever as long as all these long shots.

None of it added up.

I said, "It doesn't add up."

"True," said Jimmy, by now lying stretched out on Frank's couch, his arms behind his head. "No sense at all."

"OK," said Mrs. Willingford, her hand on the knob of Frank's door, "then what does?"

"I'm working on it," I said. "When I know, you'll know.

And I think I'll know soon."

"Until then," said my sidekick, my roll in the hay, my pal, "I'm off to keep an eye on Mrs. & Mr. Glenda."

With that, she swept out of the room like Boston out of his barn.

I gave it to him. Jimmy didn't laugh. He said, "You really think you got this figured out?"

"Some of it. Some of it. And with some of it, I'm bound to work out the rest."

Jimmy shut his eyes. "All I ask is you do it before anyone kills anyone else. One more killing, and *Harvey* could become a modern *Macbeth*. We'd have to call it that 'New York City play'."

I think I knew what he meant. Or maybe I didn't. The hell with it. I knew what I meant. I *did* know some of it.

Time to do something right. And I knew right where Jane and I were going to go to do it.

# 31

I hadn't had one of my headaches in a month. I suddenly had a beaut. All it took was me and Jimmy walking out of Frank Fay's dressing room into the chaos of cops and murder and that night's performance of *Harvey* going up in the middle of it all.

I'd sworn to myself that the Case of the Two Dead Rabbits wouldn't end up in the soup like the mess Lino'd got his reprimand for. This was the big one he kept throwing in my face whenever he felt like I might walk out on him. I knew who did it, but I never could figure out *why* the guy did it. Lino couldn't pass the buck without giving away our working arrangement and none of his guys had proof enough to convict the guy, so the creep got away and Lino got the blame.

I knew the guy's name. Mickey Cates. I knew where he lived. About a block from me. I knew what he was doing right now which was what he always did—when he wasn't getting away with four murders. Maybe even more. I always thought there were more. Cates was propped on a bar stool three blocks from both our places in Stapleton drinking beer in a strip joint called the Green Garter. Ever since I had him pegged, I'd stroll over to the Garter now and then to see how he was doing. I'd see Holly too, my favorite Stapleton neighbor. Holly didn't strip, she sang. Holly didn't strip because Holly was a man. I think. I don't think anyone else thought that. If they did, Holly could get into big trouble some night. I'd made a habit of checking on her too. Anyway, Mickey knew that I knew about him and I knew he knew. I'd show up, he'd tip me a nod, and then get on with his drinking.

Mickey Cates was the only man, so far, who tempted me to take the law into my own hands.

Here and now, every actor in *Harvey* except Fay, was on stage. The new guy playing the rabbit, as tall as Raymond, but nowhere near as tall as Maurice, hovered near the back of the stage. The stage itself was set up like someone's library: a large couch, a couple of large wingback chairs, what looked like a real fireplace, two walls of book shelves.

Josephine was knitting in one of the wingbacks, the judge, Mr. Kirk of the shrill voice, sat bolt upright in the other one. Jimmy had settled himself on one end of the couch next to Glenda who was deep in conflicted heaven. She might not of wanted Jimmy, but she sure as hell wanted his movie connections. The guy with the stogie, whose name I finally knew, Jesse, paced back and forth in front of the fireplace. Anders the doc, leaned with rather pleasing grace against a wall. His face was shining, his lashes were long, his hair was perfect, he didn't look anything like a doctor. In one of the wings, stage right or left or whichever, Mrs. Willingford was doing her best to capture and keep Cliff's attention. It wasn't hard, not even with his wife warming up to Jimmy twelve feet away. In the opposite wing, a clot of cops was having a terrific time, on duty in a live theater.

As for the stagehands, very much including Noodles and Eddie, they were doing whatever they did each night the show went up.

The curtain might rise any time now. I walked over to Josephine's wingback and knelt down. She didn't stop knitting and she didn't look up—but in a very low voice she asked me the question I was expecting her to ask someone. "Where's my Maudie, Mr. Russo? I haven't seen her all day."

In a voice as low as hers, I said, "She's probably dead,

Josephine."

"Oh Sam," she stage whispered, "I knew it. Somehow I just knew it. I knew nothing good could come of that man."

I didn't ask her what man. I already knew. I said, "The day Jane flew into your dressing room?"

Josephine was weeping as quietly as she knit, as quietly as we talked. "Yes?"

"Had someone else just been there? Moments before."

"Yes. *He* had. To see Maudie."

"And then what happened?"

"He walked out and your dog was about to go after him, when she saw Bluto. It made her change her mind. You know, like when you can't choose between an éclair and a cream puff."

I got that too. Jane hadn't smelled Bluto from across 48th Street. She hadn't rushed into the 48th Street Theater to attack what looked like a yeti but behaved like Stan Laurel. What happened was, being Jane, the sight of Bluto swayed her from her real prey. If it hadn't, I'd probably of missed the murder of Raymond LeGrand being too busy with a lawsuit concerning my dog. I might even of lost my dog. Thank you, Bluto.

Josephine placed her knitting in her lap as gently as she might place an infant. Without looking at me, she took my hand. "Oh, my poor poor show. It's just a show, Sam, something to cheer people up in the hard times. And we've had such hard times. Why would this happen to something so sweet and loving as *Harvey*? I simply don't understand."

"I don't know, Josephine. I really don't know. But *Harvey* will make it through. I promise you that."

Josephine finally looked at me. There were tears in her eyes. "I believe you, Sam Russo."

For the first time since I could recall wanting to be a PI, I didn't feel like Sam Spade. I didn't feel like Philip Marlowe.

I didn't feel like a dozen other guys on the silver screen, playing it tough but deep underneath their hearts were soft as salt water taffy. I felt like Olivia de Havilland as Melanie Hamilton in *Gone With the Wind*. I felt like a true blue decent human being.

It wouldn't last, but it was swell for now.

I looked up at the rest of them. From cop to Barney Google to Cliff, they were all acting. No one really gave a damn about who'd killed who. Except Jimmy. He gave a damn about Maurice. And Josephine. She gave a damn about *Harvey*. I had a lot of it figured now. This time, unlike that time with Mickey Cates, I couldn't let it go. I couldn't leave the killer out there. This time someone had to go away.

I was off the stage just as the curtain rose.

I got to see some of the show. Mrs. Willingford and I stood in the wings. Jane, a perfect lady, settled down with us, only to fall asleep ten minutes in. A few feet away, Cliff also watched the show. Mrs. Willingford'd already told me he stood there every night, never missed a performance.

Jimmy became Elwood P. Dowd. I'd never seen that before. In the movies, you don't see the man behind the actor. You don't even see the actor. You see who they're playing. If they're good, you believe them. Jimmy was great. I knew him as Jimmy. I saw him turn into Elwood—and I believed him.

The guy who now had the role of Harvey the Pooka sat on a chair maybe three feet back from us. He wasn't on until the last few seconds of the last act, but there he was, a rabbit from the neck down. The head was in his lap.

So what was I thinking of? Bluto. I always ended up thinking about Bluto. Poor mutt lost Maurice and gained, if you could call it that, Anders Slydel and Maudie Rivers. Anders walked him; Maudie fed him. Neither liked Bluto and Bluto didn't like them. Scratch that. I thought of Bluto edging away from Anders. I thought it wasn't so much he didn't like the guy, as it was he was afraid of the guy.

Suddenly, I had one of my Sam Russo hunches. Alright, so they didn't always pan out, but they came home more times than not.

Where was I? In a building full of actors. What did actors do? They played roles. What did the paying folks do? If it was a good play, they believed what they saw like I believed Cagney and Bogie and Jimmy.

I suddenly realized I'd been watching a damn good play.

I got what I had to do next. It felt better than feeling like Olivia DeHavilland.

It was intermission and I was on my way out Josephine's back door when a rough hand grabbed my arm.

"Stop it right there, wise guy."

I stopped it right there, turned and looked down into the mad brown eyes of Mr. Glenda. Jane, who'd been loping along, also stopped. She sat and studied his neck.

"You been with my wife?"

Had I? Oh right. I had. The two of us, alone in Josephine's dressing room when she told me about Raymond and Reno.

"Well, I wouldn't call it being with her."

"What's that mean, buster?"

Poor little man. His life with Glenda was hell.

"It means we had a talk."

He was cocking his head up at me, almost on tiptoe, sweating so much his rug was slipping. I resisted the urge to pat it into place. Jane did not resist growling. A low growl, but neither of us missed it. Cliff Winker was too worked up to worry. "A talk? I'm supposed to believe you just talked?"

"Believe what you like. You'll have to excuse me now. I'm going—"

"You ain't goin' nowheres." He pulled a gun on me with one hand and pushed me, hard, in the shoulder, with the other. He was small, but he was strong; I fell back a step.

Being in a hurry, I'd ignored a knife from Noodles. Here I was in another hurry; I ignored a gun from Cliff. I pushed him back. Me pushing was harder than him pushing. It snapped back his head, sat him down on the floor with a huge thump, and threw his gun one way down the hallway and his hair the other.

The minute I was shoved, Jane launched herself for his throat. She must of caught the flying rug out the corner of her eye, because she flipped in mid-air. She was on the rug like she'd be on a rat, shaking the hell out of it.

I didn't have time for this. "Jane! Drop it! Come!"

Hot damn. Jane did exactly what I'd told her to do. A first.

And then we both ran out the door. Neither of us cocked an ear at Cliff's going for the gun and running out after us.

Hector, in his paper hat, may not have remembered me, but he remembered my dog.

"No dogs!"

"Knock it off, Hector."

It worked for Maudie, it worked for me.

Hector had half a customer. The half was a kid. It had to be a kid. I was up to my hairline in giants, dwarves would be too much. The kid collected his ice cream and was gone, leaving Hector and me and Jane just where I wanted us to be, alone.

"You know I was in here before?"

"Yeah, with the dog."

"There was a woman already here."

"Yeah. She works in some theater."

"You've seen her before?"

"Sure. She comes here all the time."

"Alone?"

"Nah. Well, not usually. Say, who are you? A cop? I heard some guy got killed at a theater. You workin' on that?"

"Yes." It wasn't the whole truth, but it was true. I was working on "that."

"If she didn't come alone, who did she come with?"

"Well, for a dame with glasses and those clothes, it was always surprising to see her with a guy as smooth as that guy."

"What guy?"

"Some actor."

"Was his name Anders Slydel?"

"Yes. No. Hold on, I think so. I always thought he looked more like a Harvard snot than an actor. But he said he was an actor. He the one got killed?"

"No. Did you notice what happened last night when I came in?"

"Yeah."

"What?"

"You brought a darned dog."

"Other than the dog."

"Yeah. I noticed she left in a big hurry."

"Do you know why?"

"How should I know why? Maybe she didn't like you."

Hector loved that one. It made him snort with what I think he thought was laughter.

"Did you see anyone out the window around that time?"

"Did I see—well, yeah I guess I did."

"Who'd you see, Hector?"

So he told me. A minute later, Jane and I were hailing a cab. I wouldn't even put it on Lino's tab. It wasn't Lino's murder. It was mine. Or better, they were my murders. All three of 'em.

Riding uptown in a yellow taxi, I sighed. Jane hummed. I smoked. Jane hummed some more. I went over every single moment since I'd arrived in the 48th Street Theater thanks to my dog Jane.

Jimmy thought he knew who'd killed Maurice. Raymond

LeGrand did. He thought he knew why. A pitiful reason: to cover up he was cheating in those card games of his—people had been killed for less, a *lot* less.

But who killed LeGrand?

There were three good reasons for someone to kill someone like Raymond LeGrand. The first would be to avenge a lover's obsession. In that case, Mrs. Willingford was on to a good thing. Cliff was her man. The second would be to erase a debt. If that's what happened, there was one hell of a lot of suspects and the cops were welcome to chase down each and every one of 'em. The third was simple hatred.

I knew which one it was. I knew by the electrical wire.

But what could Raymond do to be that hated? As for his killer, what about the risk? To kill LeGrand in a theater full of people getting ready for an evening's performance—that part was nuts. If you loathe the guy, you catch him alone. Any self respecting murderer could see that. So what could touch you off so badly, you'd grab a length of electrical wire and wind it around his neck? Then there was Raymond's size. No one else was as big as he was, not with Oboram out of the picture.

Raymond LeGrand must of scared you or drove you so nuts, things like where you were didn't matter. Maybe just for a minute, but a minute was long enough.

Or maybe you were just plain nuts to begin with. Maybe you were born that way, as nuts as the Zawadzkis, husband and wife. And that was as nuts as it got.

But the hell of it was you got seen and somehow you knew you were seen. Was the trap open before you were taking Raymond's life? Or did Maudie Rivers hear you struggle with Raymond and open the trap? So you looked up.

I rubbed Jane's ear, right where she liked it best. "We have to solve this case, Jane. If Mrs. Willingford, or worse, some war hero actor solves it before us, I'll have to kill myself. I don't want to kill myself. It's messy and it hurts."

Honking through a tangle of traffic on 58th where it crossed Fifth Avenue, I thought about the note in the barrel on Bluto's collar which said the same thing as the words printed on Raymond's arm. *Beware the Tides of March.* I thought about Maudie Rivers' black eye and the telephone number in her kitchen. I thought about Maudie.

I think I knew what kind of body she'd been hiding under that huge sweater. The kind of body men kill for. Or die for. Although in Maudie's case, she did the dying.

## 32

It was one of those buildings you never see in a Bogart film. Maybe something with William Powell, but never with Bogie. Facing Fifth Avenue, it was doing a grand job of making Central Park look a little cheap, a little tacky. Its wine colored awning was at least as big as the one they stuck on the front of the Hotel Astor. Its silvered doors were wide enough to drive a couple of buses through, and it had two doormen, not one. For all I knew, every inch of it was made out of marble including the doormen.

I was looking at money, pots and pots of money, and the money went all the way from the basement to the penthouse thirty stories above my head.

You'd think with that kind of money strutting its stuff, it was impossible to get inside if you didn't already live there. Wrong. I knew exactly how to pass through its silvered portals. I'd learned it from one of Lino's burglars. A real friendly guy once he knew the jig was up. He'd said: watch the place until just the right guy or gal is half a block away from going in, slip alongside them on the sidewalk and make friends fast—a dog like Jane was perfect for a stunt like that— then, talking away, walk past the doorman. The doorman would assume you were a friend of a tenant. The tenant would assume you lived there. So easy it was laughable—if you thought that kind of thing was funny. Not living in a building like that and with nothing to steal, I thought it was at least amusing.

It worked just like Lino's second-story man said it would. Scary, really. Being rich didn't mean being safe. I'd say I was glad I wasn't rich, but I'd probably be lying.

So I got into the art-deco elevator with the fur-smothered, make-up slathered, elderly woman I'd chosen to walk past the doormen with. She was the perfect choice, she was a dog lover and Jane acted like a poodle even when the old lady planted her one right under her nose, leaving behind a thick smear of pasty blood red lipstick that to a dog probably smelled like poison. I hit the button for three floors above the floor I actually wanted, got out, and got spotted by someone's maid. Another perfect moment. If things went sideways, I had a witness I wasn't on the ninth floor but on the twelfth.

While I was pretending to be letting myself into Apartment 12-B, the maid disappeared into some grand spread farther on down a hallway full of so many mirrors it felt like a fun house built for the Rockefellers.

I made a dash for the stairs. Me and Jane were going on down to the ninth floor.

No one would be there. *Harvey* might be winding up for the night, its audience drifting out onto the streets of Manhattan, but the cast still had to clean themselves up, change into street clothes, and get themselves home. Home was all over town. Home for the person I intended to meet was on the corner of Fifth Avenue and East 72nd Street, apartment 9-A, right down the red and blue oriental carpet from the staircase I was hiding in.

No need to worry about Jane or me making noise. You could lose things in that carpet, large things.

We stood in front of 9-A. Not a sound from anywhere, but I didn't expect there to be. The doors to these places were as thick as vault doors, which was funny when you thought about it, because although it'd take a cannon to knock one down, it took nothing to get through the lock.

I took my time. I had plenty of it. For some reason, I felt like time had stopped for me. If anyone was thinking of leaving some other door, or showing up at some other door, I knew they'd be doing it at some other time. It was like a time warp, or one of those strange things me and Lino and Paul and whoever would read about in our smuggled-in copies of *Astounding Stories*. Jane sat at my feet, her little black nose as wrinkled as her forehead. She was probably trying to smell through the thick coat of greasy lipstick that almost clogged her nostrils. She sneezed, she pawed at it, she shook her head—until I could do something about it, it was still there and it looked like staying there.

Before picking the lock, I checked my gun. Slowly and carefully. I had all the time in the world. Cleaned and fully loaded with fresh ammo, safety off, back in my pocket where I could get it fast if and when I needed it. I thought I might need it. Jane finally stopped trying to lick the lipstick off her nose. I'd heard about lipstick like that; it was the latest thing and it was probably driving Jane nuts. But it wasn't going away—so she stopped struggling with it.

I picked the lock. It was sweet. It was as sweet and easy as George Woolf, "The Iceman," sitting chilly on Seabiscuit as they slipped on by War Admiral. That was one of the most exciting days of my life. The year before, War Admiral had taken the Kentucky Derby, the Preakness, and the Belmont Stakes. He took the Saratoga Cup and the Whitney Stakes and the Jockey Gold Cup—but he couldn't take the Biscuit or The Iceman.

I felt like Georgie Woolf. I don't know what Jane felt like, Seabiscuit maybe. But we were inside and had the door closed behind us like whoever the best burglar of all time would of done. I had no idea who the best burglar of all time was because anyone who was the best had never been caught. But that's who I felt like.

Once inside it was dark and warm and as silent as a museum in the dead of night.

Hard to tell, since the drapes—thick soft drapes, not

curtains or blinds—were drawn and the lights off, but there was enough light to know we were in one swell place.

I did then what I'd expected to do as soon as I was completely sure I knew what I knew. I found the bar. I knew there'd be a bar; these places all came with 'em, chose a nice brand of whiskey, foreign of course, snagged a glass and an ashtray—no need to make a mess in such an upscale joint—and padded over the extra thick carpet to make myself comfortable in a big soft chair. The chair faced the door. That part was to make myself safe. I intended to sit there, smoking and sipping good whiskey until the door opened and things got exciting.

Not too exciting. Back in Saratoga Springs, I'd had about all the excitement a man could take—or, for that matter, a dog—and survive.

I didn't expect to wait long. It was late. Even an actor has to get some rest now and then. But while I was waiting, I thought it might be nice to enjoy my time alone somewhere a guy like me could never afford.

Jane hopped up onto a couch. She'd given up licking her nose. Now she was back to using a front paw to try and wipe the old dame's lipstick off.

Whaddaya know? Jane was a southpaw.

The more I sat still and looked, the easier it was to see. Over to my left was a chrome kitchen. That's where I'd found his impressive stock of alcohol. Beyond the kitchen a short hall led to what had to be a dining room. To my right was an oval opening into what was without doubt the guy's study. No actual door, so I could make out a large fireplace, the corner of a desk, and a wall of books. Too bad I couldn't snoop around, get a look at those books. A man's collection of reading matter might tell me who I was dealing with here. I knew what he'd done, but I still wasn't sure why he thought killing was a good solution to life's little problems. You'd think he'd just buy his way out.

That left him as nutty as a Planter's Peanut Bar.

Behind me was a lot of windows looking out over Central Park. I know, I'd peeked. Right next to those was a second deeply carpeted hall that must lead to the bath and bedrooms. There were three of them, the bedrooms. I'd studied the building's snappy brochure before my visit. There were bigger apartments than this one with its three bedrooms. There were apartments with servant's quarters. There was a whole floor on the top of the building meant for only one occupant which included a private garden on the roof. With fountain. Some banker lived up there.

This place was for a well-heeled someone who lived alone. Or maybe with a man servant. I'd checked on that too. No man servant.

The walls were angled, high and white and covered with paintings. Even with full light, I already knew I'd have no idea who painted them. Few would. But from the way they looked in dim light, all splodges and smudges and globs of revolting colors, I knew they had to be the latest thing in how to take a sucker for all he was worth.

So really there was just me and Jane and the dark and the waiting.

Somewhere a clock ticked, gently counting off the time.

## 33

A key turned in the lock.

Jane was off the couch and crouching next to the door so fast I didn't stand a chance at her collar.

As the door slowly opened—already odd… when I came home, I flung open my door and threw myself across the room, right towards where my Murphy bed was waiting. Almost always with an enticing half-read book lost in the covers.

Not this guy. This guy opened the door as if he expected a surprise party and he hated surprise parties. I slipped my gun out of my pocket and held it gently, pointing it pretty much where I expected his stomach would be when he finished creeping into his own apartment.

I heard a sigh of relief when the door was fully open, Jane hidden behind it. Whatever he feared he might find, he figured he hadn't found. The drapes were drawn, the lights were off. I'd stubbed out my last butt ages back, so the smell of a fresh burning Lucky had to of worn off. I still had some whiskey in my glass but the whole place had smelled a little like booze when I got here.

Relaxed, he shut the door a lot faster than he'd opened it, slipped the bolt home which would of made my breaking and entering a little bit harder if he'd been inside when I came calling, and took off his dark wool coat and his gloves. He tucked the gloves into the pockets of the coat, unwound his fine woolen scarf, then hooked both coat and scarf on the coat-stand just inside his door with all the finesse of an English butler.

He didn't hang his hat, he tossed it. It landed perfectly and spun a little while Jane was sitting right there, looking up at him.

I knew he felt safe, safe enough not to notice her. I might of noticed her. She was pretty obvious, but he was headed straight for the bar I'd headed for earlier.

The rich seemed to have a thing for carpets. The carpets here were almost thick enough for buffalo to range on. Jane's toenails, following him, were soundless.

He flipped on a small light, giving just the right amount of glow to all those bottles he owned. It made the rest of the place all that darker.

Jane once again sat and watched as he mixed himself a Gin Rickey. I hate gin. Nasty stuff. Then, glass in hand, he turned to do exactly what I'd also done: sit in his big soft chair.

Trouble was, someone was already in it—me.

"Evening, Anders. Good show?"

Jesus. Ever hear a pig squeal? I had. Once. At a racetrack. The pig's name was Cuddles and he was the best friend of a damn good sprinter called Four Below.

Anders sounded exactly like Cuddles getting his tail caught in Four Below's stall door.

"You!"

"Right on the first guess."

"What are you... how did you... is that a gun?"

"It is."

"A loaded gun?"

"The best kind."

Anders Slydel collapsed on the nearest leather couch while I turned on a table lamp. By its light he looked, as Mister used to say, a mite peeked.

He finally managed to speak in a short but full sentence. "Are you alone?"

"No."

That almost turned his hair white. It certainly drained the rest of him of his usual healthy color. "Who... who... who... ?"

"Jane."

"Who's Jane?"

"My dog."

Jane jumped onto the couch next to Anders Slydel so she could steadily glare at him, while Slydel came close to weeping on his own furniture. "Oh, thank god."

Observing all this from my side of the gun, all I could think was he'd expected the cops. I would if I were him. But seeing only me was a relief.

Jane and I watched him while he had his little weep and then a little Gin Rickey and then another little weep and then some more gin. When he'd finally gotten tired of all that, he said, "How'd you get in here?"

"I have my ways."

"I suppose you would. You've come for the truth. You know, don't you?"

"I know. But whether I know the whole truth, well, that's where you come in. You're going to help me with that."

I didn't expect him to look confused. I expected him to look nuts. And guilty. He looked confused. I didn't expect a confession. No matter what you've heard, very few confess, even the insane. But if they do, they either leave a lot out, or take it all back later with the advice of a lawyer

I'd bet Anders Slydel had a dilly of a lawyer.

His eyes slightly crossed with gin, weeping and confusion, he didn't confess, he said, "It's like this. I don't really know if I can help you. I honestly don't know everything. And I certainly don't understand everything. Actually I doubt even if I did know everything, I would understand it. To understand all this would require a degree in psychiatry, and maybe twenty years practice in Bellevue."

Or twenty years as a guest. Me, I had no idea what he

was talking about. But that didn't make me lower my gun. I kept it aimed right at his belly.

Jane didn't move a hair. She already knew about knives. Since then, I'd taught her about guns. One thing I couldn't of stood after all we'd gone through, was Jane getting shot.

I said, "I'd still like to hear you make a stab at it."

There he went, weeping into his gin again. "If I told you what I know, I'd be a dead man."

"You already are a dead man, Slydel. Three killings usually do that to a guy—once they're caught."

Anders sat up, sloshing his drink on his perfect pants and his perfect couch. "You can't think, you don't think—"

"That you killed Maurice Oboram, Raymond LeGrand, and Maudie Rivers?"

"Ye gods, man! Why would I do that? What reasons would I have for any one of them?"

"I was hoping you'd tell me."

By now, he was leaning so far back, if I'd shot him high, I'd catch him under his chin.

"Do the police think that? For God's sake, I'm an actor. I don't kill people. I might take a part as a killer, actually I'd kill to play a killer, much more interesting than—no, please forget I said that. Tongue got away from me. But why would I, Anders Slydel, do a thing like that—in real life?"

"That's what I'm here for. So you can tell me why you'd do a thing like that."

I leaned back too, but only a little, not too relaxed, but not too keyed up either. Anders' whiskey had a nice kick to it. Not too hard, not too soft.

He seemed so lost, so out of his depth, I gave him a little as a gift. "The cops could be thinking anything. They usually do. Jimmy thinks Raymond killed Maurice because Maurice had the goods on him for cheating. Mrs. Willingford— "

"Mrs. Willing... ?"

"Never mind. She thinks Mr. Glenda killed LeGrand

because he was sticking it to his wife, Mrs. Glenda. They both think Maudie was in the wrong place at the right time, and was killed by one or the other of the Glendas to save their own skins."

Big surprise. I was fascinating Anders. He'd stopped weeping and was now leaning toward me, gun or no gun, his eyes shining with interest. "I've always liked Jimmy. He gives me tips, helps with my lines. But you, you don't think what he and Mrs. Whoever think, do you?"

"I think maybe Jimmy is on to something."

Did Anders Slydel smile right there? Hard to tell in the soft light. But, strange as it was, he might of smiled. I know one thing he did. He said, more to himself than to me, "I wish."

" ...but I don't think the Two Glendas killed Raymond."

"Why not?"

Sitting there in a swell apartment with a guy in swell clothes, both of us sipping swell booze, I found I didn't mind being the one answering the questions. It seemed kind of right. Considering I thought the poor little rich bad actor was way off his rocker, and I was the one with the gun.

"First because if Mr. Glenda really *had* killed Raymond, Glenda would have killed *him*, not Maudie. She really loved the big palooka. And second, because you killed Raymond LeGrand. And when Maudie saw you do it, you had to take care of her 'cause she'd either peach on you or blackmail you—which is precisely why you killed Raymond. He'd already threatened you. You owed him plenty. I know. I've seen the record he kept and your total was steep, very very steep. Plus you were sweet on someone who'd never suit the Slydel family and I'd bet anything he said he'd tell. I checked you out. The family owns half of Maine which means most of the trees and all the paper mills for miles around. Your father is on the board of half a dozen companies in three major cities and your mother's the biggest snob since Mrs. Astor.

And that's saying something. They've already threatened to cut you off if you don't stop pretending to act."

"Pretending to—?"

"Forget that part."

Anders'd lost his color again. "I loved Maudie."

I said, "I know. But not that much." I thought: You loved her enough to make her think she was going to be rich when she married you, but not enough to let her live when she got up the nerve to tell me about you. She was afraid of you, Anders, afraid to lose the apartment you paid for, afraid to lose her hope of living someplace like this place, but she was terrified when she saw who you really were while you were garroting LeGrand.

Anders must of felt safe. He was acting safe, lighting up some foreign smoke he'd removed from a silver box. "It's true. I once did. I once loved her enough to say to hell with my family."

"But not after she saw what you did."

"Wrong. Not after *I* saw what *she*—"

From behind us came a soft warm voice. "Shut up, Anders, you dolt. Hello, Sam. I have to say: you're one dumb dick."

Anders opened his mouth to make that pig sound again. I didn't blame him. The woman had her own gun and it was a lot bigger than mine. Her hair was down and it hung around her face like the roses hung on the shining back of a Kentucky Derby winner. She wasn't wearing glasses. In fact she was hardly wearing anything but the gifts a generous God had given her.

I couldn't see everything, but I saw enough. Maudie Rivers was built better than Ava Gardner. She wasn't better looking, but she sure could of been a runner up in "all the rest" department.

I suddenly understood what had happened to Anders Slydel. He didn't stand a chance.

I should of been ready.  I should of known Jane wasn't going to stand for any of this.  She'd heard the sly threat in Maudie's voice.  She knew Maudie was supposed to be dead. Last, she knew what a gun meant.

She leapt for Maudie Rivers.

It took three bullets to stop me up in Saratoga.  It took a single slug to drop Jane.

## 34

I'd never felt worse. Not when I found Jane on the blood splashed floor in a pink hotel in Saratoga Springs stabbed eleven times, not when I was shot up close by someone I thought was my friend, not when I found out my mother was killed by a maniac when she was only a kid and I'd played for years on her make-shift grave. This felt worse because this time I'd brought Jane here. I'd put her in harm's way. It was all my fucking fault.

I was out of that chair and on the blood wet carpet by Jane's side, gun or no gun aimed by Maudie Rivers, back from the dead and looking good.

"Jane," I said, placing my hand on her chest, "Jane, don't you die, don't you die on me."

Jane, who'd been nicked in the shoulder, had no intention of dying. What she intended to do was go for Maudie again. I grabbed on and held her for all I was worth, which meant dropping my own gun under the coffee table.

"That mutt comes at me again," said Maudie, "I won't miss twice. Now Anders, what's all this about Bellevue and you *did* love me. I'm not real happy with your use of the past tense. It makes a girl feel sort of unwanted. You still want me, of course you do. And I'll always want you and what's yours. So let's kiss and make-up right here and now."

I thought Anders had pissed himself. Either that, or he'd spilled his Gin Rickey in his lap.

"But you were... ," he said, "I thought you were, I mean, even this fellow here, this private dick person thought you were... "

"Dead? Too funny, honey bun. Although I suppose I was dead just as long as I needed to be. Fooling ol' Dick Tracy over there was about as hard as fooling Maurice, the poor sap. Socking myself in the eye, pretending I was being chased so I had to leave the soda shop real quick and you showing up right then so the soda jerk saw you, that last part was plain good luck. Leaving my address book for him to find, messing up my apartment, going to that muddy place on the river so I could 'die,' placing my glasses and my sweater on the mud just so was plain good planning. I watched from a telephone company window as he and his high tone woman and that damn dog thrashed about in the mud, and laugh? I thought I'd get sick laughing."

She showed us what she meant by going off into what I'd heard described as "peals of laughter" while I went off into what I'd describe as furious thinking. Furious, because she had fooled me and she'd fooled Mrs. Willingford, but most amazing of all, she'd fooled Jane. It was Jane who'd led us to the same place Maurice had been killed.

She hadn't smelled Maudie in Anders' place. That one made sense. I figured all she could smell was that old woman's lipstick. Bad luck for us both getting in the wrong elevator at the right time.

But mostly I was thinking about what she'd just said about Maurice.

"You killed Maurice Oboram, didn't you Maudie?"

She was still laughing. If I thought Anders was off his rocker, I was now looking at someone who wasn't even on a porch. This one could give Flo and "Mister" Zawadzki a run for their money, anytime, anywhere.

"Now that wasn't easy, Mr. PI man. That was one huge chump. And he didn't exactly trust me anymore. I mean, he didn't trust me at all. But he was weak. I've discovered that all nice people are weak. They just can't believe that someone else could be, well, not so nice. Even when proof is staring right at 'em.  So me getting him to dress up like that and getting myself all dressed up just like him so he'd think I was helping him rehearse wasn't easy.  But what a moron.  What a pushover.  Going somewhere with me.  Not to mention his thinking he'd ever get to play Shakespeare again.  And then there was the getting him to go somewhere where I could be taller than him.  So I said practicing outside would give us more room, and so's we wouldn't have an audience we'd need somewhere nice and private.  And where else but the docks?"

I saw it happening.  I held my struggling dog, her blood seeping out of her just as it did once before, and I watched Maudie get Maurice down near the river, saw her gay Shakespearean leap up onto the pier to be above him.  I watched her raise his double headed axe and I watched her bring it down.  She missed the first two times.  One miss took his thumb, the second his whole hand, and then... fuck.  The poor man.  The poor doomed enormous man.

Anders was silently weeping.  "Maurice was my best friend, Maudie.  I loved him like a brother."

"I know," she said, "that's why I had to get rid of him.  He loved you too, the pansy, which is why he was going to tell you something about me I didn't want you to know."

"What?  What didn't you want me to know?"

"Oh, for heaven's sakes, Anders.  You think I'd tell you what I stopped someone else from telling you?"

Me, I imagined what she didn't want him to know was that Maurice wasn't her first kill.  Or even her second.  Or third.  How Maurice found out, only Maudie could tell us.  I didn't expect that to happen.

Maybe it wasn't wise, but who said I was wise?  "And you killed Raymond too, didn't you?  Anders here saw that when he looked through the open trap door."

It'd all fallen into place.  Maybe too late—but better late than never.  Noodles had lied.  He hadn't seen who'd opened that trap. All he wanted was money. He thought I'd be sucker enough to believe his story.

Noodles was right. I did believe him. Until right this very minute.

Maudie turned her big brown slightly unfocused eyes on me, the black eye fading, batting her lashes. "Why sure I did. Honestly, before Maurice was even gone, that bastard LeGrand takes his apartment off him. The rotten nerve of a man who cheats at cards. But Raymond also winds up with that dog who didn't raise a tooth to help his giant friend. Bluto's how he knew the address in the first place, from that barrel around his neck, the one I left my little note in I signed by Raymond. Which of course I didn't do until after Josephine was stuck with Bluto, which meant I was stuck with Bluto." Suddenly there was this huge smile plastered all over her deadly mug. "Now that was really clever. Like Dorothy Parker. You know, the Jew poet? I've often thought I might become a poet like her, hang around with those smart guys at that hotel dropping bon mots. Well, anyway, the big dumb cowardly mutt drags Raymond to where he last saw his master. Bad luck for Raymond, because then he has to go and find Maurice's hat. That's not like me, to leave anything behind. I must have eaten something, probably one too many of Josephine's damn Tootsie Rolls. So LeGrand isn't stupid like Anders here, 'cept he wasn't too bright telling me about the hat. Anyway, he works it all out what with finding the hat and playing those cards with Maurice, and having Maurice moaning at him about awful me and about his good friend Anders, and everybody knows Anders is worth a mint, and thanks to Maurice he knows Anders is still keeping our love from his people and he also knows I hate that, all of which brings him to what happened to Maurice getting in my way like he did, so he comes to talk to me, expecting me to get him money off Anders—or he'll tell. Well, we all know about blackmailers. They never stop, do they? They think they've found a piggy bank and they just can't help themselves—they keep shaking it for more. So I had to stop him too. And let me tell you, killing a big strong man like LeGrand took everything I had, a lot more than killing Maurice. If I'd tried any other way than that wire, I'd be the one dead. But, of course, once again, something goes a bit wrong. I'd left the trap open so they'd find Raymond really soon and I could be sure of an alibi. But which boob of all those boobs looks through it? Mr. Slydel here, my soon-to-be. I wrote what I wanted to write on the lug's arm anyway, fiancée or no fiancée. Didn't I, Anders?"

"Yes, Maudie."

"The Tides of March. Get it? Not the ides but the tides? That must have confused our little shamus here."

I'd been moving my foot under the coffee table as she talked—she really liked to talk now she could be who she really was and not Josephine Hull's dresser—when I heard something that chilled my blood.

"Anders, stop being useless. Go get a blanket so you can wrap up that nasty little dog and throw it in a closet. I have some interesting plans for Mr. Sam Russo here. Plans Mr. Russo himself helped me dream up with all his talk about those nags over in the Philippines and how they wound up dinner on a plate."

Anders didn't want to stand up for more reasons than one. He tried to stay put, but it was like keeping your balance in the face of a wave twenty feet tall.

"Anders! Now!"

I was this close to my gun when he threw a blanket over a snarling Jane, wrapped her up as tight as he could, kicking my gun farther under the table while he did it.

He did exactly what Maudie told him to do: he tossed my dog in a front hall closet.

The racket she made in there, even wounded and with part of the blanket stuck in the door, ought to of alerted the entire building. But not this building. The rich have to go and soundproof things.

Maudie stuck her head around the kitchen door. "Bring him on in, Anders. Tie him up. Use your ties. You have a million of 'em. You know I'm not very good with knots."

I said I get these headaches. The one I got now was really special.

Anders tied me to a kitchen chair and all the while he was doing that—better than Maudie could of, but not well, yet not badly enough to make it easy to slip out—Maudie was going through his kitchen drawers. What she finally found made her whoop with delight.

For the one moment she was caught up in her find, Anders leaned in towards my ear. I was right. He'd peed himself. I could smell it. But who could blame him? "I'm sorry. I'm so so *so* terriby sorry. If I get out of this alive, I'm going home to Portland, Maine, no more acting for me."

"What about me?" I whispered back.

He looked as mournful as a clown. Clowns made me uneasy. Anders made me feel a lot worse than that. "I would if I could, but I can't help you. I'm afraid— "

"Anders! Hurry up. Momma's found a toy."

He pulled the last knot tight, so there I was, bound to a chair in a kitchen with some broad who belonged in a padded cell in *The Snake Pit*, and all I had was a rich ex-actor, forever idiot. But what I really cared about was the sound Jane was making in her hallway closet. Was it getting weaker? If it was getting weaker, I had nothing to lose. Maudie Rivers could do her worst, and her worst was looking pretty bad, but she wasn't killing my dog. Me maybe, but not Jane.

Trouble was, I didn't know how to stop her.

"Pull his head up, Anders. I want him to see what Maudie's going to do."

Anders pulled my head up. It figured. She was holding a large kitchen knife, the kind you see in the best stores for fine kitchenware.

"Now Sam," she said, "I don't want you to think I'm going to use this to stab you. That's so common. No. This is for Anders in case he wants to join in. What I'm really going to do is pretty good. I've thought about it ever since I knew what you did in the war. First, you'll note I've turned on the oven, and that I've put on a huge pot to boil— "

"Maudie?" I said.

"Yes, Sam?"

"Do you still expect to marry Anders?"

"Of course."

Behind me, I heard Anders breathing speed up. But he did nothing.

"So what happens to Anders when they find what happens to me all over his house? Won't that spoil the wedding?"

"You have a point and I have a solution. A delicious solution."

I knew what her solution was. I knew it as soon as she said the word "delicious."

I was leaving the very nice apartment of Anders Slydel as food. Prepared and packaged. For dogs or for cats, or maybe for the hopeless helpless veterans who now took up most of the space in the Staten Island Home for Children.

Sam Russo knew when he was beat. And he was beaten fair and square. No point asking for mercy. No point telling her I never ate my horses. A lot did, but not me. All I could do was one last thing. "I'd like to ask for a favor, Maudie. You did Maurice a favor. You 'rehearsed' with him. His last moments must of delighted him."

"Oh, they did. He didn't like me. He told Anders he shouldn't like me. And yet he laughed and laughed and laughed, not thinking for a moment why I'd climb up onto that pier. I'll bet he thought we were switching from *Hamlet* to *Romeo and Juliet*. So what's the favor?"

"When you're finished doing what you're doing, would

you please have Anders take my dog to a vet?"

"Why sure, sugar. What do you think I am? I've never hurt Bluto, why would I hurt your doggie? The ugly little thing, who somebody must have really hated, I've never seen so many scars on one animal in my life, was only being loyal to you."

"Thank you, Maudie."

"Think nothing of it. Anders, you ready?"

Out in the hall Anders Slydel had a grandfather clock. Big old thing, as ornate as one of Louis the Fifteenth's wigs, probably a Slydel family heirloom, one you had to wind to keep it going. Obviously Anders kept his clock wound. Even in the kitchen, if we hadn't been so preoccupied—I sure knew I was—we could of heard it ticking. Suddenly it began tolling the hours, all twelve of them.

It was midnight on the isle of Manhattan.

I'd always wanted to live in New York City. I hadn't given much thought to dying there.

## 35

"Anders, dear, I need his arm up on this wooden block. You'll have to loosen that knot there. Not that one, *that* one. Just one arm. I swear, sometimes I think you haven't the brains of a fly."

Anders untied my arm. As it happened, it was the left arm.

Maudie handed him a rolling pin. "Hit him with this, hard, really hard, on the bicep. Don't want him doing anything, do we?"

Anders sighed, and then hit me with the rolling pin right where he was told to. He hit me hard, really hard. Which left my arm dangling as useless as Anders Slydel while Maudie prepared the butcher's block, setting out various carefully chosen kitchen utensils.

Oh God, it hurt. It hurt a lot more than being shot. That's because being shot shocks you, protects you. Getting smacked with a rolling pin is like, well, getting smacked with a rolling pin. The ache went down to the tips of all four of my fingers and up to and over my shoulder.

My bicep was throbbing in grievous agony.

I didn't make a sound. I don't know how I did that, but I did. OK, so I made one small short whimper.

Anders himself, after he'd done as he was told, fell into a chair near the window. What he could see from his window was what the back of his building faced. Another nice building like his. Turning his back on me and Maudie, a Maudie who'd begun singing *You Always Hurt the One You Love*, he stared out at it.

That's when I heard a sound I understood immediately. It both thrilled me and terrified me. It thrilled me because maybe there was a way out of this. It terrified me because maybe there was no way out of this and Jane wasn't going to a vet like Maudie promised.

It was the sound of Jane pushing open the closet door. I knew as soon as I saw the blanket that the door wasn't entirely on its latch. And I knew Jane, no matter how wounded, would push at that door until she died—or got out. Now I knew she'd gotten out. I knew she was headed my way. Anders was staring out his kitchen window, blanking things out, pretending none of this was happening; Maudie was placing things just so on the wooden block. Singing, I'd bet across the board she heard only her own voice.

Me, I heard the slick click of Jane's toenails as she left the carpeted hall and entered the tiled kitchen.

I took a chance and looked down. There was Jane all right, getting her doggie blood all over Anders Slydel's nice little Upper East Side home. I saw what she carried in her mouth. My gun. As I've said, Jane knew what a gun was for. So she'd brought me mine, the one that'd wound up under Anders' coffee table.

I only had the one arm and the one hand. My aching, almost useless, left was going to have to do.

One second more, I'd have the thing in my left hand, I'd have my hand up if I had to scream with pain doing it, and I'd be pointing it at Maudie Rivers. Only thing wrong with all this was Jane. She stood right where she was. If things went wrong, and things were always going wrong even in the movies, she was in the way. I couldn't ask her to leave. I couldn't make a sound.

I didn't have to.

I'd been listening to more than *You Always Hurt the One You Love* and the click-click-click of Jane's nails on the floor. There'd been another sound, one I knew as well as I knew

Maudie's song. Someone was picking Anders' front door lock and they were picking it well.

As soon as the last tumbler fell, the whole door was kicked open with the bottom of a boot. The door splintered on its hinges, the sound of it rattled the dishes.

Anders would of leapt out his window if it wasn't barred.

Maudie's song came to a dead stop as the both of us looked up at the exact same moment. In the door stood Woody, Mrs. Willingford's "chauffeur." Beside him stood Rudy Hiller, my old teacher from Bayonne, New Jersey, with a set of picks in his hand, and behind Rudy stood Mrs. Willingford in a small hat, a cute one all made of bright red feathers that curled round one side of her gorgeous face.

"What the fuck!" said Maudie, the song dying in her throat as she reached for the cleaver, third along in her row of cutlery. "I won't… "

What she "wouldn't" died in her throat. Woody drilled a neat little hole right in the very middle of her forehead.

"Of course, I was worried," said Mrs. Willingford. "The way you left and all on your own. As soon as I saw which way you were headed, which had nothing to do with Mr. & Mrs. Glenda and nothing to do with mud, I knew we'd better come prepared."

"You and Jimmy?"

"No, me and Woody. Although it was Jimmy who rustled up your locksmith for you, right after his last bow in *Harvey*. You missed a great show, and by the way, some of your friends are expensive. All the way from Bayonne? that Mr. Hiller asked Jimmy. But he was worth it. And he really did make time. I knew we'd need him as soon as I had a word with the charming boy in the soda shoppe— "

"Charming?"

"If you'd be so good as to shut up. I'm on the phone

here."

Mrs. Willingford'd been saying all this around the mouthpiece of Anders Slydel's telephone. Her vet was on his way if he had to fly.

Once paid, Rudy Hiller said a quick hello and a quicker goodbye. If cops were involved, Rudy Hiller wasn't your man. Woody was guarding the door to the kitchen with his arms folded across his chest. And I was holding Jane in my arms, one of which was useless, the both of us lying on Anders' other couch, not the one he'd pissed himself on. After checking, it was Mrs. Willingford's professional opinion that Jane would be fine, not even a limp.

Anders Slydel was lying in a heap in the kitchen along with Maudie. Only one of them was dead. Anders had fainted.

Now, after a heated discussion about calling the cops—after all, they already thought Maudie was dead, why bother reporting it again?—the clearer head prevailed. Woody said if we simply skipped out, Anders could come to, take one look around, and would surely concoct some wildly imaginative story to save his own skin, not from the cops, but from his family—who knew?

So, along with Mrs. Willingford's vet, the cops were also on their way.

Waiting, Mrs. Willingford did something very unlike Mrs. Willingford. She sat on our couch, Jane's and mine, eased my head into her lap, and held me.

"Sam," she said, "I might not say this again so you'd better hear me now."

"What's that?" I didn't trust her. Not for a minute, even as Jane hummed and licked my neck while Mrs. Willingford gently pushed my hair out of my eyes.

"You're a better PI than I am."

"You're not a PI."

"But if I were to decide I was—— "

"I'd still be better at it?"

"Very possibly."

"Thank you."

"You're welcome."

The sound of a lot of flat feet out in the hall made me remember something.

"You had to pick the lock to get in here. OK, I understand that. But how'd you get in the building?"

"Sam, darling, I'm not Mr. Glenda, out on the sidewalk waiting for you in the cold. By the way, Woody took his gun away. I'm Mrs. Joker Willingford. Why would it even cross anyone's mind to keep me out?"

I was left with only one nagging question. Why did Jane attack Bluto? Only way to know was to ask her and the only way to do that was to look deep into her wild Egyptian eyes and say: "Why Bluto?"

Jane answered me. No doubt about it.

She went for Bluto as soon as she smelled him. Jane could smell Maurice on Bluto, the dead man she'd smelled in Mort's morgue, the man he didn't protect. She could smell Bluto's guilt and his fear.

Jane had decided he'd been a bad dog.

**Enjoying the adventures of Sam Russo, Private Eye?**

**Turn the page to preview the first chapter of Sam's next case:
THE GIRL IN THE NEXT ROOM ...**

**THE GIRL IN THE NEXT ROOM and other books in the Sam Russo Mystery series are available from:**

**www.eiobooks.com**

**And your favorite bookseller.**

Follow Ki Longfellow on the Internet:

Blog kilongfellow.wordpress.com
Facebook Ki Longfellow
Twitter @KiLongfellow
Official Website www.kilongfellow.com
Sam Russo www.eiobooks.com/samrusso

I was calling on my new neighbor, the goober in room 4-C. 4-C was old Nate's room before old Nate curled up his toes and died. When the new guy answered my knock, it was like watching a rock roll away from a hole. The rat inside was enormous. He had a glass of something brown in one hairy paw and a glass of something less brown in the other. I figured one of 'em was a chaser.

About then his smell came out and punched me right on the nose.

I stood there, Jane at my side, trying not to inhale. I said, "Hello. My name is Sam Russo."

"So?"

"I live in 4-A."

"So?"

"I wondered... have you seen Holly?"

"Who?"

"The girl in 4-B. That's the room between us."

"Girl? Beat it bub, before I give you what for. Or her, if I *did* see 'er." With both hands full and a wet smoke stuck in his wet mouth, there wasn't much he could do to keep his pants up. They were dungarees: old, encrusted with filth, and slowly sinking.

I thanked a slammed door.

Goddamn you, Nate. Dead, you're a pain in the ass. You let this guy into my building. Here for a week now, he played his radio half the night. Obviously fond of a drink or ten, coming or going he'd slam between the stair rail and the wall. He dropped his used butts on the stairs. A coupla times he didn't make it to the top, and we were supposed to step over him. I admit it: I stepped *on* him. As for Jane, she never missed.

But worse, much worse, he was sharing the bathroom.

With Nate newly underground, Holly and I'd had a nice long run with just one or the other of us in it, but now, like Joe Louis and boxing, our run was over. I was thinking of moving. Out of Stapleton. Off Staten Island. But then, I was always thinking of moving.

Manhattan was only a ferry ride away. If I couldn't get off Staten Island—yet—I could at least find a room with a better view of New York City.

But Jane and I were sailing pretty close to the wind money wise. And then there was Holly. I didn't want to leave Holly alone in a room next to the room with a guy like the new guy in it.

Holly who? I didn't know her last name. I didn't know her first name either. I just knew the one she used. Basically, I knew sweet diddly about Holly in 4-B. Where she came from. What it must of been like for her growing up. Who her people were. Why someone as smart and funny as she was worked the streets. And why, of all places, did she work them in Stapleton? Holly could do better than Staten Island. Even I could do better than Staten Island.

What I did know was that Holly hadn't come home for two days and three nights. The first day wasn't bad. For one thing, it was the first Saturday in May and I was glued to my radio listening to the Kentucky Derby. I can't remember when I named myself Sam but I can remember when I decided that the day the Kentucky Derby ran each year was my birthday. Of course this meant my birthday fell anywhere from the 1st to the 7th of May, but I liked that part. It messed with my horoscope. On this year's birthday which, as it happened, fell on May 7th, I'd put my money on a colt called Capot, but Ponder, a "come from the back of the pack" closer, took it with a run called "relentless." Ponder'd been dead last and then he was suddenly a rip-snorting first. But hey, I figured losing a few bucks to listen to an unexpected win by the son of Pensive—the horse who should of taken the Triple Crown in '44—was well worth my loss.

On Sunday I began to worry. And Jane began to worry as much as me. Holly'd missed not only the Derby—something she'd promised to try now we were pals—but my birthday. It wasn't like her to break a promise. Also, I liked to think she'd remember I was getting old.

Twenty eight. Thirty wasn't far off.

When we'd pass Holly's door, Jane'd stop and sniff all along the bottom edge. Doing that, her tightly curled tail would unfurl.

It was the tail that did it.

After our latest scrape, the one in Manhattan where Jane got another scar to go along with her growing Sam Russo knife and gun collection, and I'd been *this* close to being Russo soup, I'd taken only "safe" cases. No one was famous, we never got covered in oily mud, it just about covered the rent, and no one died. Just ugly little human nature stuff. No matter the job, jealousy and greed lay at the bottom of most of it— and a sort of basic human fear lay at the bottom of jealousy and greed. I'd find myself standing around knee deep in some mess someone had made of his life, or her life, or in the lives of others, or all the above—usually all the above—and wonder what they were scared of. It all boiled down to who the hell knew? That was the problem. None of us really knew what we were doing, or why.

It was making me sick. But it was better than making me dead. And twice as better for not making Jane dead.

My Manhattan adventure down two different rabbit holes still worried me though. I'd tripped over who did it, even survived the fall, but I never did discover all there was to know. I might of learned more—I was sure there was a *lot* more to learn—but a neat black hole through the killer's neat black brain put a stop to that. That brain contained a whole lot of things I wish I'd learned. Too bad I wasn't going to learn it.

Mrs. Willingford was off in California somewhere, buying a shiny new racehorse. And if I knew Mrs. Joker Willingford, which I did, sort of, she was also busy bumping into good-looking strangers and blocking doorways with her hats.

Anyway, for a few months there, it'd been just me and Jane and a lot of getting to know Holly. We'd spent our idea of Christmas together. For Holly that meant a small hurtful tree and a present for Jane and one for me. I suppose the tree hurt because it was the first one I'd ever sat by on a Christmas Eve listening to Bing sing Christmas carols. Where I'd grown up—the Staten Island Home for Children—we celebrated Christmas like Scrooge celebrated Christmas.

Holly gave me a book. Holding it was like holding a paving stone. Reading it was like wading out into a swelling sea and practically drowning there. *Raintree County* was some book. Jane got a new leather collar. Attached to the collar was a metal disc. The disc said JANE, and under that was my Saint George 7 phone number.

"In case she gets lost," said Holly.

"Jane's never lost," I said.

"Never say never," said Holly.

Jane said something in her own language neither Holly nor I understood, though we were both working on it.

Jane and I gave Holly a silver locket. It wasn't shaped like a heart. I might be that sappy but Jane wasn't.

We'd actually laughed, Holly and I. And Jane. When Holly wasn't working the Victory Boulevard edge of Tompkinsville Park, or singing in the Green Garter, she was great to be with. We went to the movies a lot. We liked the same movies, the same radio shows, the same books. Besides my Christmas present, Holly'd borrowed a few things from the Stapleton library I'd never of thought to read if she hadn't. I could of done without a strut of a guy called Hemmingway but Scott Fitzgerald and Charles Dickens really had something to say.

Because of Holly, I was getting elevated.

Jane and I liked her. We both liked her a lot.

So where was she?

She'd better not be dead. Besides liking her, my being a Private Investigator was turning out the most dangerous job in the world. Two big cases in '48, Summer and Fall, each a mess of multiple murders, and each almost winding up with me or Jane dead. Or both of us at the same time.

Did Holly's disappearance have something to do with me?

If so, I was through as a private eye. For a PI, I was the bunk. I wasn't Poirot with his little gray cells whirring around in his head, working out whodunit all by his lonesome. I wasn't Bogie playing Sam Spade or Philip Marlowe. Bogart didn't really have cases exactly, they were more like sticky situations where he'd get hired, get sapped, get kissed by a great looking skirt, get sapped again, or for variety, pistol whipped, and somehow turn out right side up in the end. I wasn't your ordinary real life police detective—which did not include my old friend Lino Morelli because Lino Morelli wasn't ordinary. Lino, detective with the Staten Island police, was dumber than a sack of Idaho spuds. I mean your *real* ordinary police detective who took fingerprints, tapped phones if he was lucky, had files and files of convicted and yet-to-be-convicted bad guys to look through and finger. I wasn't anyone I'd ever heard of or read of or seen on the silver screen. I was Sam Russo, and if Holly was dead, I'd rather not know she was dead.

As I said, we liked her.

So maybe we ought to move out first thing in the morning. Then I could go on with my life believing Holly'd been off visiting her old mom somewhere, say over in small town New Jersey, or maybe even in upstate New York—a place she'd come home from just as my cab was turning the corner. And Jane and I hadn't looked back.

Only I wouldn't move out in the morning. I wouldn't go anywhere until I knew about Holly.

I got the call at dawn. Fell out of my Murphy bed to answer it. Knocked Jane off her personal pillow. I'd been dreaming of Mrs. Willingford. We'd taken a whole floor at the Plaza which somehow became one enormous room and we were dancing like Rogers and Astaire. Only I was dressed like Ginger, all white and black froth. Gorgeous, really. The frock, not me. And Mrs. W was dressed as a jockey, whip included. No time to let that one sink in, I was listening to Lino Morelli on the end of my line.

He was saying, "Sam? You awake?"

"Uhh?"

"Good. You remember the nance I saw in your room that day last November? The time I came to tell you about the giant floater?"

I was suddenly awake, so awake my grip on the phone came this close to cracking the thick black plastic. Jane growled. Jane didn't like Lino. But then, who did?

"Yes," I said through terrified teeth. *She's not dead. She can't be dead. Don't tell me she's dead, you miserable little weasel.* "What about her?"

"She's in intensive. She's askin' for you. Get over here. Fast."

I couldn't bring Jane. They didn't allow dogs in hospitals. It killed me to shut the door in her surprised face, but I did it.